Runaway

Runaway

Luanne Smith, Michael Gills,
& Lee Zacharias
editors

MADVILLE
PUBLISHING

LAKE DALLAS, TEXAS

Permissions
Madville Publishing
PO Box 358
Lake Dallas, TX 75065

ACKNOWLEDGMENTS:

- "The Anchor Song" by Maurice Carlos Ruffin was first published in *So to Speak: a feminist journal of language and arts* (fall 2014), https://sotospeakjournal.org.
- "Daphne: The Aspen Version" by Erica Soon Olsen appeared in *Menacing Hedge* (2016) and in Girlmine (Bull City Press 2019).
- "The Fishing Dog" © 1999 by Bonnie Jo Campbell first appeared in *North Dakota Quarterly* and later in *Women and Other Animals* (U of Mass Press 1999).
- "Kansas" by Emily Chiles was first published in *Blackbird* (Spring 2019).
- "Lost Her Way" by Jen Knox was previously published in *Juked Magazine* and in *Resolutions: A Family in Stories* (AUXmedia, 2020).
- "Lubbock, 1974" © 2018 by Bobby Horecka first appeared in *Amarillo Bay*. It is also included in *Long Gone & Lost: True Lies and Other Fictions* (Madville 2020).
- "Reapers" by Jeffrey Byrem was first self-published in *The Promise*.
- "Sugar" by Misty Skaggs was first published online by journal *Fried Chicken & Coffee* (2012).
- "Vivian Delmar" by Louise Marburg was first published in *Joyland* (2019).
- "Willie's Crucifixion" by Rick Campbell first appeared in *Kestrel: A Journal of Art and Literature*.
- "Xmas, Jamaica Plain" by Melanie Rae Thon first appeared in Ontario Review and was later included in the collection First, Body, published by Houghton Mifflin.

Cover Design: Jacqueline V. Davis
Cover photo: Lori Beneteau, licensed through Shutterstock, Inc.

ISBN: 978-1-948692-26-7 paper, and 978-1-948692-27-4 ebook
Library of Congress Control Number: 2020931918

Contents

Foreword

This anthology grew from a message thread between Luanne Smith and Madville's publisher, Kim Davis. It was already a notion as Luanne and I sat over lunch in Portland, Oregon, exchanging childhood recollections about running away. Why else would the subject have come up? I'd never shared mine, and I was struck by its similarity to the memory Luanne had relayed to Kim. Both of us had run away often and young, seemingly with our mothers' blessings, neither of us traveled far, and we always returned unharmed. Luanne's grandfather told her that it was illegal for five-year-olds to cross the street, that those who did would be arrested and put in jail. Still, every time she got mad, she packed a shirt and stuffed animal in her Barbie case and departed for the front yard, her mother waving goodbye. Because the only sidewalk was on the other side of the street, her side bordered by a ditch deeper than she was tall, her journey consisted of pacing back and forth with her dog Spot, who pushed her back whenever she got too close to the ditch. On the one occasion she was angry enough to risk arrest and slipped past the dog, Spot grabbed her shirt with her teeth. In Luanne's words, "Between Grandpa, fear of prison, a big ditch, and my dog, I never made it out of our front yard."

My mother never waved goodbye. Instead she would offer to help me pack my suitcase, and once I stepped onto our front stoop, I would hear the formidable click of the door lock behind me. Apparently, I never chose to run away in summer, for this was in northern Indiana, just outside Chicago, and in my memory it is always winter, always cold, always dark. But we had a sidewalk, and so slowly I walked to the end of the block, where the widow of a police officer who had been killed in the line of duty still lived. Though I often crossed the street beyond in daylight—to visit playmates or on my route to kindergarten, later first and second grades—the fate of the policeman brought my expedition to a halt as inevitably Luanne's ditch, for he had gone out one night, crossed that street, and never returned. And so I turned around to walk even more slowly home, where I sat on that cold concrete stoop until misery and hopelessness forced me to knock and beg to be let in. Always my mother won.

But just as neither of our childhood threats ever came to fruition, neither Luanne nor I have chosen to develop these memories into stories, not yet. Though they have pattern, they remain at the level of incident. They are anecdotes, nothing more.

What follows in this anthology is a collection of stories, real or imagined, that have been carefully crafted into works of art on the theme of running away. Most of the characters travel much farther than we did, and certainly the stories do, into consequence, awareness, and resonance. In many of them absence becomes presence—the absences created for those left behind or the absences created within those who leave, or even think about leaving, others behind. In every one of these stories something is missing, a parent, a feeling, or some essential part of the self.

It is no surprise that many of these stories are motivated by abuse. Those characters older or less fortunate than Luanne or I were often run for good reason, though doing so frequently traps them in even more desperate situations. In one case a teen mother sacrifices herself by returning to an abusive father to let her baby daughter go for what she hopes is essential medical care. Not many of us know where—or even how—to run, and though a few characters run *to*, most of them run *from*. But to or from, one thing comes clear to them and to the reader: you can run from yourself, but no one ever completely escapes.

The two prize-winning stories* both involve rituals, one mysteriously invented, the other ill-conceived. And though both of the honorable

---

*   "Ritual" by Aden Albert and "Willie's Crucifixion" by Rick Campbell are the winners.

mentions* begin with young women barely into adolescence hanging out with friends, the tone and atmosphere of those tales diverge. That these are all such different stories should give everyone heart. As similar as my childhood memory is to Luanne's, my recollection ends with humiliation, hers with sweet humor. No one's running away story is quite like anyone else's. Perhaps no one's circumstances are quite like anyone else's. Memory and imagination never spin exactly the same way. More importantly, the art one creates from such circumstances, or the circumstances imagination creates, is unique. These fully realized stories speak in diverse ways to a nearly universal desire. Who has never wanted to run away from something? Every one of these stories has been selected because it contributes to a larger narrative. Every one of them speaks to the questions that belong to that larger narrative. Who are we if we refuse to be shaped by our pasts? Who are we if we choose no longer to be ourselves? Who are we, whether we are left behind or gone?

My thanks to my co-editors, Luanne Smith and Michael Gills, for the wisdom and care they brought to their reading and our deliberations, and to Kim Davis for guiding the collection into reality and giving it a home. It is an honor to work with them.

Lee Zacharias
January 6, 2020

---

* "Neighbor Boys and Cousins" by Jodi Angel and "Nothing to Light Our Way" by Emily Hoover" are the honorable mentions.

Neighbor Boys and Cousins*

Jodi Angel

Bobby said Wayne could get Black Cat firecrackers—the real ones—and maybe some M-80s, too, but it was Tony Guiterrez that finally came through, and they all came over to my house that afternoon and Wayne said I could hang out and blow things up if I'd practice "doin it" with them, which wasn't a bad trade since doin it for real meant taking off our underwear, and none of us wanted that yet, but practicing doin it just meant pulling our pants down and me letting them climb on top, one at a time, and rub on me until I could feel the small tight knot between their legs.

Wayne and Tony Guiterrez lived in the cul-de-sac around the corner from my street, the one that dead ended at the orchard, and Bobby had biked over from the Forward Addition, and all of them were standing on my front porch, sucking on Rocket Pops, and Tony Guiterrez had a grease-stained paper bag in his hand, with the words *Holiday Market* printed in green on the side, and he raised the bag up when I answered the door and he said, "I got 'em," and we'd been talking so much about Wayne's plan of robbing a trucker from Mexico that I wasn't quite sure what might be in the bag, but then he shook it and I could hear things inside jump around, and Wayne said, "boom," and I knew Tony Guiterrez was talking about bricks of Black Cats just in time for the 4th of July.

Behind me, the living room was a cool, dark cave of air conditioning and cartoons, and my little sister was on the couch with a can of Pringles, and I knew at any second she was going to threaten me with telling mom if I didn't close the door, come back inside, stop letting the cold air blow across the porch and into the yard.

"I gotta get my shoes," I said, and I pushed the door shut and went into my room, and there was a part of me that didn't really want to go practice doin it just to get to stand and watch them light firecrackers and blow things up because I knew they'd probably only let me light a few

---

* Honorable Mention

1

fuses, and maybe let me make a few suggestions about what to watch explode, and part of me already had a feeling that it wouldn't be as great as I'd imagined, and we'd use them all up before the day was over, probably even before it got dark outside, and in the end we'd probably all get in trouble somehow by somebody for something.

I told my sister I'd be back soon and not to tell mom if she called, and not to call mom first if she didn't, and when I went back outside, I sat on the top step of the porch and tied my shoes, and I said to Wayne, "I'll go but only if I get to light as many as I want," and he started to say something, to probably tell me no way, or barter me down to lighting just one, but before he could say anything, Tony Guiterrez said, "you can light all that you want if you really do it with us," and nobody else said anything, but Wayne and Bobby dropped their eyes and started picking at the frayed legs of their cutoffs, and I thought that maybe Bobby might speak up then, what with him being my best friend that year, but his eyes acted like they were coated with grease the way that they slid around in his head without looking at anything, and I just kept tying my shoes as though they required more concentration than I was capable of giving. Tony Guiterrez was older than us—already heading to high school after the summer, but he was kinda slow in things—had a hard time reading, had almost been held back a couple of times, and he'd lived around the corner for years, rode my bus, but he hung out with us even though me and Bobby and Wayne were just starting the 7th grade.

I finally finished looping rabbit ears and double-knotting, and I looked up at them standing around me in a half-circle, and I said, "no way," and Tony Guiterrez unrolled the top of the bag and tipped it toward me, and in the shadow of the opening I could see the "T" shapes of M-80s, with their wicks sticking out of the sides, and bundles of Black Cats still wrapped in their cellophane, and I said, "What about the M-80s?" and Tony Guiterrez smiled and said, "all you want."

Bobby's bike was on its side in the piss-patched lawn, and we left it there and set off toward the end of the street where the houses trickled off, and instead of turning into the orchard, we climbed a small embankment of hard red dirt and then we were in a field of stubbled weeds and star thistle, and we broke down the stalks as we walked so that the air was full of sharp green and I could feel the spiked flowers bite into my bare ankles, and we cut across toward the edge of the field where the trash was tangled, and then we crossed the double lanes of Live Oak Road that was already so hot we could see the heat lifting off the asphalt in shimmering sheets, and it was empty in both directions, and unusual in its quiet and stillness with most people either at work or the city pool or on their own couches with cartoons and Pringles, trying to avoid the heat of a Tuesday, and school had only been out for two weeks, but it felt like two months, and I was glad to be out and doing something.

We kicked through the weeds on the far side of the road and then we started the descent toward the slough, where the water was slow and green on top, something thick we could smell before we saw it, and we stepped over dirt bike tracks that had been cut into the muddy bank when the rains came, and were now hard as cement in the dry heat, and then the trees closed in, and before too long, we were in cool damp shade, and we kept walking the trails that ran parallel to the water that we still couldn't yet see, and then we pushed our way deeper through the overgrowth and came out in a small clearing where the grass had been tamped down by a hundred pairs of shoes and there was some flattened cardboard to sit on and the tossed remains of Styrofoam ice chests and broken beer bottles and wrinkled cans rusting in the dents, and there had been times when there was the burnt smell of firewood that someone had gathered and tried to light, and one time a busted TV, but it was still early in the summer and nobody had been hanging out much yet.

Wayne found a rotting lawn chair and set it upright and he sat down and pulled a dirty piece of cardboard toward him and asked Tony Guiterrez to give him the paper bag, and Tony Guiterrez handed it over and Wayne unrolled the top and dumped the bag upside down onto the cardboard and Bobby and I watched the bundles pile until the bag was empty.

"Where'd you get it?" Bobby asked, and we all looked toward Tony Guiterrez who despite being slow had a way of getting his hands on things that we weren't supposed to be able to reach.

3

"Redding," Tony Guiterrez said, and we knew he wouldn't tell us more unless the story was good, so we waited, but he didn't say anything, and I remembered that he had a stepbrother or a cousin or somebody who lived up there and had once given Tony Guiterrez a sandwich bag of dirty weed that we had all smoked despite the fact that it looked like a small sack of dead lawn that had been mowed together with twigs and leaves, and even though I couldn't really tell if I felt anything, I kept saying over and over again that I was high, really high, fucking high, and I only had to let them feel me up over my bra in order to get there.

"Can we light some right now?" Bobby asked, and we all looked toward Tony Guiterrez to see what he said. Bobby was my best friend and I had spent a lot of time at his house after school instead of riding the bus home because he lived close to Bidwell and his parents had money and his next door neighbor had a pool that we were allowed to swim in as long as somebody was home. Bobby liked to watch *Mommy Dearest*, and he knew all the words, and one time when I was at his house, we were watching it and he made us sliced up beef stick with a kind of mustard that I had never had before, and I thought for a minute that I could probably fall in love with him.

"Not yet, not yet," Tony Guiterrez said, and he raised his hand like he was a teacher trying to get our attention. "We don't want to make noise."

All around us there was noise—the sound of birds in the trees, calling and answering, and frogs near the water, expressing their anger at the heat, the shift of branches overhead, rubbing leaves against wood, the sound of cars on the freeway in the distance, on the other side of the water.

"I got something good first," Tony Guiterrez said, and he dug into the front pocket of his cutoffs and pulled out a flat bottle, and he held it out toward us so that we could read the red and white label, *Smirnoff.*

"Vodka?" Wayne said. "Hell yes." Wayne would've been in eighth grade, but his dad went to jail a couple years ago and Wayne ended up missing too much school because no one could find his mom, and he had to stay back a year with us to make up for the time. He was shorter than Bobby and Tony Guiterrez, with a lot of shaggy black hair that fell into his eyes, and he used to go around with no shirt on all of the time until Tony Guiterrez started calling him a chicken hawk, like in the Looney Tunes cartoons, and now Wayne always had a shirt on even if it was dirty, but Wayne was the craziest one among us, and there wasn't anything that he was afraid of or wouldn't do if it meant that somebody said he was cool, and once he broke a bunch of car windows and stole what he could grab, and he almost went to juvenile hall, but in the end nobody could prove it, and he had only kept one thing—a braided gold bracelet that he wore on his left wrist.

Wayne took the Smirnoff from Tony Guiterrez and unscrewed the cap, and he tipped the bottle back and took a mouthful, and I could see his throat working and his eyes started to water, but he swallowed hard and handed the bottle to Bobby. "Smooth."

Bobby smelled the opening and then made a face, but Tony Guiterrez shot him a look and Bobby took a small sip and swallowed, and coughed a little bit, and put his hand over his mouth. "Tastes like gas," he said.

"More like ass," Wayne said, and he and Bobby slapped hands and Bobby passed me the bottle and it was warm and I held it up and looked at the liquid inside and I was surprised that it looked thick despite being clear as water, so I lifted the bottle to my mouth and put my tongue over the opening and pretended to drink, but some of it seeped into my mouth and I could taste it—too hot and thick and like some kind of medicine, and I closed my eyes and moved my tongue and opened my throat and poured until Tony Guiterrez yanked it out of my hand and told me not to bogart the bottle. For a second my throat went warm and I could feel the last swallow all the way down until I imagined it landing in my stomach and coating it all over like in the Pepto Bismol commercials.

Tony Guiterrez drank twice and then the bottle went around and around the circle until it was empty and Bobby almost tossed it into the weeds before Wayne grabbed it and set it on the cardboard and said maybe we can blow it up later, like a bomb, and we all agreed, and my head suddenly felt a little lighter, as though it could float away if only my neck weren't like a string.

We sat down on the cardboard and all of us joked about our hot ears and buzz, and in the distance I could hear a semi blow its horn in one long breath and I remembered when there had been an accident there once, and a logging truck had caught on fire, and we had climbed up on my roof to see it all better, and we stayed up there for a long time, watching the flames licking the sky in the dark distance until the fire shrank and went dim, and if I closed my eyes I could still feel the warm shingles under my jeans, the way that they were rough as nail files and sticky underneath, and we watched the fire and the neighborhood, the comings and the goings, and we could see into backyards and windows that I never even knew were there before, and I wished that I could always be on the roof and looking at everything, and maybe we would have stayed up there all night if my mom hadn't told us to come down.

"You change your mind yet?" Tony Guiterrez said, and I knew he was talking to me even though he was watching a line of ants carry a dead moth into the weeds.

"I don't know," I said, and I wished there was more in the bottle or that Tony Guiterrez had that sandwich bag of pot again, or we had something to do that might help widen the distance between my body and my head.

"Last chance," Tony Guiterrez said, and I could feel Bobby beside me, breathing slowly. "You can light all you want," and he pointed toward the small pile that was still in the center of the cardboard as we sat in a loose circle around it.

I wanted to reach out and pick up a brick and feel its weight and count how many firecrackers were on a string, and I wanted to hold an M-80 in my palm and wrap my fingers around it and know that if it were to explode, it would take my arm off to the shoulder, but Tony Guiterrez had already slapped our hands away and told us we could look with our eyes but not with our hands.

"What about if we just practice?" I asked, and I was hoping he might be willing to barter, but he just shook his head slowly, back and forth, and said, "for real," and I pretended to brush some dirt off of my bare knee, and said, "you have to let me have some to keep," and I could hear Bobby and Wayne shifting around on the cardboard, but I didn't look at them, and then Tony Guiterrez took a deep breath and said, "okay."

As soon as the decision was made, the birds went quiet, and I thought I could hear footsteps in the weeds, and I hoped that it meant that more people were coming and maybe we'd get run off by some high schoolers, and maybe they'd threaten us a little bit, and I could see Tony Guiterrez tense up, and he took the paper bag and scooped everything up in quick handfuls and I hoped that it would be mean high schoolers who showed up, the ones in Dio shirts and dirty jeans, and they'd take the bag from Tony Guiterrez, maybe chase him if they had to, and our circle would bust up and we'd all run back across the road until we hit the neighborhood and I'd pretend to be pissed off at the loss and the missed opportunity, but really I would be happy to go home and ignore my sister and eat what was left of the Pringles and watch afternoon TV until my mom came home from work, but in the end, there was nobody coming, and maybe it had only been an animal roaming around in the weeds, and Tony Guiterrez stood up and pulled his T-shirt over his head so that his sunburned chest was exposed, and he told Bobby and Wayne to go keep watch because he was going first.

I wanted Bobby to say something then, maybe stand up for me and say this was all a stupid idea, but he just got up and didn't look at me and he went to the edge of the clearing where a trail cut through toward the road, and he stood there for a second, checking around, kicking at an empty Lay's bag, and then he turned his back on the cardboard and Tony Guiterrez and me, and Wayne pulled a pack of Merits from the pocket of his cutoffs and lit one with a book of paper matches, and I could smell the smoke, and then he walked toward the opposite side of the clearing where the weeds bent in the direction of the water, and he turned his back, too.

"Pull your pants down," Tony Guiterrez said, and I thought about getting up and saying something mean, telling them to fuck off, but there was a lot of summer in front of me and these were my friends, and I had been wanting Black Cats for a long time and I never thought I'd have a real M-80, and my girlfriends from school were all at the pool, lying on sticky towels and comparing swim suits and paddling around without getting their hair wet in the water in front of boys from school, and there was no way I wanted to spend the rest of my free summer days doing that with them, and I wasn't really scared about doing it because someday I would anyways, so I might as well get it over with here and now with someone I knew when it meant I could get something back for it, rather than wait for some other time with some other boy I didn't know when I probably wouldn't get anything back for it at all.

I popped the button on my shorts and pushed them down until they were around my thighs and then I leaned back on the cardboard and pulled my underwear higher, like I did when we were practicing, and I could feel the cardboard move around underneath me, and for a second I could imagine the damp pressed dirt underneath it, and I bet that if we lifted the cardboard, the ground would be full of roly-polys and worms recoiling from the air.

Tony Guiterrez dropped his cutoffs to his ankles, and I had seen him like that before, more than once, in his red or blue or white underwear, and I could already see his penis, and I thought of that word suddenly, *penis*, as though I was reading it in a Judy Blume book like I had last year when I had discovered that word in print, and the word *come*, and I had read them both together over and over again until the pressure between my legs was too much and I had to rub myself against the wood corner of my waterbed until I felt something shiver inside of me and there were flashes of light behind my eyes and everything got tight and then went slack and I had to bite my lip to keep from making any noise even though my breath was trapped in my chest and all I wanted was air, and while I was thinking about how many times I had rubbed against the corner of my bed since that first time, I could feel Tony Guiterrez put his body on top of mine and I could feel him against my thigh, his tight hard knot, and then instead of putting his arms next to me and rubbing himself back and forth, he slid one hand under the elastic of my underwear and I could feel his fingers stumbling around until he got one against me and I sucked in my breath, and he pushed at me with his fingers, rough and blind, and then suddenly his hand was gone and he took mine instead and slid it down his stomach to his own waistband and then forced it underneath, and there was hair, and I

8

wanted to jerk my hand back, but then I was touching him, and I could feel him breathing against my neck even though his face was turned away, and he whispered to me to hold onto it and move my hand up and down, and I did, and he pushed into me, harder, until I could feel all of his weight on top of me, and for a minute I felt strong and full of control, like I could make Tony Guiterrez cry, or close his eyes, or hold his breath just through the power of my hand, and then he reached down and stopped what I was doing and he panted hard for a second, like he had just come in from running laps, and then he was shoving his underwear down with his right hand, and whispering at me to do the same with mine, so I did.

From the corner of my eye I could see Bobby with his back to us, and I thought maybe he would turn his head and look, but he just kept staring toward the distance and the road that he couldn't see, and the smell of Wayne's cigarette had long faded, and above me I could see the tangle of branches and small windows of sunlight as it strained to come through, and I could hear the birds again, all of them it seemed, gathered in the same tree.

Tony Guiterrez shifted his weight back onto his knees and he leaned up a little bit and part of me wanted to look down so that I could see, but instead I watched the sun and branches and breaks of sky in between, and he just guided me with his hand, moving my legs apart wider and then wider still, and I could feel him naked against me, poking and pushing and moving his hips and shifting around again, and I watched the trees above me, watched the leaves move, and beyond the weeds, something splashed in the water, and Tony Guiterrez paused for a second and listened, and then he pushed forward again and dug his shoes into the cardboard, and I closed my eyes, and there was a pinch and sharp pain, and I remembered once when I was walking with my cousin, Billy, out on our grandpa's property, and we were at the pond, heading back to the house, and his mutt dog had scared up a rabbit that had been hiding in the deep grass near the shore, and in the shock of us coming up on it so quickly, the rabbit had flung itself into the water, and when I closed my eyes, I could still hear the splash, and the dog

9

had tried to follow it, but Billy held the dog back and let it whine and bark itself into a frenzy while the rabbit kicked away from the shoreline toward the center and the deep, and I ran toward the water to jump in and save it, but Billy had grabbed me by the arm, hard enough that his fingers bit into the soft skin beneath the muscle, and he held me there while we watched the rabbit swim, and it didn't take long—just a few kicks farther from the shore and then a panic went into its eyes, and it swam in a small circle as its head started to dip below the surface, and I struggled against Billy's too-tight grip, but he was older than me, and bigger, and he was laughing at the rabbit, saying bye bye fucker, and I wanted to break loose and swim, and I wrestled against him again, but not very hard, not as hard as I could have, and maybe I could have broken free if I had really wanted to, but in the end we just stood there on the shore, our shoes sinking into the dark mud, and the rabbit's head dropping below the waterline, coming up once, and I could see its wide eyes searching around for something that we couldn't see, and then the head went under and stayed, the thin brown surface-water like a window until it disappeared into the murk, and Billy took a long time to let go of me.

Around us the cardboard dipped and shifted and rubbed against the ground, and Tony Guiterrez was breathing into my neck, and everything felt slick against me, his skin on my skin where my shirt rode up, and I could smell him, dark and damp like sweaty clothes in a hamper, and I could see the hair in his armpit when he raised up on his elbow and then suddenly he stopped moving and he pushed back and lifted himself off of me and rolled onto his back and pulled his underwear and cutoffs up in one quick tug, and I laid there for a second, naked below the waist, my own underwear and shorts around my ankles, and we were done.

I pulled my clothes back on and sat up, and Bobby and Wayne turned from their posts and walked back toward the cardboard, and Wayne was staring at me and Bobby wouldn't look at me at all.

"You're next, Wayne," Tony Guiterrez said, and Wayne fished another cigarette from his front pocket and lit it with a limp match that took a while to strike.

"I gotta go home," I said. "It's getting late," and I stood up and brushed the loose dirt off of me.

"That wasn't the deal," Tony Guiterrez said. "You're not going home."

"I have to," I said, and Tony Guiterrez moved next to me, and then behind me, and I could feel his hands on my arms, and he was squeezing them.

"You want me to hold her down?" he said, and both hands tightened, and I had never realized how strong he was, and how much older.

"Get off me," I shouted, and above us the birds went quiet, and I turned and walked toward the trail, and for a second I thought that maybe Tony Guiterrez would chase me, or that Bobby might follow me back, but with each step I took I could tell that mine were the only shoes breaking the weeds, and when I finally ascended from the trees and the grass, the sun beat down like a hot fist and pinned me to the dirt, and Live Oak Road was alive with cars, and I had to squint until my eyes adjusted and wait for them to pass before I could cross and walk the rest of the way home, and I let the star thistles chew into my bare legs, and I pretended I didn't feel anything.

My sister was still on the couch when I opened the front door, and I didn't know how long I had been gone, but part of me felt like maybe it had been a year or two, and *He-Man* had given way to *Inspector Gadget*, and Penny and Brain were pulling Gadget out of the fire again, and I didn't say anything to my sister, and the air conditioning swallowed me and I went straight into my room, and for a minute I stood and looked at myself in my mirror on the closet door, and maybe I thought that I might look different somehow, but I just looked the same, and my legs were all scratched up and there was dirt on my shorts, and I took my clothes off, all of them, and looked at myself again, and still there was nothing that I could see except for the blood in my underwear, and I just shoved them into the back of my closet, at the bottom of my pile of dirty clothes, and I knew my mom would never notice, and even if she did, she wouldn't say anything because it was my fault I hung out with so many boys.

When I was done inspecting myself for change, I got dressed in

11

clean clothes, slowly, feeling each piece as it covered another section of my skin, and I thought about going into the bathroom and getting a washcloth and wiping the dirt and the blood from the scratches on my legs, but my feet felt heavy and all I wanted to do was maybe lift the covers on my bed and climb inside and say I was sick, and maybe I was sick, maybe I was coming down with something, and I wondered how quickly getting pregnant happened, and maybe I would be, maybe I already was, and I wasn't afraid of that thought, or maybe I would have to spend the summer in bed, suffering from a mysterious sickness, but then my sister yelled from the living room, "mom said you have to clean the kitchen before she gets home," and I left the darkness of my bedroom and shut my door and I knew that nothing inside would ever look the same to me again.

"Did you tell her I wasn't here?" I asked.

"I'm not a tattle tale," she said, and I wanted to laugh and say, yeah, right, but my voice was too tired to fight her.

I went into the kitchen and started stacking the dirty dishes to the right side of the sink, and then I opened the cupboards to put the clean dishes away, and in the distance I could hear the sound of firecrackers, the quick pop pop pop of a string going off, and I knew they'd find some good things to blow up along the water, the glass Smirnoff bottle, piles of wood, old cans, empty ice chests, the torn couch cushion that had been rotting in the clearing for months. Those were the things that I would pick to blow up, but I was a girl, and I knew that they would find other things to destroy, and that they would want to blow up something different.

I had forty-seven dollars in a jewelry box under my bed, and I could travel easy, sneak out of my house before the sun came up tomorrow, and I could be past Redding while it was still dark outside, while the sun was still tucked on the other side of the world, and I could stick my thumb out and point it north toward someplace new. There was nothing here that I would miss—especially Bobby not looking at me— and there was nobody that would come looking for me for long—my mom worked two jobs, had a boyfriend that lived in Gerber, was only ever home to change clothes and leave again—and I imagined what it would be like to watch the oak trees fly by outside the windows of a semi, watch the mile markers and the billboards and the dead yellow hills roll back and flatten with distance, and I knew that by tomorrow I would be gone, but for now I would stand in the kitchen and listen to the little explosions in the distance, and wait for the big one, and line the glasses up in the cupboard into even straight lines, one after another, just the way they were supposed to be.

Kansas

Emily Chiles

"I cannot understand why you should wish to leave this beautiful
country and go back to the dry, gray place you call Kansas."
"That is because you have no brains," answered the girl.
—L. Frank Baum, *The Wonderful Wizard of Oz*

Dorothy pulls the bedclothes off the children in the cold morning dark.

"I have a secret surprise for you, but you have to promise to be very,
very quiet, and you have to hurry."

Mary begins to cry but Robert shushes her. Dorothy helps them
dress and promises them if they are quick there will be sweets and a train
ride. She has already packed the suitcase she now tugs from under the
bed. Robert pulls on his boots and asks if Papa is coming. Zeke, their
father, is out in the barn with the cows, though his sour-sweet breath
still lingers in the air.

"It's a special place only magical children and their mamas can go,"
Dorothy answers.

Robert grins at his sister—they remember their mother's stories.

"Race me through the fields," she says.

They will make it to the train station before daybreak if they hurry.

Out the back door they go, through the mile of frozen fields that leads
away from the barn where Zeke is hunched in the damp hay, half asleep
against a warm flank, chewing, always chewing, just like the cows. The
children can feel the hard earth under their feet. The corn stalks crackle
as if they might disintegrate. It hasn't rained in weeks.

The station is empty, except for a stooped old man sweeping the
platform, stirring up little dust clouds. Occasionally he stops to puff on
his cigarette and look at the mother—young, but already the lines on her
face—and her small children, who huddle close on the bench. Dorothy
gives the man an unsmiling nod.

The boy coughs. "I'm cold, Mama."

Dorothy takes off her blue Sunday overcoat and drapes it across their laps. Mary rubs her eyes and pulls her hair into her mouth. The sun begins to show in pale streaks above a bank of low clouds that remind Dorothy of weak, twice-wrung tea. Waste not, want not. Try to make the water taste like anything but dust. All she could ever taste was dust, her whole life.

Dorothy looks down the track, her feet resting on the suitcase. She can feel her feet trembling on the hard leather. She thinks of everything she left behind. She hadn't thought to bring a warm blanket. There was the water to haul for the horses, the slop for the pigs. Everything not done would now never be done.

The train can be heard in the distance. Dorothy stands and rights the suitcase. Robert stands too. She tries to hold his hand but he pulls away.

"Where we going?" he asks.

Dorothy takes in the long slope of his nose, the flat cheekbone. Zeke's profile. "We'll see when we get there."

She picks Mary up and lets the girl, who is almost too big to be carried, wrap her sleepy body around her. The train rumbles into view. Mary holds her hands over her ears. Robert counts the cars—one, two, three, four. They start to go by so fast he loses track.

"Will the train stop?"

"It will," Dorothy says. "It's got to."

If it doesn't—she wants to shudder the thought loose, like flapping the dust out of her clothes at the end of every long day in the fields. God's will in that dry, gray earth.

But the train slows, and she lets a breath out. It feels like she's been holding her breath her whole life, since she was young and believed in something. The brakes screech as a passenger car door slows to a stop in front of them and opens. Mary slides out of her mother's arms and takes Robert's hand, and they climb up the little steps, their eyes wide. They've never been on a train before. Dorothy follows with the suitcase. The old man is leaning on the broom, smoking.

The car is empty, so they take up three rows. The children are bouncing, waving to the crows out the window. They name the crows after the characters in their mother's stories. The stories are about good and evil, and what happens to girls when they dream and then grow up. When the train lurches forward, Mary scurries into Dorothy's lap and buries herself in her coat again. Robert looks out at the fields, crusted with frost. They go by slowly at first. Soon he settles in next to her and leans his head on her arm. Dorothy watches for the farm and the barn and then closes her eyes until the train begins to pick up speed. They pass the mill, a silo, a crumbling chimney standing alone, the white clapboard church. Horses running.

"What about Papa? Isn't he coming too?" Mary asks.

Zeke will be back from the barn by now. He will pick up the cold coffee pot, holler for her. Holler again. He will find the empty bed, see the drawers gaping like mouths that must be fed. Feel around under the mattress for the bundle of money. He will strike a fist against the door frame. He'll see the row of shoes gone, including Dorothy's Sunday shoes. Her work boots still standing by the door, caked in mud. He will see the small empty oval over the fireplace where a year ago she had hung the pale photograph of the baby boy they lost and the wisp of straw-colored hair tied in a black ribbon. And her ring on the mantle—perhaps he will pick it up and notice how dull it is now, how bent, how far from a circle.

He will throw her kitchen chair, her basket of mending. He will get in the truck. Turn the key. Turn again. Pound the wheel with the flat of his palm. In the exhaust pipe, he will find the potatoes she had dug up the day before, the bitter smell of half a year's labor spoiled by a late frost. He will curse her, up into the lightening sky.

"Maybe Papa will come look for us," Robert says.

Perhaps days or weeks or months from now, she thinks, Zeke will find them.

They pass through new towns she's never seen, over rivers whose names she doesn't know, so she makes up names for the children. They have never seen a river. The corn fields are replaced by green hills, blue mountains. They blink at the colors. It rains a bit. Mary sleeps now, and even Robert eventually closes his eyes. Dorothy begins to drift too. She dreams of the pigs. The rustling corn. She dreams of the farm where she grew up, miles away from here, of the mute faces watching the sky, of the swirling dust. She dreams of his chewing, the spurts of rusty spit.

They pass factories, smokestacks. Dorothy wakes the children. She opens up the packed lunch of bread and ham and they eat quietly. They are so quiet. They see people waving from their porches in the shacks on the outskirts of the city that go on for miles. The children wave back and bite into their sandwiches. They watch her.

The train enters a tunnel. In the dark she closes her eyes. For a moment, she's back in the root cellar, with Robert and Mary huddled close. She can see the tears streaming, their mouths open, but she can't hear them. The train's howl is the swirling muscle of wind and dust scraping the fields, wrenching trees and houses out of the earth like a fist. The rattle of the train cars on the tracks becomes the clatter of the jars on the cellar shelves, all she could put by for another hard winter. There's the taste of blood and dirt, there's Zeke with the broken broomstick she always used to fish laundry out of the scalding tub. The smell of dust and liquor and lye. The terrible clank of his belt buckle.

She opens her eyes and allows a small idea to grow into a prayer, a spell:

Zeke set fire to the barn.

Set fire to the animals.

Let the smoke mix with dust.

Set fire to our room, to the bed where I bore my babies, where I bled, where my last child died in my arms.

Take that rifle off the rack and sit down in your chair.

Remove your right boot.

Hold my ring in your left hand, rifle in your right.

Finish it.

The conductor calls out, "Next stop, Indianapolis."

Dorothy opens her eyes. The late afternoon sun spills through the window, clear and cold. A different light. She smiles at the children and gathers up their things.

Ritual*

He was short and skinny, shorter than the others, and never wore a shirt when he ran. His thin arms flailed as he kept ahead of us and we all wondered how. He was so fast. But mostly we watched the bouncing scars on his back and thought about how he got them. We called him the Wizard. It was because of his hair, wild black mass with a white shock hanging in the front. That's how I thought of him. The Wizard. I wish I knew what names they had given him but I never asked.

Between us, there was an unspoken rule: everything would remain unspoken.

I started running because I saw the others doing the same. I was the fourth to join up. The kid who came immediately after me—I called him Five because I wasn't imaginative enough to make up a nickname for him—he smiled too much. He was generally second place, after the Wizard. Thicker build and with strong legs, big legs with the hard definition of an athlete. I guess I should have called him Two, but I didn't like his face, didn't like the way he smiled so much.

Ghostly, expressionless, the Wizard commanded my respect. He was small, so small and thin, and had I not run with him—night wind in my ears—I would have thought he was fragile. He looked fragile. Clumsy. Like a bunch of broomsticks tied together with the skin stretched tight over him, dark jeans and brown sneakers. Pale skin with yellow-brown, not tan, but sick. The Wizard was invisible except for the contrast under the harsh lights and the starless skies.

I didn't think much about the other kids. The Wizard stood out, Five bothered me, but the other three were just present. Standing on the edges of things, two of them last after me, and one just between me and Five. I didn't know their names either.

One of them went to my school and looked like an Ethan. I had

---

*   Winner

18

heard the name before on my mother's television shows, gossip shows about celebrities, and his face was smooth, pretty enough to be a star. I gave him a snotty name but he carried himself quietly. He knew this was the Wizard's show, knew he couldn't beat him. He beat me but never smiled about it. Just ran the laps and I felt the wind over his shoulders. I thought for a long time Ethan and the Wizard were friends, the way he waited with the smaller boy for the rest of us to arrive. Always wearing black sweatpants, a tight black shirt, black running shoes. Stylish, black and white. He was definitely an Ethan.

One time he'd worn aftershave, and it was cloying with a hint of blue that clogged my nostrils. I had to breathe through my mouth and the cool air with its taste of asphalt came up in my lungs harsh and burning. The lack of oxygen held me with heavy hands and the wind pulled at me with a thousand fingers. My legs were lumpy, loaves of dough. I thought the heat welling up in me would have baked them hard, cooked the heaviness from them. But it didn't.

That was the only time Ethan wore aftershave, and the only time I came in last.

The other two, well, they fell behind. We all started on an even keel—wouldn't have been fair otherwise—we all started at the same spot and ran the same tracks. By the end of the hour, with thirty or forty laps in us, my feet were so hot that the last two boys should have fallen in the molten steps I left behind. They didn't. They slapped across the parking lot back and forth. With graceless noise, they followed me. I heard the sounds of their breaths and each one a deep suck, taken in through the mouth. Their nostrils were thin and their noses cold by the end of the run, cheeks shining red and full of blood. They looked in decent shape but I was more toned, I guess. If you asked me, I would have said they knew each other, and their camaraderie kept them in the last places. I called them Tom and Jerry, thinking about them in secret whispers as we ran.

It was never about winning. I knew that. But the two of them never even tried. I always made a decent effort, tried to maintain my place in the pack. Just behind Ethan, watching him flow over the black pavement.

A mop of bright blonde hair waved at the top of his head, absurd over the darkness in which he dressed. The backs of his hands were scratched and tough. They moved in glimpses, arcs of flesh, weaving bobbing lights I followed.

Five ahead of us, moving in the long strides of the seasoned. A half-hour into the run he would start lagging. Ethan and I would creep up on him, slight but noticeable as he grew larger. His chest gleaming with sweat or dew, hard muscles stark in motion. After the first run, he'd taken to ditching his shirt by our starting line. His body was massive. His muscles were balloons straining against the smoothness of his skin. Five was unmarked by time or gravity. I focused my attention on the streaking scars of the Wizard far ahead, instead of Five's queasy symmetry. Hypnotic. Feeling the slight gain, Ethan would run faster, pump his legs for thirty feet to recover the lead. I thought when I first saw this, that he wanted to be second.

The third time, it was ritual. Ethan closed within a yard of overcoming, and with a too white smile Five pulled forward. The distance grew until he chased the Wizard's shadow, but try as he might Five did not catch up.

I always thought of Ethan as Two.

Even the first time I ran with them, keeping pace just behind, he was second. The Wizard streaking ahead, turning at the end of a lap and running past us silent swift. His draft blew cool in my face, carrying only the slight salt of sweat. The night air was always cool and in a parking lot took up the smell of ozone. It could scour if you weren't careful. You had to breathe in through your nose, to keep it moist enough, to keep your pace over the run.

The parking lot was long, maybe a football field and a half from one end to the other. It belonged to our local movie theater. They never started a movie later than nine-thirty, and by the stroke of midnight when I walked across the lot, I could easily see Ethan and the small shape of the Wizard standing next to the towering floodlight set dead center in the lot. Anyone who'd seen a movie had long since driven off, headed home or farther downtown, and the empty lot gave us all the space we needed. The pattern was the same. We started at the leading edge of the movie theater from the road, the right-hand side, aligned to the same white stripe. Settling into easy, expectant silence. You heard the sound of a long, drawn breath, and with its whistling exhalation we started.

The first lap was the slowest. We ran alongside each other, conscious of the rules. You did not run faster than anyone else. This lap was not about winning. There was no winning. This lap was keeping pace, was maintaining the slow up and down that everyone could manage. The first time I ran with them, I thought the whole run would be like this. Equal.

But as we hit the halfway mark and turned in a lazy semicircle, the Wizard would change. From the loping jog to a full-on sprint, without drawing a deeper breath. He was so quiet, that first time, I wondered if he was even breathing at all. And when he started running, we all started running. He was just getting us ready, getting the blood flowing, and then all we saw were the bouncing scars and his pale yellow-white back, and the bottoms of his shoes as he kicked.

I can't say how long they'd been running before I showed up. It was a month or two ago that I joined them. I came out of the theater from a late-night showing, started as late as possible I mean, around nine-thirty. The movie lasted two and a half hours. What it was about, I don't remember. More remarkable was crossing the double doors into the night—brighter than the theater had been—and seeing a line, seeing the three of them cutting back and forth across the lot. Their rhythm was fluid, their paces were easy. They ran like I wanted to.

My mom came and picked me up in her old station wagon. I got in the right-hand side and watched. Running to the edge of the pavement and turning back. Running to the sidewalk. My mom asked me a question about the movie but I didn't hear. It was so strange. I wanted to know why. Maybe they were racing, maybe it was a bet. Maybe they were a gang.

Secretly I wanted to run with them. The vinyl seat was cool to the backs of my legs and she asked me again. Seeing my attention elsewhere, she turned and looked into the parking lot. The Wizard shot past in a blur and my mom's eyebrows came down. Her mouth turned at the corner.

She didn't ask me any other questions that night. But the next morning, as I sat eating cold pancakes made soggy with syrup, she looked at me from the sink and said, "So is that what your friends do late at night?"

I must have looked as confused as I felt.

"Some parents will let their children do anything. I've dealt with that before. Staying out all hours. Don't you get any ideas."

With that reminder it was sealed. I pleaded with her to send me to the same movie. Another two and a half hours I could spare in the theater if I saw them again. I wanted to know if it was regular or a one-time chance. The image of three boys running scarcely left my eyes for the remainder of the week. I don't know what made it stick. Why it was I wanted to run. I didn't particularly like running, even. The days of gym class and the warm-up around the basketball court bothered me, and I lagged toward the end of the trailing line of students. There was something in the Wizard's pace, something in the way he moved.

He ran so fast, he could run away from anything.

Never had two and a half hours seemed longer. The theater wasn't bright enough for me to read—my mom hadn't let me bring a book, either, that was too suspicious, but there was a rack of cheap newspapers standing by the ticket counter in the night. On a second viewing it wasn't a total bust. But the excitement came from leaving the lighted screen and walking out the doors into the summertime night. My mom waited for me in the parking lot at the first row. As I came outside she waved, and as she waved the Wizard ran across my line of sight.

The lope. He must have run his entire life. So natural. He flowed from step to step.

When the next Friday rolled around the two of us were watching television on the couch. A police show about a murderous celebrity, guaranteed to hold her interest. I begged off at ten and went upstairs to my room. Our little house in this little subdivision was close enough for me to walk. If I was too tired to run, then I could still watch.

My mom went to bed soon after and when her light went out, I knew it would stay off. I wore a loose shirt, running shoes, soft blue jeans. The night was smoothly cool and walking would not warm me enough to wear shorts, I knew.

Shadowed, the streets around your home are different. Painted in grayscale, everything is exotic and new, everything shares your secrets. The trees whisper to you warnings about parents, being caught. I could have walked in the shadows off the street, but the sidewalk called my name. I spent the mile to the movie theater slipping from bright streetlight circle to streetlight circle. My head was empty. I wanted to conserve energy.

I didn't bring my watch to the theater. I didn't even know if they'd be there. But as I walked the gentle rise of the hill and looked out into the lot, not a hundred feet from me they were there. Ethan and the Wizard, standing at the floodlight, the smaller boy leaning against it with a bare shoulder. I slid down the low landscaped slope and when my shoes struck pavement it was electric. The charge growing like static and buzzing up my knees to rest in my stomach—a new battery. I felt nauseous and strong.

The Wizard kept his faraway stare fixed in the distance, though Ethan dropped to his haunches and gave me a little smile. My nerves settled somewhat. At least one of them was welcoming.

My first impression of the smaller kid, pale and off-white, was not dislike. I didn't think he didn't like me. I didn't think he wanted to run alone. He was just somewhere else, looking in a different parking lot, maybe, or looking for more people. But we waited an eternity in the quiet night until Tom arrived.

As he crossed the far edge of the parking lot there was something in the air I could touch, some clue in the Wizard's posture. Ethan stood and the pair walked to the right-hand side of the lot, leaving me no choice but to follow. Tom glanced at me once or twice as he recovered the distance but gave me no expression. He was blank and unthinking. For whatever reason I didn't like him as much as I felt comfortable with Ethan, his little grin, and the Wizard.

We dropped to runner's stances—as if we had blocks—and then came the starting breath. We moved across the lot in that starting easy jog and I wondered if this would be it. But as my feet touched the last painted line I heard the accelerating steps of the others, and with my heart pounding I willed myself faster. Overtook Tom easily, but the Wizard was always so far in front that I never even hoped. Ethan I could keep pace with, could keep the distance between us fairly regular.

We ran for an hour and by the end of our laps my legs burned. My feet ached. I knew my arches would collapse and with every twitch in my thighs I felt lightning. When the Wizard stopped on that last line, when Ethan slowed as he approached, I didn't feel all so much different. We ran back and forth, we crossed this same space again and again, and now it was over.

But walking back in the deeper streetlights I touched something untouchable. I don't know if I just walked across a long spider's web, or caught some minor breeze. But there was a brush of silk across my body and I was restored. Empty of the unnecessary energy but in the pit of my chest I felt whole.

I came back to the parking lot next week, and found the Wizard and Ethan waiting again. This time Five came, for whatever reason, and Tom brought Jerry. The second night I ran with them it felt like racing. Like some unknown audience watched us from just past the floodlights' edge, from the deepening blue-black of the tree stands and the mulched shadow fields. But the Wizard kept in first, and I kept up with Ethan, and everything was all right.

Every time I ran after that, I noticed something different about the pavement. Some little gulch washed microscopically deeper by the rain, or rolling tires. Some oil slick painting that had changed its loops and whirls. But I did not keep my eyes down for long. Watching Ethan in front of me and the Wizard beyond was more enthralling than erosion.

As I walked to the parking lot, I thought about the nights leading up to this one. Streetlights kept me company although they passed me from one to the next. I stayed in their receiving line lost in my memories. The sky overhead stirred and moved, a deep purple, the stars lost above a carpet of clouds. The air was tight, straining to pull floodwaters down. The forecast was grim. We were supposed to catch the last threads of a hurricane that unraveled over the coast this week.

When I started to climb the gentle hill, I felt a drop of rain. A drop fat and full. It spattered against my head and laid my hair down. But the first drop was just the first, and in a breath the night opened up and let out all its water. It poured in thick slashes and gathered on the lot faster than it could run out. An asphalt ocean that rolled with every new raindrop, if only for a millisecond.

The clouds threw lightning around. I stood on the slope above the parking lot and the others were waiting, huddled at the floodlight. I made my way down to them. As my foot struck its first step against black asphalt, blue-white struck down hard into the horizon and lit up the world. Halfblind I made out their silhouettes walking toward me and knew despite the weather we would run. Blinking the last of the lights out of my eyes I counted them again.

There were only four, all of them taller than the Wizard. I crossed the distance quickly and with each step my shoes squelched. Water squeezed out of the soles and soaked my socks. The rain obscured but I searched Ethan's face for some clue. It was still and inexplicable. Even Five's glance was faraway. Tom and Jerry looked vacant, but that was no different. Unease slid around my throat.

We waited a long time, in the crashing thunder and the deepening rain. The last gasp of hurricane scattered storm above us. The floodlight flickered against the weaving drops that came down in long lines, stretched out glasses and bottles of water. The angels poured their drinks onto our parking lot as the five of us waited for the Wizard.

I don't know how long we stood there. We were all soaked to the bone. Tom and Jerry fidgeted by themselves. Ethan squatted and Five was his gleaming statue counterpart. Their faces betrayed their thoughts, and I knew mine did too.

He came from behind the movie theater, walking slowly, his left arm held against his side. The rain had plastered his white shock against his forehead, and tangled as it was in the black mop it was hard to find. Glasses spotted with rain. His shirt was a nondescript blue, though the collar was ragged on the right side.

We watched him walk slowly to us. With a wince and a low breath he took the shirt off and laid it on the floodlight's base. Never once did he meet our eyes. The Wizard just turned and walked to the starting line, our glances magnetized to his back. Above the mass of scars we had already mapped, there was a new line, purple and smeared with the brown of clotted blood. A long, rectangular bruise and then a bright blue splash that must have been the belt buckle. Ovals on his arms traced the rough figure of fingertips. From his posture, his shoulder might have been strained.

None of us said a word.

We followed. We took our places at the starting blocks and dropped into our stances. The white line painted at our feet wavered in the shimmering waters. A slow inhalation broke quivering from the Wizard. His teeth held his lower lip and his elbow shook. He shifted his weight to his right hand and the quivering dropped to the inaudible. We let our breaths out, stood, and started the first lap.

The Wizard couldn't manage the jog. I made my feet heavy, my steps clumsy and slow. He was faster than I was. It shouldn't have been a problem. But the heavy slashed scar must have weighed a thousand pounds. Our lap was the slowest it had ever been, and the Wizard breathed hard. His mouth stained the clean draws with a gasp, a trembling in his throat.

It was raining, so I couldn't see him cry.

We crossed the lot slowly and I dreaded reaching the other side. The last line and the sidewalk stood solid, though I wanted it to sink into the dark distance. I threw my will at it. I prayed. With my hands swinging, uselessly clenched at my sides, I wished the lap would never end.

The sidewalk was stubborn and the last line more so, shining an ivory reflection in the rainwater that sliced over it. The storm drain sucked down the rising lake with the noise of loud conversation. My feet hit the last line and I turned slowly, waiting to hear the splashes that signaled the beginning. The splashes that would leave the Wizard behind.

There was nothing.

I looked to the side and saw the Wizard leaned over, holding his sides, his left arm limp. He gasped and choked and the violence of his sobs unnerved me. Eyes squeezed tight. The rain washed away his tears but the thunder was not loud enough to disguise the sobbing.

Lightning stabbed down quickly and the thunder broke in the horizon. Five moved first.

I watched his brown body, so visibly muscled, so much better built than the Wizard. I had watched him taunt Ethan with the promise of second place, seen him run hard with eyes to the Wizard's scarred back and cutting steps. I had never liked him or his smiling face.

I saw him break the line we had formed, standing on the solid stripe on the pavement, the rain coming down and splashing off his broad chest. He was shirtless as well, his skin unmarked. With an unsteady hand he pulled the Wizard's limp left arm across his shoulder and turned.

They stepped in time ahead of us, one foot after another, the Wizard leaning his weight on the bigger boy. There was no hint of a smile on Five's face, no smug look now. Only eyes that might shatter. I watched them move toward the far side. Ethan moved silently, his feet casting waves in the puddling water, and he took up the Wizard's right arm.

The three of them stepped in time, slowly, easily. The grayish puckers, long strikes, the blue and bleeding bruise stood out starker when I had a basis for comparison. The boys became minutely smaller and I followed, stepping slowly, staying behind them. Tom and Jerry did the same after a moment.

I came up to Five's side and measured my steps, left and right, left slow right. He looked at me once and I nodded. The six of us made a straight line and we walked the same laps we always had, the rain around us and the thunder deafening.

I can't remember how long we walked. How long Ethan and Five kept the smaller boy's weight. How long Five's arm held across the Wizard's waist to take the strain from his shoulder. The bruise trickled a few lines of crimson but mostly scowled from the yellow-white flesh alongside. I can't remember how many laps we made. But the rain never stopped, and the lightning came down in forks and spears to drown out his brittle sobs.

We made our last lap and approached the starting line. With a foot separating us from equality Five and Ethan stopped. Tom and Jerry looked empty toward me but my eyes were on Five, and his set toward the Wizard. Ethan stood drenched in black and let the smaller boy's arm slip from around him. Five gently lowered the arm he held and with a slight pressure moved him forward.

The battered Wizard took a sinking step and crossed the finish line first. He broke into a long high wail and fell to his knees. Ethan's face was fierce and Five kept his straight ahead, jaw set. I saw it shake but I didn't do anything.

We stood there for an eon. The rain never slackened.

I went running for six more Friday nights, a month and a half, after the cataclysmic rain. Our town got the brunt of it, with downed power lines and branches scattered over the streets. The first Friday after the hurricane I came late. Cresting the hill I avoided looking at the others, but when my feet hit the pavement, I knew he was there. His presence was heavy. Lifting his shirt overhead we glanced at the foundations of new scars. Last week's belt was fading, and laid over it were crisscrossing tracks. Maybe from fingernails.

Ethan and Five carried him without complaint, and we jogged a slow first lap before walking. The Wizard soaked up his pain with a few sighs but no tears. He fell across the finishing line and stayed on his knees as we scattered.

I walked home, unease balled in my gut. I was glad he hadn't cried.

Every weekend was the same as those before. I left my room late, and each of my steps was longer than the last. It was easier. I found excuses in every streetlight but they didn't have the cure for the nerves that boiled in my stomach.

The Wizard was there. His stare faraway. He peeled his shirt off and it cracked with dried blood. His back was a maze of welts, long raised rectangles of blue and red above the fading yellow of last week's work. I didn't know who put those there but I guessed it was his dad. The rules stayed the same. I didn't ask.

Neither did Five or Ethan. They carried him that night more stiffly, their arms harder and pace more unforgiving. We jogged and I felt my breath quicken in my chest, felt my heart surge. The adrenaline was welcome and I walked step for step next to Five, his big body shifting under the floodlights. Blood dripped from the Wizard's arm across his shoulders and in the cool night air it steamed, a little.

The first lap put fire in me, and burned me carelessly. Lost in the sounds of my footsteps and the shining asphalt below my feet. Running I had never gotten to know it, as it blurred underneath me. I knew its general shape but now all the little details came out easy. I watched as my running shoes sank at the heel with every press, and how the canvas tops wrinkled as I stepped with my toes.

I stepped again across the white line and started to make my easy turn.

Looking at the others I realized what I had done. Five and Ethan held the Wizard at the finish line, the small boy's head down, hair matted. His hand on Five's shoulder was bruised and blue, the knuckles swollen. Tom and Jerry looked at me blankly. Ethan's face I avoided. I knew what I had done. The lot was quiet except for the crackle and buzz of the floodlights.

I had crossed the finish line first. We stood there taut and frozen. I looked between my shoes at the glittering asphalt.

A floodlight burst apart in a sharp snap and a flurry of sparks. My heart jumped in my chest and I turned from them and ran. I ran up the slope and onto the sidewalk without slowing. The wind whistled in my ears and I ran hard. I had to get home. Streetlight after streetlight passed and I crossed roads and through stoplights. My feet ached. My lungs burned. I wheezed breath after breath and I ran harder. I didn't stop running until I got to my backyard and I opened the door quietly as I could, blood thumping through my body and banging in my legs.

In bed I stared at the ceiling until my body calmed down, and then I slept.

Tonight I crested the hill with a weak heart and a sinking stomach. I looked out over the rise and saw the five boys waiting at the floodlight. Keeping my head down, I stumbled along the slope and over the pavement until I crossed the Wizard's shadow, held upright by Five's steady arm. None of them looked at me, except the Wizard. Blood trickled from the corner of his mouth. "What took you so long?" he said.

Running Toward Away

Richard Jay Goldstein

You can easily imagine a tranquil summer afternoon, in the Mission Hills neighborhood of San Diego, in 1959.

He is twelve.

He finds a thing under some bushes in the little pocket park a few blocks from his house.

What he finds is a thin metal pole—a rod really, cylindrical, the diameter of a curtain rod. It is made of light springy steel, pointed at one end, flat on the other, perhaps three feet long. He only stands four-foot-ten himself, so the rod seems a good, strong length. It has been painted white, but the paint is peeling and powdery, and there are many rust spots.

The steel feels alive in his hands as he hefts it. He has no idea what it was originally intended to do or be, but he can easily imagine it is a weapon—probably magical, if he had to guess. He thrusts with it, like a sword. Shadowy enemies fall, pierced through. He throws it, like a spear. It traces an inscribed arc in the air and lands point down in the grass, thrumming.

He carries his prize home, taking his secret short-cut—over someone's lawn, between tall hedges, down someone else's side yard, and across his own quiet street. His new magic weapon is loose and ready in his hand, like an enchanted sword should be. His feet fox-walk lightly, his heart a warrior's heart.

And now he makes a serious tactical error.

He brings the rod into the house and props it proudly in the corner of his room. He flops down onto his bed, pleased with himself and with the world. He picks up a comic book. His mother comes in.

"James, *what* is *that?*" she asks, pointing. She only calls him *James* when she is displeased.

"I found it," he answers obliquely.

"Well, get rid of it," she says. "It's dangerous. And filthy."

Under his mother's keen gaze he takes the steel rod out behind the garage, to where the trash cans live. He places it gently amid the rubbish. It will be taken away in the morning by a garbage truck. His cheeks burn red with something like *dishonor*—more than disgrace, less than shame. The universe dished up a magic weapon, but it seems he was not worthy of it.

He trudges dispiritedly back into the house.

"Fine," says his mother. "Now go and wash your hands, and then set the table."

As he is carrying dishes and silverware into the dining room—with clean hands—he considers the possibility of sneaking outside after dark, reclaiming the steel rod, hiding it somewhere. But, no, that would be totally undignified, unworthy of a warrior, and might only lead to pointless confrontation. This is too deep for that, has already moved beyond the rod itself. Something has changed, shifted, tipped.

He conceives a better plan.

He will run away.

Meanwhile he imagines flipping the plates and silverware across the table with a careless hand, and having them land exactly right, perfect place-settings.

The alarm slices through his tumbled dreams, muffled by his pillow. He reaches under the pillow, switches off the alarm on the little wind-up clock he has hidden there. He rises into the two AM chill, his room made strange by the unfamiliar hour. He can hear his father snoring in his parents' room down the hall.

He doffs his pajamas and pulls on the clothes he laid out at bedtime— jeans, tee shirt, high-tops. He hefts his school back-pack, which he has filled with run-away essentials—rain jacket, flashlight, his yard-work savings of $42, a bag of cookies filched from the pantry, Swiss Army knife, compass, a pair of socks and a change of underwear. And his worn copy of *The Three Musketeers*. He considers adding the little clock, then decides against it. He has his Timex wristwatch—*indestructible*, according to John Cameron Swayze. *Takes a lickin' and keeps on tickin'* just like a warrior.

There is no cellphone included in his gear—because, of course, those did not exist in 1959.

He does add his little plastic flute—the kind called a *Tonette*. In the movie playing in his mind, vagabonds—such as he means to be—often play a lonesome and plaintive harmonica. But he does not have a harmonica and wouldn't know how to play it if he did. He can, however, play *Three Blind Mice* and *Mary Had A Little Lamb* on the Tonette, and he figures he has plenty of time to learn sad and lonesome vagabond songs as he goes.

He tiptoes down the hall to the kitchen, where he leaves on the table a note he prepared the night before.

I am running away. I will write. I love you. Sincerely, Me

He steps to the back door, opens it silently. There comes a sharp moment then, as he thinks of his parents' sorrow and regret when they find him gone and read the note. The house whispers to him in a sweet voice of familiarity. The warm dark kitchen, the good old cluttered back porch—he wonders if he will ever see these things again.

But he swings his pack up onto his shoulders bravely, steps through the doorway, closes the door with a soft click. He thinks briefly of retrieving the steel rod he found, but no, it would just encumber him. And besides, it is not really a magic weapon, only some discarded junk. What it did was to prod him into putting aside the poignant things of boyhood. But it was high time for that anyway and did not require any magic.

He slides through the shadows of the back yard, and out to the street—*his* street, but which he happens to know leads to other streets, and to boulevards and highways, and to distant cities, like New York and Chicago, and to foreign lands, like England and Spain. He knows all this because he has read a lot of books.

His street, like his room, is transformed. It has become a different street—empty, pools of yellow light under the streetlamps, the houses turned to ominous black shapes. He imagines people dreaming inside the houses, then waking fitfully, not realizing a heroic vagabond is passing by, bent on his mysterious way.

He has a vague plan of heading downtown, where the Greyhound station is, and buying a cheap ticket to *somewhere else*. LA maybe—that would be a good start. He's been to LA, to Hollywood, and to Knott's Berry Farm—when it really was a berry farm.

Downtown drapes around San Diego's busy bay, like a bright *serape* below the hills of Mission Hills and Hillcrest and Loma Portal. So he steers generally downhill, past the little park where he found the steel rod, and into strange new neighborhoods.

A pair of headlights glimmers in the next block, winking toward him. A moment of fear prickles his skin. Could it be his parents? He crouches in the lee of a hedge in a yard, peering through the branches. The car passes by slowly. It is a police cruiser. He can see the faces of two bored-looking officers in the front seat, lit by the dashboard lights. They do not seem to be looking for runaway fugitives. Anyway, it's way too soon for his parents to have missed him. Still, he's never hidden from the police before—*the cops*, as vagabonds say. Is he an *outlaw* now, as well as a vagabond? And so what if he is?

When the cruiser has taken its lights around a corner he stands, shoulders his pack, and strides on.

He crosses a wide boulevard—usually a cascade of rushing cars, but now empty and silent—and enters a neighborhood he does not know at all, especially at night. The houses are bigger and grander than in his neighborhood. The trees are taller.

Ahead of him a lit window gleams, like a beacon, a rising sun amid the dark hulks of the houses.

As he approaches the house with the lit window his steps slow. His high-top sneakers are soundless on the sidewalk. The house is an imitation California Spanish Colonial *hacienda*—gated archways, two stories, a red tile roof. The lit window is on the upper floor, protected by a tiny wrought iron balcony. The window is beveled glass, multi—paned like an insect eye. At the top is a half-round transom. The light streaming through is rosy and golden. A gauzy curtain hangs in soft folds.

He comes to a complete stop, stands mesmerized—uncertain, uncertain why he is uncertain, drawn dumb as a moth.

A figure in silhouette appears behind the gauze curtain, pulls the curtain aside. It is a young woman—young, but older than he is. She is perhaps eighteen, though of course he has no way to judge this. She is wearing a sheer white silky nightgown, which shines like water in the room's golden light. She steps forward and opens the window casement to the cool dark night in which he stands. The light behind her flows through her gown and illumines her body. He sees the curves of her, the swell of her breasts, mysterious shadows. Her long hair moves in a small breeze, hair black as starless sea.

The young woman stands staring out at the night, leaning on the sill of the window. From below, hidden, he watches her face, and thinks he sees an expression of *pensive sorrow.* These are emotions unfamiliar to him, and he certainly would not use those words. But he does know she is the most beautiful thing he has ever beheld, and that she is sad. Suddenly he understands, with a capacity of his understanding he has never before used, that this sojourn of his is longer and farther and richer and deeper, already, than he ever dared imagine. That what he feels is reverence, and this is prophetic vision, though he would not use those words either.

Before he quite realizes what he is doing, or the nature of the offering he means to make—or even that it *is* an offering—he has quietly shrugged out of his backpack and pulled it open. The Tonette is in his hands and he puts it to his lips. As wistful and plaintive and lonesome as he can, he plays *Mary Had A Little Lamb.*

The young woman starts, quickly pulls the window shut with a bang, jerks the curtain closed. A moment later the sweet golden light switches off and the Spanish house stands as dark and unknown as its neighbors.

But Jimmy finishes the melody, to the last lonely note.

If That Isn't a Sign from God, then I Don't Know What Is

Philen Bradford

I'm from the red clay of the North Carolina Piedmont. From the loins of my Mama. It don't matter where I'm from, because it's for sure I can't go back, so I'm always thinking, here we go.

Now I'm in Vegas, driving a limo I rented from a Chinese dude named Chu out in Henderson. And one night, this one guy down at the Venetian that I know calls me and says he has a guest I might want to pick up. It was almost midnight.

I say: "What do you mean 'might want to pick up.'"

"Bill Joe," he says. His voice is raspy, and he puts you in the mind of one of them Italian mobsters from the movies. "Take it or leave it. We're all just trying to make a way out here, you know?" The world is full of interesting characters.

When I pull up to the lobby driveway, he nods to me and then gestures to a woman standing along the curb. I figured she wasn't a day over thirty and everything she wore was tight and red. Her hair's thick and dark and little freckles danced on her olive skin. I get out all business-like and open the trunk. There's her red leather duffel bag on the hotel luggage cart. It's heavy, but not too bulky, not like what most women carry. I put it in the trunk and walk over to get the door for this woman, and as she steps toward the car, she reaches her arm and then her hand behind my neck, like to pull my head down like she wants to hug me, and sure enough, she does and then she plants a kiss on my cheek and says, "I've been waiting for you." It's more like a wet kiss and a whisper, and I think, here we go.

I nod to Little Miss Red and say, "Well, I'm here now." When I open the door, she slides into Chu's limo like she owns the thing and then she kicks off her high heels. The wind is whipping at me like it's God Himself telling me to mind.

Once I get into the driver's seat, I call her through the back-seat speaker. "Ma'am," I say, "where to?"

She sighs and waits, and I start to repeat myself, but then she says, "Darryl, no games tonight. Let's go home."

Here's a question: what's heavier, Divine Intervention or Sin?

I think I know the answer, so I push the Speak button on the control board, clear my throat, and say, "Ma'am, I think you have the wrong," but before I can finish she goes, "Darryl," and I'll never forget how she called me like that, like I was the surest thing in the world.

I power the cabin window down and look at her in the rearview mirror. She's so cute and pretty, I think, watching her reapply her lipstick, and I hadn't thought of a woman like that, in that way, in a long time, and she goes, "we made a lot tonight."

I hadn't done nothing wrong yet. I don't say anything.

She goes, "I need a bath, a foot rub, and a brandy. Let's go home, Darryl."

Chu's limo has one of those fancy Sirius radios so I put it on the Jon Bon Jovi channel and turn that sucker up. I bet Little Miss Red was a 90s Rock type of gal, and anyway, who can't get into a song like "Living on a Prayer" going twenty miles an hour on the Vegas strip where all the neon makes the world feel like cotton candy. I didn't right know where *home* was—or who this Darryl was—but that didn't stop me from driving. I was in it then, or decided I was jumping in it.

I get almost to Circus Circus and Little Miss Red must have gotten antsy because she says, "Darryl, where are you going now?"

I say, "Sugar," not hesitating one bit, "the night's young. I thought you might've wanted to go one more round at the Riviera or the Sahara."

"Not tonight, Love. I'm tired, and we won't make it to L.A. until morning.

"L.A.?" I say, although I didn't want to say it like that. I retrace my tone. "I mean, you sure you want to go all the way to Los Angeles tonight?" I look at her then through the rearview mirror.

She gives me a look. "Home. Darryl," she says. "Home."

If you could talk to God and actually hear Him talk back like you could hear His voice and you knew it was His for sure, what would you ask Him? That's a question I think on when I'm juggling like I was with Little Miss Red.

I pull into a gas station and park. "You want a coffee or a Coke or something for the road," I say. She nods no and then I fiddle in the glove box and pull out the GPS. "Honey," I say, turning around to her through the cabin window, "you think you can plug in our address on this thing while I get some snacks. Remember how I got us next to lost last time."

At this point, I thought I had messed the whole thing up, but what else was I going to do? What do you think, God? What else was I going to do? She stares at me hard, like she's testing me, but then she finally sighs like those she-she-foo-foo reality bitches on television do when what they mean to say is *I'm worth more than a hundred yous*. She leans toward me, takes the GPS, and says, "Darryl. Hurry, Love."

If that isn't a sign from God, then I don't know what is. I hurry quick as all get-out, and inside the ARCO station I buy her two bottles of the Evian water (the expensive type), a few Organic granola bars and a thing of Greek yoghurt which I thought she might like, and a Red Bull, a pack of Beef Jerky, and a pack of Twizzlers for me. When I get back to the limo, I open the door, and she's sleeping. Out cold. I get the black fleece blanket from the trunk that this real old rich lady left in the cab recently and draped it over Little Miss Red. I almost kissed her on the forehead in that soft way I'd kissed all the lovers I'd had in my life, but didn't. She did type the address into the GPS: 5690 Wilshire Drive, Beverly Hills, California.

When I reach the gate to the driveway, it's 4 a.m. and still dark. There's a code lock, and for a minute or two I mash buttons like I know the dang code. I get out, open Little Miss Red's door, and ease my hand back and forth on her forearm until she starts stirring.

"What is it," she says, waking up. I wonder if I'm still Darryl.

"It's the gate," I say, "I can't get the code to—"

"It's your birthday, Darryl," she says and sighs. "Remember?" She gives me a look then.

"Right." Well, I'm thinking, damn, now what?

I close her door gently and take out a cigarette. What I'm about to tell you makes no more sense than the man who hammers a nail up his nose. After I smoke half of my smoke, I go ahead and mash in my birthday 0-4-0-1 in the code box and the dang gate opens. Dag on, I think. I try not to act too surprised, thinking she might be looking at me through the limo window. I play it cool, like always, smoke the rest of my smoke, and get back in the driver's seat.

I'd never been to Beverly Hills before, and, well, the houses are about as big and uppity as I expected. 5690 Wilshire has a circular driveway with a fountain statue of a little angel standing tippy toe, spitting water from her mouth. When I pull around to the front of the house the motion light comes on and lights the home, which is more modest than uppity. It has two stories and is painted some fancy hipster color name for light brown, something like Flirty Mocha or Burnt Tortilla.

Little Miss Red steps out of the limo barefoot like she'd been in a long dream. "Darryl," she says, "don't forget the bag."

After I get her heels from the limo floor and her duffel bag from the trunk, I turn for the house, and she takes my free hand in hers. Our fingers intertwine like it's something familiar.

The front door's not locked. I let her lead me into the house and I drop the duffel bag at the foyer. She hands me her purse then and motions for her heels so I hand them to her. "Make us drinks," she says. "I'm going for a bath." She walks up the stairs then, one hand on the staircase bannister, the other holding her red heels.

I'm just a Bill Joe. That's all what I'm thinking, watching her move up the stairs smooth-like, like a fierce Cat Woman. What would you do with a name like Bill Joe? She turns her head once at the top of the stairs to look down at me. She smiles. I stole 83 bases my junior year on the Varsity baseball team and that record still holds at our dinky high school ball field. William Joseph Ackley. Now, I'm just Bill Joe. I look up at Little Miss Red until she's out of sight and then I take her red purse and walk through the living room and on to the kitchen until I find the bar.

I pour myself a quick shot of Johnnie Walker. I don't particularly care for Johnnie Walker, but it's Blue Label Johnnie Walker so why wouldn't I? I open the purse and it has all the typical Little Miss Red paraphernalia, like lipsticks and a little mirror and mints and a make-up kit. There's nothing else worth looking at except her wallet. Little Miss Red is: Stacia Evie Worth. Eyes: Brown; Hair: Black; Height: 5'8"; Age: 30. She's not a donor.

I'm exhausted and don't know my next move, but then I hear her yelling down to me from the upstairs so I rush to the foyer to hear her better.

"Stacia?" I say, taking a chance. "Honey?"

There's a pause and then she says, "I said, bring some chocolate."

"Oh," is all I come up with.

"Water's warm. I'm just waiting for you."

Next thing I know I'm upstairs rubbing Stacia's feet. She's *ooh*-ing and *aah*-ing and saying how her heels had been too tight. I'd be lying if I said I didn't look at Little Miss Red's bare body between the soapy suds. You could dream a long dream about all the splashing and skin slapping that tub water was making on a girl like Stacia. All her innocent self there, fragile and naked in that tub. Why couldn't I have just jumped in there with her? Wouldn't you, God? Wouldn't you? I didn't know just how sad it all was. We clink glasses and sip brandy, all the while I'm sitting on a stool there next to her by the tub. She looked so comfortable and I had a million-and-one questions that I couldn't yet just ask.

In between sipping and eating chocolates, she says, "Tell me a love story, Darryl, about us."

I decide to tell her a true story. I tell her about the time she almost sliced off her thumb cutting onions one evening in the kitchen.

She looks at her thumb then. "I did that?"

"Yeah, Honey, don't you remember?"

She looks again at her thumb and then at me.

"Honey," I say, with a convincing tone, like I'm trying to convince her, make her as sure as she called me like *Darryl* back in the limo in Vegas that this really happened. I'm awful. "It was my birthday. You were

40

making your famous meatloaf. I was watching television downstairs and then you were yelling bloody murder from the kitchen."

"I did that?"

"Yeah, you did," I say. "I tried to take you to the hospital, but you said you didn't want to ruin my big day. Remember?"

"I," she says, and I think she's bothered and confused, but really she's just putting that memory to life in that sick noggin of hers because she goes, "oh yeah, I mean, I guess I did. I mean, you're sure, right?" Her skin is glistening wet and innocent in the tub water, and it's all beautiful and smells like pink and lilac and like your first time in bed with a woman. I'm awful and I think God has something to do with it. What makes a man make up something like that for a sweet girl like Stacia?

"Well," I say, "maybe you don't remember it like I do. I tried to take you to the hospital again and again and you finally told me to get the superglue from the garage."

She starts to smile then, like she remembered the whole dang thing.

"I went and got the superglue, and, well, you know the rest."

She looks at her finger again. "I didn't even cry, did I, Darryl?"

"Not one tear."

"Kiss me, Darryl," she says, and she's got that certainty in her voice again, like I'm her man.

I lean over the tub and soap bubbles wet my chin. She leans forward and we kiss and it's all mushy in her mouth and our tongues start to peck love pokes and jabs back and forth. After a while, Stacia pulls back and says, "Darryl."

"Yeah, Baby Doll," I say.

"It'll always be like this, won't it?"

"Yeah, it is," I say, pouring a look over her. I'm like a bear sitting in a pool of honey.

She smiles. "Let's go lie down now."

She starts to stand then. The water's sprinkling and dripping everywhere. She's got the body of a goddess. I can't help myself but to look and then the strangest thing comes out of my mouth. It's like God was punching me in my throat. I say, "You want some eggs?"

41

She's not throwing her body at me, not that any woman ever has like that or ever will, that's just all fantasy isn't it, God, but she's looking at me and her look is doing a few different things: one is asking for something to dry off with, another is wondering why I'm asking about eggs, and then another is wondering why I'm still in my dress pants, shirt, and blazer after we've been home already and she's been all relaxed in the tub and whatnot.

I hand her the bath robe that's hanging on the door. There are two there.

"Carry me to bed, Darryl."

I can hear my Mama telling me I'm no good as I try to swallow whatever God is trying to make me say.

"Come on, Stacia, you're not hungry?"

"Carry me, Darryl, like on our wedding night."

"I mean I can make a mean scrambled egg."

"Take me, Darryl. I'm ready for bed now."

I reckon I deserve a sick woman. All the hurt and worry I've put on everybody all my life.

"Let's lay together, Darryl. Please."

She's looking so pretty, and, dang, the way she said *please* like that. I take off my blazer finally and hang it where her robe was. The Man With No Past Making Scrambled Eggs for The Insane-in-the-Membrane Crazy Lady. Together at last. "Giddy up," I say and I hold out my arms like to carry her. The water in the tub is talking as she starts to step up and then I lift her into my arms. All her wet innocence smeared on me like that, like it's another type of Baptism. I can tell her stories for ages. I'll just leave out all the heartbreak and she won't know no difference.

I carry her to the bedroom and notice the floors are hardwood, but everything else in the room is white. White walls, white bedside tables and white clothing drawers, even the California King is draped by a white-curtain canopy. I wonder if this'll be my deathbed one day.

"Darryl," she says, as I lay her down.

"Yes, Baby Doll."

"Meatloaf," she says. "Can we make meatloaf tomorrow?"

"Of course, Stacia," I say, and just like that, she's sleeping again. I tuck her in bed, make sure she's snug and warm enough. After that, I know what I have to do.

In high school I had a girlfriend who everybody thought was crazy. Her name was Darlene. I thought she was just unique. Someone interesting. More interesting than the rest of the world. She hated school worse than I did. She barely graduated. After lunch, she'd pick up the empty trays and trash students left on the cafeteria tables. Every day. I'd try to stop her, but she'd say, "you can tell a lot about people by the messes they make." Just strange stuff like that she'd say all the time. When I told Coach Taylor I was going to marry her as soon as we were both eighteen, he looked at me and said, "you know she's on the spectrum." I didn't know what that meant. He said, "she's as crazy as you are quick at running the bases." On a bet at a party the night of graduation I smoked 83 cigarettes because I was crazy about doing stupid shit. You can't help who you love or who you are, and that's the truest truth I know in the world. You can't help who you love or who you are. Let's just say it never worked out with me and Darlene but that's only because of how she died.

I go downstairs and finally open the duffel bag. It's full of cash, pills, and casino chips. Fifty thousand in cash or more, I figure. The pills are Vicodin, Sertraline, Risperidone, Donepezil, Memantine, and Zyprexa. I know the last one because my granny had dementia before she died, and that's the saddest death in the world to watch.

Daylight is probably another hour or so away. There are too many unknowns. What if the neighbors come around? Or relatives? Shit, I'm not even for sure if this Darryl might be on a jet plane or in a car coming back to 5690 Wilshire at any moment.

I take to the leather sofa in the living room because I need some shut-eye myself to think on things. I don't know why some memories stay with a person and some don't. Another lover I had had a broccoli-shaped

43

birthmark on her inner thigh that I liked to nibble at and suck on, but I can't—for the life of me—recall what she really looked like. Wasn't she the redhead? What's weird is I remember everybody's phone number I dial. Why can't I trade that memory for the good stuff I've done in my life?

I fade away to sleep for a bit and dream of lightning bugs floating up to heaven. When I wake I have a stale taste in my mouth. The sun's beginning to shine through the big bay windows. It's quiet. That eerie quiet that's some sort of calm before the storm. I decide to call Mama.

After it rings for a while, she picks up.

"Mama," I say.

There's a pause that's like a wave getting ready to break.

"That you, Bill Joe?"

"Mama."

"You in trouble again?"

"No," I say quick. "How you doing, Mama?" I get up off the sofa and start to walk around the house.

"I'm fine. Just fine."

"Well, that's good, Mama." I make it to the foyer and then start down the long hallway that stretches to the back of the house.

"Where in the world are you anyway, Bill Joe?"

Framed photographs of a younger Stacia line the wall.

"Oh," I say, "I've been driving a limo in Vegas."

Mama exhales hard in the phone. There's Stacia in between her Mom and Dad at graduation. Stacia wears a navy-blue gown, her smile charms the hell out of the camera.

"How's Tommy and June Bug?" I say.

"I've been worried about you," Mama says. "It's been a long time."

In another photo, a toddling Stacia sits on top of a yellow Labrador, like she's wanting to ride him. Her hair is lighter then and her skin is sun kissed.

"I know, I know, I know. Don't worry on me, Mama. How's Tommy and June Bug?"

"They're fine, Bill Joe. Everybody's fine. Everybody." She exhales again, but it's a little softer. She wants a cigarette and so do I. I can hear

Mama flipping through either a calendar or a notepad like she always does when she's sitting at the kitchen table on the phone. Like how I always remember her doing. In front of me is a picture of Stacia—probably nine or ten—holding a handful of blue ribbons at a swim meet. She's got buck teeth that look normal.

"*That's* not today, is it?" Mama finally says.

I know what she's talking about. In another photo, Stacia is in a sequin green dress, hugging onto a boy with the worst acne I've ever seen. He's in a tuxedo too, in one of those cummerbunds.

"No, Mama, that's not today," I say.

She keeps flipping through whatever she's flipping through.

"Mama."

"What, Bill Joe?"

"Mama, can I come home?"

She stops flipping. I can hear her so good, it's like she's there in Beverly Hills at 5690 Wilshire Drive looking at me. Like I could reach out and touch her hand. I smile and think about driving back across the country in a limo I'm renting from a Chinese named Chu. Tommy and June Bug would laugh at how I'd tell it all. I could take a little bit of Little Miss Red's cash and send it on a money order to Henderson and just buy the dang thing. Dag on. I could set up something. A limo service to and from the State Fair. Or to a ball game or even to Kings Dominion and back. Everybody wants to ride in a limo at least once.

Mama says then, "I don't think that's a good idea, Bill Joe."

I hear Mama breathing like she means it. I start to say something, but don't.

I should have taken a picture of me and Stacia last night by the tub. With her in my arms like we were married. Or, even better, like we were just in love with nothing else in the world. One of those selfie pics.

"Well," I finally say, and then after a few beats, I hang up on Mama.

I do take some of the cash, but that's all. I could have taken all of it, the pills and chips and whatnot. I could have done a lot of things, if you think about it, and what do you think about that, God? When a man does what's not expected, and considering what the woulda, shoulda, coulda is, it's way better. Is that still sin or divine intervention? I can't tell, because I don't hear God like that. I just feel him when he grabs my throat.

I'm The Man With No Past. Even my own Mama doesn't want me to come home. I write Stacia a note and leave it on top of her red duffel bag in the foyer. *You can't help who you are. Forget me not. Love, Darryl*

Here we go.

Sugar

Misty Skaggs

On a hilltop faraway, in another time, I had a pony. Papaw tethered her to one of the tall, thin maple trees situated in the dead center of the bright, green acre of clover we called the front yard. And I stood, hypnotized at the picture window, pressing the chubby, pink flesh of my cheeks against the warm plexiglass. For hours, I watched her lope lazily in wide, steady circles stopping to snap up mouths full of sweet, tender grass. Her long pink tongue tickled me and when she'd stomp her feet and throw up dust, I'd stomp mine, too. Mommy said I was too young for a pony, and at four years old, I was. But she was a gift horse, an unplanned present from the absent father to his bastard daughter. The only thing he'd ever brought me before was a Cabbage Patch Kid without her adoption papers and half of a Reese's peanut butter cup.

My young busty, bumpkin of a mother couldn't quite bring herself to refuse when Frankie brought his beat-up, pickup down our long driveway with a sparkle in those blue eyes of his, eyes wide and clear like mine. She had a big heart and he had a palomino pony prancing around the bed of his truck, tethered to a toolbox. The loose ends of a big, pink bow tied in a knot around its neck got trampled and tangled in the shit around its feet. A shock of shiny mane fell across her forehead and the chocolate brown splashes of color in her tan coat caught the springtime sunshine. And I called her Sugar.

"Now, sweetie, sugar..." Frankie began when he stepped down out of the dusty, black Ford.

His snakeskin boots crunched gravel as he strode toward the two of us with purpose, grinning to reveal a row of small, white, perfectly fake teeth. The stiff collar of his plaid, Western shirt was open wide across his chest and a thin, gold crucifix glinted through the bramble of hair there. Absentmindedly reaching up, with a thick thumb and index finger, he smoothed down his full mustache. It was like a blonde Burt Reynolds had swept down all the way from Hollywood, into the hills and out to the Ridge, especially to visit us. We were both blushing.

Mommy was harder than her curves would lead you to believe. She put her hands on her generous, soft hips and shot him one of her squint-eyed, scathing looks. The kind of look that makes you feel guilty and you're not even sure why.

"I know what you're thinking, sweetheart," he continued. "But you worry too much! I broke that pony myself, just for my baby girl!"

I seem to remember the pitch of his voice being a little high. But somehow still thick and rich and dripping honey. I definitely remember he was a smooth operator. Confidently sliding one arm around my itty-bitty body and the other around my mother's waist, he lifted me up to run my baby fingers over Sugar's coat. I buried the other little girl hand in the golden curls at the nape of his neck. When he smiled, we wanted to trust him.

The Whiskey Monkey

Maureen O'Brien

Last night I took a pair of dull scissors, chopped off all my hair, then flushed it down the toilet. I thought it would keep the men from staring but with my long neck exposed throughout the breakfast rush at the Bagel Bin, I only felt more naked in front of the strangers folding pennies and dimes into my palm.

Now I'm drinking here at Gools again, the dive bar down near the lumber supply store that sells chicken feed. Every night someone tumbles ass-first off the broken deck into the icy crust of the harbor. I'm waiting, waiting to disappear into the thickening secondhand smoke, here for their Rolling Rocks, three for $1.

"Buy you a drink?"

I recognize him as one of my customers, and I know who his friend is, the town fool. When men buy, I get top shelf. "Boodles."

"You a student?"

"Nope."

"Where you from?"

"A galaxy far, far away." He doesn't find this clever, because it really isn't.

"I'm Bobby. I've lived here all my life," he replies somberly.

"I can vouch for that," the Whiskey Monkey adds.

I gulp my gin. "So, can you clear something up for me? Cayuga Lake is a Finger Lake, right? And the story is that Great Spirit lay down his hands and the lakes are the imprints of his fingers."

They wait to see my point.

"But there's *eleven* Finger Lakes."

They wait.

I ask, "Is God deformed?"

"Whoa," the Whiskey Monkey exclaims. "She's even more cynical than we are."

"We grew up in Trumansburg," Bobby says.

The Whiskey Monkey snickers. "His approach is *limp* dick. At least with me, chicks know right away I intend on porking them."

"Are you always such a pig?" I ask.

"I am." The Whiskey Monkey lifts his glass, slurps his ice cubes then slams air-guitar power chords on a pool cue.

"He gets that all the time." Bobby appears to be about twenty-seven or so, but could be thirty, or even thirty-five. His eyelids are junkie-pink and he slouches, a graceful twist, a juniper tree.

"Diamonds and Rust" quivers out of the jukebox. He peers inside me the way Joan Baez looked into Bob Dylan to write the lyrics:

Where are you calling from? A booth in the Midwest.

"What's this from?" He taps my forehead like picking stale crumbs off a table with your fingertip.

"Get the hell out of my face!" I slap his hand and rush off, bursting into the December night. I head down Cayuga Street to downtown. All the stores are dark, only the XXX adult bookstore is lit and I glow in its sallow light. Then I skid across ice in the Woolworth's parking lot, scanning to make sure no torso suddenly runs toward me.

I live in a dump called "The Home."

"THE HOME"

is actually chiseled in concrete above the front door. At the turn of the century, it had stashed unwed mothers. My room overlooks the crossroads of Route 96 and Route 89, the curve of lights called The Swan. I'm dizzy with rage and gin. It's been a year since the surgeon peered into my file and said, "That last scar will become less visible with the passage of time. It will subside." Subside. Like a wave going from high to low tide.

A few weeks later on the Commons, little girls with parkas unzipped chase pigeons in the January thaw. The sun is like warm water poured on my eyelids when I close them, savoring my fifteen-minute work break. When I open my eyes, Bobby is aiming for me in a gait like an egret.

"I'm sorry for that night," he begins. "I never want to scare you."

I keep my focus on the butter-stained tips of my shoes.

"So Happy 1983?" He asks uncertainly.

I stand up. "Happy New Year? More like should auld acquaintance be forgot."

"You know, you—"

"What? Say it."

He accuses, "You think you're the only one who's ever been shit on?"

We hold one another's gaze but this time there's no folk singers, only girls shrieking to the rhythm of pigeon wings.

I scoff. "A junkie's going to offer me that insight?"

The girls toss crusts, legs swinging in red tights. I remember that. Being a girl. Extra material around my ankles, all bunched.

A gorge zigzags through this town, with Cascadilla River freezing in white humps one minute, frothing and gliding smoothly the next. Bobby tugs at his mustache and coughs nervously.

"So what do you do?" I take a swig of beer.

He's sitting on the rock staircase, his long bird-legs bent up. With beige hair and chicken-broth eyes, Bobby blends in like camouflage. "I'm a—landscaper."

"Let me guess. The Whiskey Monkey is also a 'landscaper.' You scrounge around for odd jobs when the rent is due."

"Actually I only work when the rent is overdue." He scratches off the label of his beer bottle with his thumbnail. "So maybe you could tell me how you ended up here?"

I'm embarrassed to say. I shrug. "That bumper sticker."

ITHACA IS GORGES

"Here I am," I sweep my arms.

He tosses a handful of dry leaves into the water. "You're a runaway, aren't you."

"It's none of your business." The leaves take on water and sink, stems spinning. "Anyhow I'm nineteen. Too old to count as a runaway."

"I want to ask you something. Don't get pissed. Do your people know where you are?"

"My people?"

"Your folks. Your family. Do they know you're okay?"

I shrug.

"You don't call them?"

"No."

"A postcard?"

"No."

He picks at the bark of a twig until it's scraped bare. "You just fucking up and left. Jesus. Your family must be worried sick." He puts his hand up. "I'm not going to pry."

"Really. Could have fooled me." I pull a joint out of my sock and cup my hands for him to light it.

"Phoebes," Bobby grunts, holding in a good long hit.

"What?"

He exhales. "Phoebes. That's the kind of bird. Hear that? It sounds like they're saying fee-bee, fee-bee."

"A song of only two notes?" I blow out smoke. Further down, another phoebe responds. They whistle an eager duet, two notes becoming four. Mixed with the burble of the river, it's very beautiful. How I long to be like them. To have wings and carry no memories.

There are clocks and watches, ways of telling time. Noon, afternoon, dinnertime, but mostly there are the long hours past last call. Bobby and I crouch on my fire escape, trace the twinkling lights of the Swan.

"Do you see the neck or the wing?" Bobby asks.

"Both."

"I see a beak, up there." He places a candy heart in my palm. The red foil smolders in the dark. "Happy Valentine's Day."

"Thank you."

"I could touch you," he says.

I down half my beer, dribbling on my mittens. "I can't. I was robbed."

But that's strange. I don't mean to say, "robbed." I just can't get my lips to say the right word out loud.

"I figured it was something like that. You know I fought in 'Nam, right?"

"Whiskey says you both came back—misshapen."

"We 'came back' different, all right. For lots of reasons. One of them being I got busted for possession of opium and sent to prison. I was robbed. Not exactly robbed." He goes quiet as our breath rises as soft white light.

I press my mitten to my scar. "You know what the worst part was?" I choke on the words. "My mother came to the hospital and she said, 'You're lucky he didn't kill you.' And then when the cuts and bruises faded she's like, 'You're lucky he didn't get you pregnant.'"

I tip my empty Rolling Rock bottle so the wind blows into it and makes a lonely sound. "You want to come on in?"

"Really?" He's eager.

"We lie down. That's all." We climb in through my window, unlace our boots and kick them off.

"I'm going to sleep with all my clothes on, even my jacket," he announces.

"You're a gentleman. I don't care what the Whiskey Monkey says about you," I tease.

Bobby wraps his arms around me with sleeves the scent of canvas tent. He takes a deep breath, lets it go. "I just remembered something I haven't thought about in a long, long time. A buddy of mine, we slept like this once, but up to our chins in mud. He kept watch while I held onto him like I was a baby. He's on that new wall. The one they just opened."

Then he's silent.

"Bobby?"

As if he's safe now, with me, inside.

It's been a damp spring but the honeysuckle has pinkened early. Besides being a counter girl, I now have a part-time job working for Hello Notes Singing Telegrams.

I auditioned on the deck of Gools for the owner, Rick. When I belted out a Patsy Cline song people actually thought it was an old 45 that had been slipped into the jukebox. On the lines "I've been so wrong, for so long" I received a round of applause from the snobs across the inlet at that prim restaurant with curlicue French words on the outdoor umbrellas.

Rick drives me to hoity-toity restaurants. Sometimes he sings harmony, but usually I disturb everyone's meals by myself. At first I performed in a pressed white button-down shirt and a black engineer's cap. Now I make more money, especially with the Cornell grads, if I deliver the telegram in a costume. I'm glad my face is covered with a mask. I sometimes dress as a chicken. The head is made of foam rubber covered with white feathers. Other times I am Kermit the Frog, and occasionally, a gorilla. I hate the leather gorilla headpiece! It weighs a ton, it's airless, and my voice cannot project through the mouth hole. I made decent money this whole month of May. The father of the graduates throws back his head laughing at me, then slips me a fresh twenty-dollar bill.

Tonight Rick is dropping me off for a birthday telegram at a new restaurant, "Yankee Doodles."

"Just ask the hostess for the Manzoni party. She knows you're coming," he instructs. I step out of his Toyota into rain. "Don't forget," he calls after me, "Really pour on the charm, you know, rub up against the guy, they love it when you ma—" I slam the door on his pep talk. He flashes me a thumbs up sign.

I am ashamed to say I am actually dressed as Miss Piggy, wearing a shoulder-length blonde wig and pig mask with eyeholes way too small. I wrap my feather boa around me and enter the Yankee Doodle doorway. As I wait by the cash register, my breath condenses into water and drips inside the plastic nostril holes.

My palms dampen my opera gloves. No hostess comes. I won't get paid if I don't deliver this telegram. Should I look for a dark-haired Italian family? I swish over to a table and blurt, "Is this the Manzoni party?"

Three preppies in the next booth laugh. "No, Piggy."

I traipse to another booth, tripping on my velvet hem.

"Is this the Manzoni party?" I ask frantically. A child giggles, "Mommy, what is that?" pointing a French fry at me.

Suddenly all chatter in the restaurant ceases. Families and couples stare. Through my eyeholes all I see is a pair of cold eyes. It's one of the preppies, peering in. "Hey! Who's in there?" he demands. "Is there a real pig underneath too?"

Faceless men are laughing. I grope along the salad bar, rush under the Exit sign, and crash into Rick's arms, where he's been lurking under an awning. "What the heck are you doing? Did you deliver that telegram?"

"Fuck off!"

"I have connections," Rick threatens. "You'll never work in this town again!"

Suddenly the pop and sputter of a Harley Davidson motorcycle explodes past me, tires squealing, and it crashes, sliding horizontally across the asphalt. Orange sparks sizzle. The driver is wedged under the rear axle of a car, and then he slithers out, stands up reeking of gasoline. I pluck off my wig, grab the snout of my mask to tear it off, and realize it's Whiskey, teetering. The back of his scalp is pushed down around his neck like a sock slipped down around an ankle. "Is that you?" we both ask each other at the same time. He reaches to the back of his head and I try to warn him. "No!" But he touches himself, his palm so dark with blood it looks like shiny black satin.

"Tylox is good shit," Whiskey mutters as Bobby and I tiptoe the next day into his hospital room. The drapes are drawn because any light is too bright for him. Even in the dimness, the whites of Whiskey's eyes glow garnet red.

"Brain swelling," the nurse offers, reading the shocked expression on our faces. There's only one chair so I sit on Bobby's lap. The nurse checks Whiskey's blood pressure.

"I'm flying high in my taxi," he sings a line from the Harry Chapin song.

The nurse grins. "You're pretty chipper for a man who just got 57 stitches in his head."

"Gettin' stoned ..."

She writes on her clipboard. "He's beat up pretty good. Dr. Morgenstern anticipates a long, long recovery. Your friend is—this isn't the medical term—but he's scrambled."

"Bobby, baby, I'm all fucked up," he laments. "Remember after your Ma left you?"

Bobby tenses. "Of course."

Whiskey continues. "Remember when you got suspended for calling the shop teacher a dildo?"

We all laugh at how random that is, but when the nurse leaves, Whiskey asks him again, "Where's your mom?"

Bobby shrugs. "You know."

Whiskey says to me, "He looks just like his old woman. Except she had freckles." He turns his blood-eye gaze to me, "Who do you look like?"

"Hey. Enough." Bobby warns.

But I want to answer him. I think for a moment. Big green eyes, pretty "M" shapes on our upper lips. "My sister."

"See, she's fine, Glumpkin."

Bobby laughs. "Oh please, no."

Whiskey addresses me. "His nickname was 'Glumpkin' 'cause his front teeth were too big for his head." He keeps talking, dreamily. "Summer days we'd cool off by dancing around in the sprinkler pretending to be Indians. Remember Glumpkin? The water spraying up in the shape of a harp and we'd pretend to be angels?" His fingers flicker in the air as he mimes plucking a harp then drops his arms in a painful groan. "Before our voices changed I could shriek higher than any girl. They called us pansies and fairies. But we were just little goofballs. Just goofballs."

The nurse returns, takes his pulse and adjusts the tape of his IV, and visiting hours are over.

"I'm in love with you, Miss Piggy," he confesses.

56

I reach out and very gently cup his face on the darkest part of his five o'clock shadow. I call him by his real name. "Bye, Carmelo."

And he bursts into tears.

"I can't stand seeing him like that." Bobby drives back to town from the hospital.

Now I want to throw back some fast Kamikaze shots.

We spin around the Swan.

"I want to go to the Wall. You in?"

"When?"

"How about now?"

I nod. "Let's fly south."

"You know why he hates himself so much? Because he lied to a buddy in Phuoc Lon that everything was going to be all right. What the hell was Whiskey supposed to say as the sergeant lay bleeding out and died rambling about his daughter named Peanut? Whiskey got a medal for that. He swallowed it."

I think about this. "What happened to it?"

"He shit it out and flushed it away."

"Are you sure? I think it might still be inside him."

At this, we laugh as we drive for hours. The rain spatters in circles on the windshield as we enter Maryland. Bobby stops for gas, buys a tin of sardines. By five a.m. we're both singing full throttle to a duet I've pulled in on Southern radio. Bobby is George Jones. I'm Tammy Wynette.

At first sight, the Vietnam Veterans Memorial Wall is a horizontal black line sprouting the vertical trunks of flowering trees. But up close, the line enters your heart and lances it. Bobby and I are mixed in with all the children on field trips. The rain is rinsing and rinsing the Wall as teachers direct red umbrellas. I wonder if any of these kids have the same names that I'm touching. Jimmy, Wendell, Jesse, Luther, Lynn, Billy.

John.

Jack.

Jerome.

Thunder suddenly cracks above us and lightning splits the sky apart. The teachers try not to show their panic and the children rush, holding hands in pairs, back onto their busses.

Bobby flips open the lid of the sardines, "I have to find Panel 42 E." He doesn't have to say who that is. I know it's the man Whiskey once held. As he marches deeper into the deluge his sweatshirt and jeans become soaked, turning dark, then shiny. The pale bouquets left behind are blowing apart and I chase the rolling carnations. I run, and just as I leap up and become a spray of Baby's Breath, Bobby steps into the wall, vanishes into the granite, completely disappears.

Vivian Delmar

Louise Marburg

For twelve years, Eleanor had been telling people her parents were dead, but the chance of that being true anytime soon was slim. Her mother had given birth to Eleanor at twenty-one; her father had been twenty-three. Now, at fifty-six and fifty-eight, they traveled around the country in a derelict RV, stopping in random towns whenever they needed money and taking what temporary work they could find. They had been living this way since Eleanor's junior year of college. Her roommate at the time referred to them, too often, as "recreational hobos." Eleanor had killed them off in a crash the summer after graduation and arrived in New York City an orphan.

Their number was identified on her cellphone by the name Vivian Delmar, which was their first names combined, and Eleanor wouldn't pick up their calls unless she was alone. "What," she'd say in an unencouraging tone. They didn't call on any particular day or time, and sometimes not for long stretches, so she always jumped a little when "Vivian Delmar" lit up the screen.

They called one evening when she was at a restaurant with a guy named Nick who she'd been set up with by a mutual friend. The restaurant was a fashionable spot, and the crowd at the bar was deep. She looked at her phone, set it to vibrate, and dropped it back into her purse.

"It's just someone boring," she said as she dug into her pasta. It was past eight and she was ravenous. She was always eating or thinking about eating; it was a miracle she wasn't fat.

"Boring how?" Nick asked.

The question surprised her. "Oh, I don't know." She thought about an acquaintance who really was boring. "She just had a baby and can't talk about anything else. Don't you hate that?"

Nick raised an eyebrow. He had fabulous eyebrows, dark and full, and his eyes were truly green, not blue-green or brown-green; she would almost say they were emerald. He was handsomer than she was pretty by far, which she hoped he wouldn't realize. "Don't you like children?" he said.

"I adore children," she said. "I mean talking constantly about *any* subject is a bore." Mostly what she felt about children was that she needed to give birth to one soon because she would be forty in only five years. Every guy she went out with was a possible mate; she wasn't fooling around anymore. She imagined a dark-haired, green-eyed child, the product of Nick's dominant genes. Her hair was blond by way of the bottle, mouse-colored in its natural state. Though her eyes were identified as blue on her driver's license, they were as gray as an overcast sky.

She felt her phone vibrate where her bag touched her hip. She excused herself, went to the bathroom, and locked herself in a stall. Vivian Delmar had called three times since the day before. She sat on the toilet and listened to the voicemail.

"Eleanor sweetie?" Vivian's voice sang with eagerness. "Call us, okay? It's important." Eleanor had arrived at the opinion that Vivian was a twit when she agreed with Delmar that becoming a vagabond would be fun. She'd been a stay-at-home mom all of Eleanor's childhood, family-centric and involved in the community. "I know Dad's making you do this," Eleanor had said as plans were made and possessions sold. "Maybe *I'm* making *him* do it," Vivian had replied.

"What's the matter?" she said when Vivian answered.

"Nothing's the matter," Vivian said. "We have exciting news."

"Yeah? What?" Eleanor said. She examined her fingernails, which had been manicured that day, and was irked by a minute bare spot in the pink polish near the cuticle of her thumb. The last "exciting news" her parents had imparted was that they had traded in their RV for a slightly less run-down model.

"We're coming to New York!" Vivian said.

"You can't do that," Eleanor said in a rigidly calm voice. "RVs aren't allowed in the city." This wasn't true, but she thought it should have been.

"The RV isn't going to be a problem. Wait, your father wants to talk to you."

"Eleanor? We're going to leave the RV in New Jersey and take the bus into the city."

"Where would you stay?" Eleanor said. "Hotels are expensive, you know."

There was a silence before Delmar said, "Well, I figured we'd stay with you."

A toilet flushed and a pair of heels clacked across the tiles. Eleanor heard water running, then the *rip* of a paper towel. Occasionally she talked to her parents using Facetime, but it had been a decade since she'd seen them in person. Early on, she had made an effort to visit them, sneaking away to wherever they'd landed and staying uncomfortably on the narrow couch in their RV. Then one year she decided to use her vacation days to go where she pleased and had such a good time that she never visited them again.

"I'm at dinner, Dad. I can't talk about this right now."

She hung up without saying goodbye. She flushed the toilet as if she had used it and washed her hands at a row of sinks beneath a long mirror. Dampening a paper towel with cold water, she pressed it to her burning cheeks. She thought of herself as a generous host: she had a pullout couch where her out-of-town friends often stayed.

"No fucking way," she said to her reflection. "Not in a million years."

She sat at her desk in the art gallery where she worked, eating an orange to keep from falling asleep, and wondering how long she and Nick would have to be together before she could rightfully call him her boyfriend. Like her, he was thirty-five, but that was still young for a man. He might be playing the field. Beyond the gallery's front window, pedestrians walked past in the late afternoon sun. Vivian Delmar lit up her phone for the second time that day.

"Go *away*," she said to the phone as she tapped "decline." She should have turned it off but didn't want to in case Nick called. They had plans to go to a play that night at a small theater in the Village. Dinner before or dinner after? she wondered. She could never decide which was better.

"Why are you telling your phone to go away?" a tall, gray-haired gentleman said. Eleanor looked up. She hadn't seen him walk in.

"May I help you?" She stood and smoothed the wrinkles from the lap of her skirt. She gestured toward the signage on the wall that read, Henrik Pitzer: Reimagining Dimensions, and said "Have you seen our latest exhibit?"

"Yes, I bought that painting over there at the opening," he said, pointing to a large canvas that was smeared and splatted with various shades of yellow. "I was coming in to see it again. But now I'm much more interested in why you're talking to your phone." He smiled charmingly, a seventy-something imp. His eyes twinkled beneath the drooping flesh of his eyelids; he wore a dark jacket and tie despite the heat of the day.

"It's not that interesting. Just my parents." She shrugged. "They won't stop calling me."

"And you won't answer," he said.

"It's not important," she said. "Why don't we go look at your painting?" She led him over to the wall where the canvas hung. "It's the best one, in my opinion. My favorite, really."

"I'm sure you say that to every buyer."

"I don't." She did. They stood a while in silence, looking at the painting until Eleanor's eyes throbbed. "They want to come visit me," she said.

"Your parents," he said. She nodded. "And you don't want them to."

"It's hard to explain why, but everybody I know thinks they're dead."

"Because that's what you've claimed?" he said.

She wrung her hands. "Yes. Is that really awful?"

"Pretty bad," he said. "I'm going to assume they're embarrassing in some way."

"You have no idea," she said.

He smiled. "Tell me."

"They live in an RV—I mean, that's their *home*—and take menial jobs to get by. They used to be perfectly normal. My dad was an accountant. My mom was president of the PTA. But now they're trailer trash."

"And here you are, their elegant daughter," he said. "Living in Manhattan and working at a chic art gallery."

He was mocking her. She stepped away. "Obviously you think I'm ridiculous for being ashamed of them, but I knew them when they wouldn't have considered living this way."

"Life is long," he said. "If I showed you a film of your future, you'd be surprised by the choices you'd see yourself making."

"What does my future have to do with my parents?" She was impatient to be rid of him now.

"Very likely nothing," he said. He tipped an invisible hat to her, then walked out of the gallery and into the street, where he disappeared into the teeming rush hour crowd.

Missy, Eleanor's boss, came over. "Who was that?"

"The guy who bought this painting," Eleanor said.

"This painting? It hasn't been sold," Missy said.

"You're kidding. Then why would he come in here and say that?"

"People do all sorts of strange things for no reason," Missy said in a world-weary voice. She was in her late fifties and had worked in art sales all her life.

"He was amusing himself at my expense," Eleanor said angrily, thinking of her parents, who had never explained their wanderlust other than to say they were "having the time of our lives." What about the time when they were raising her? What kind of time had that been?

Her phone rang. It was Vivian Delmar again. This time she blocked the number.

By Eleanor's reckoning, the theater held no more than twenty-five seats. The stage was tiny, a rectangular black box, and the only prop on it was an upright piano. Arriving late, she and Nick crabbed across a crowded row. An enormously fat man entered stage left, with an old-fashioned cassette recorder hanging from his neck by a cord. A woman wearing a tuxedo entered stage right, and primly sat down at the piano. Just as the man pressed a button on the recorder, she began to play a quiet melody. It was hard for Eleanor to understand what was coming from the recorder. Words, but not sentences; a background clatter; the keening of some sort of animal. The man lifted his arms and slowly twirled to the music. The woman changed to a honky-tonk sort of tune, banging her hands unnecessarily hard on the keys. The man stopped twirling and, opening his mouth wide, made a whale-like sound that was even louder than the piano.

"Why on earth did you choose this play?" Eleanor whispered irritably to Nick. It was hotter in the theater than it was outdoors. "It's so weird."

He turned in his seat and looked at her. She could barely make out his features in the dark. "I chose it because I wanted to see it. You're kind of uptight, you know that? A little weird now and then might do you some good."

Eleanor sat back as if punched. She had no idea he was so haughty. "I'm not uptight," she whispered. "Today I told a stranger the deepest secret of my life."

"Telling a stranger your deepest secret is easy," Nick said. "Try telling a friend."

"Well, aren't you the judgmental one."

The guy behind them leaned forward and said, "Pardon me for interrupting, but would you shut up?"

"You're the one who passed judgment on this play less than two minutes in." He turned and faced the stage. She had ceased to exist.

The fat man was talking about memory, comparing it to smoke. "Whoosh!" he said and clapped his big hands.

Eleanor closed her eyes. A tear of sweat trickled down her spine. Abruptly, she stood up and inched across the aisle—"excuse me ... pardon me ... sorry ..."—and went out to the theater's dank-smelling lobby. She waited a minute to see if Nick would follow before banging out the glass doors to the street. She stopped and stood, momentarily disoriented, and looked up at the sun's final blue glow in the sky. The hot little theater and all that had occurred inside it seemed like a dream from which she had just woken.

She walked the few blocks to the subway entrance. When the train came, it was so packed that the doors opened to a wall of passengers. She squeezed in and held onto a pole. Near Times Square the train slowed for a minute, then came to a full stop. The lights in the car dimmed; the air conditioning shuddered and sighed. The conductor's voice came over the loudspeaker and said something unintelligible.

"Sounds like he said 'time minds the nutty rack,'" said a woman standing next to her.

"I heard 'don't throw the deal,'" Eleanor said. There was no indication they were going to move soon, or ever. As the heat in the car began to rise, she realized she was very hungry. She had decided on dinner after the theater because the performance wasn't meant to be long. You didn't tell me Nick is an asshole, she imagined saying to their mutual friend. What would he say about her? Uptight, judgmental, a bitch.

"Do you have anything to eat?" she said to the woman.

"Excuse me?" the woman said. "You want me to give you something to eat?"

"I'm starving," Eleanor said.

"Begging is against the law," the woman said, she flipped her long, beaded braids over her shoulder with toss of her head. She was so tall that Eleanor had to look up at her. "Not only that, you look like you can afford your own food."

"I'm not begging," Eleanor said. "I have low blood sugar. I was just wondering if you had anything like a bag of chips."

"A *bag* of *chips?*" the woman said. "Do I look like someone who carries junk food around?"

"No, of course not," Eleanor said. "I can't believe I asked. Forgive me. It's just been, you know, a really strange day."

"Yeah, okay," the woman said. "I can relate to strange."

"I've been told I could use some weird."

The woman laughed. "Have some of mine. I got enough weird in my life for the both of us."

The lights flickered bright, and the air conditioner heaved back to life. Finally, the train moved. Through the windows, Eleanor watched the stations fly by, familiar and yet startling. She felt untethered and a little scared for herself, much as she had all those years ago when her parents drove away for what turned out to be forever. She took out her phone and unblocked their number. She half expected it to ring.

"This is my stop," she told the woman as the trained pulled into her station. "I'm sorry about before."

"Oh wait now," the woman said. She dug into her purse, pulled out a small bag of potato chips, and handed the bag to Eleanor.

"What? No," Eleanor said. She tried to return the bag.

"Pay it forward, honey," the woman said in a jolly voice. The car doors closed and the train growled out of the station. Eleanor looked at the bag: Salt and Vinegar flavor.

Her building was in the middle of the block midway between two streetlights; she was always nervous approaching it after dark, careful to look behind her. She stopped several yards away: there were a couple of vagrants blocking her door. Get away from there, she almost cried out, but stopped herself when she saw who they were.

They sat on the stoop with two suitcases at their feet. Vivian was thinner, Delmar smaller. He looked, she thought, like a troll. Both had gone completely gray, which she'd known but hadn't thought about. They wore tee shirts and shorts, and flip-flops, like a million other people at that time of year, but the clothes looked like cast-offs they might have cadged from Goodwill, one tee shirt advertising an adventure park and the other emblazoned with the word "whatever."

"What are you doing here?" she said. "I didn't say you could come." She stood before them with her arms spread, as if to block them from escaping her question. She thought of her neighbors stepping past them on their way into the building. She hoped no one had asked them who they were. But of course people had asked, or tried to shoo them away. "How long have you been sitting here?"

"Since midday," Delmar said. "We figured you'd come home eventually."

"I wish I'd known."

"If you'd known, you would have told us to get back on the next bus," Delmar said.

"I would have," Eleanor said. "Why are you here if you know I don't want you?"

"The RV is on its last legs. Basically, it's dead," Vivian said. "And we haven't seen you in nine years, Eleanor. You look so different, so … urbane."

Eleanor sat down between them and put her face in her hands. "Shit," she said.

"Don't cry," Vivian said. "We can go to a motel."

"That's not it," Eleanor said. She turned to her father. "You left me and you shouldn't have." She looked at Vivian. "I missed you, you know that, Mom? Did you miss me?"

"Sweetie, yes," Vivian said, and stroked Eleanor's hair.

"Then why did you go?" Eleanor said.

"Oh, that is a long conversation," Vivian said. "Days, weeks, of talk."

"I told everyone you were dead," Eleanor said.

"Not far from it at this point," Delmar said.

"What do you mean, are you sick?"

"He's joking, sweetie," Vivian said. "He just means we're worn out."

Eleanor sighed. She felt worn out, too. She leaned into her mother and breathed deeply. She smelled the same as she always had, like sugar and laundry soap. She took her father's hand, freckled now, and ropey with veins, not the hand she used to know. It made her sad that they looked so old when they weren't even sixty yet.

"I don't forgive you," she said. She reached into her purse and found the bag of chips, offered the bag to her parents before eating the chips herself. A cab drove by, then a bicycle messenger. The street was unusually quiet. "There were times I needed you. Just because your kid is grown doesn't mean you can disappear."

"We didn't disappear," Vivian said. "You could always call us."

"What good is calling you when you're two thousand miles away?" Eleanor said. "I needed you in person."

"Maybe we needed you, too," Delmar said in voice clotted with emotion.

"Obviously you didn't," Eleanor said. "I'm not feeling sorry for you."

"We need you now," Vivian said. "But if that's not okay, we understand."

"I have to think about it," Eleanor said. She wanted to punish them. She stood up and walked into the pool of light cast by the streetlamp. There were no cars coming, no pedestrians, only Vivian and Delmar and herself. She ate the last of the chips and crushed the bag in her fist. She was still hungry for something, she didn't know what.

Nothing to Light Our Way*

Emily Hoover

My sweaty thighs stick to the vinyl school bus seat like the hardened chewing gum underneath my desk at school. I try to adjust myself, but it is the same as peeling bandages off a cut. The movement tugs at the curly, blond leg hair my mom thinks I'm too young to shave, and I wince. I keep my backpack on the edge of the seat, near the aisle, because I'm saving it for Liv, my best friend, who's been shaving her legs since last year. I hope she makes it to the bus in time. She spent almost all day in detention for losing her language arts homework again.

Dotty turns on the bus and it roars; the vibrations pass through me and continue to rattle under my feet. I keep them grounded, enjoying the feeling of the bus's engine, until the Plantar's wart on my left heel begins to throb and sting. Then, I place my knees on the seat in front of me and allow my feet to dangle.

I say hi to T.J. and Carter as they pass me. T.J.'s been my neighbor since sixth grade, but he hardly talks to me. I've known Carter since kindergarten. He's been nicer than normal since I started wearing a bra.

"Hey," Carter says. He joins T.J. in the seat behind me. "Do you and Liv want to come over and play PlayStation after school?"

I turn to face them. "Do you have SSX Tricky yet?"

"Yeah." Carter settles in the seat. "I stole it from my brother. He's been traveling for football. It'll be months before he notices we've been playing."

"Cool."

"Cool," Carter says, nodding, and we exchange big smiles. Warmth rises from my belly to my chest. When I breathe, it climbs to my cheeks, and I feel them reddening. I look at T.J. He's silent, wearing headphones, and looking out the window, as if he's looking for someone.

"Mary," Liv says, out of breath. She throws her bag down on top of mine and slides it into the center of the seat, where the seatbelts should be.

---

* Honorable Mention.

"Hey. How was ISS?"

She sucks her teeth. "How do you think?" She blows a bubble with her gum, one that almost reaches her nose. "Old man Wilson was in there again, and his breath smells like farts."

We both giggle.

"You missed out in science," I say, trying to talk over the loud chatter as Dotty pulls out of the bus loop. Dotty beeps her horn at Principal Beech and the two women wave at each other. We turn onto 100.

"What?" Liv says.

"*I said* you missed out in science."

"I heard what you said, Dumbass. What did I miss?"

I hate that she calls me dumb, but I don't say anything. "Mrs. Pittsford taught us about covalent bonds, how when the electrons become attracted to each other in different atoms, they bond instead of staying separate. She showed us how hydrogen bonds with water to become H_2O."

"Wow." Liv smacks her lips together. "That actually sounds kinda cool, the way you explained it."

"I can show you in the book."

"I wonder if I have to make it up?"

"Since when are you a goody-two-shoes?"

"Since now," she says flatly. She takes the gum out of her mouth and sticks it under the seat. "Mr. Huckabee says if I forget my homework again I'll fail language arts and I won't be able to go to eighth next year. He says they'll send me to Pathways, where they send all the trailer park girls when they get pregnant."

"But you're not pregnant. Or from the trailer park."

"That's what I said."

"So does that mean you're not going to copy my homework anymore?"

"I might sometimes." She giggles. "I gotta study, though, seriously. If I get sent to Pathways, I'll just die." She starts rummaging through her backpack. "I'm gonna start right now. Mr. Huckabee gave me a butt-load of make-up work I have to get done."

I decide not to tell her about Carter and T.J. inviting us over and look out the window instead, watching the lines in the center of the road as they stretch and shorten and blend into one.

The bus turns into our neighborhood and everybody shifts to the left. Sterling and Tanesha stop singing for a second; then, they continue playing the Slide hand game in the back seat. *Slide, baby, one, two, three, four.* Their hands clap together. *One, two, three, four.*

"I heard you got in trouble for fighting," Carter says to Liv, peeking his head over the top of the seat.

Her eyes are moving quickly over the textbook; she's rereading a chapter on sentence types. "Shut up, Carter, I'm not in the mood." When the bus stops, she's pushed forward, almost into the seat in front of us.

"What crawled up your ass and died?"

She turns to face him. "I'll shove this pencil up your ass if you talk to me again."

He looks at me and shrugs. I don't say anything.

When Dotty stops at our bus stop, the brakes squeaking and the red lights flashing, Liv shoves her book into her backpack and moves into the aisle. She carries her backpack in front of her instead of strapping it to her back like she always does. Her shirt rises up, showing her lower back and love handles, and I decide I like her love handles more than mine because they add to her shape. Mine just take away.

"See ya later, kids." Dotty's voice is raspy. It reminds me of the way Liv's mom's voice used to be after too many cigarettes and cups of boxed wine.

"Bye, Dotty." I smile at her. The old woman smiles at me with crooked, yellow teeth.

Liv steps off the bus without speaking.

As my knock-off Adidas sneakers hit the pavement, I'm attacked by hot, thick air—the kind of stickiness that happens right before rain. Carter asks me if we're still on.

"Still on for what?" Liv asks.

"Still on for SSX Tricky at my house is what. With bagel bites, bitches!" Carter moves next to us, laughing, while T.J. lags behind.

"What?" She elbows me. "I thought we were going to my house to do homework."

"We are." I try to avoid Carter's eyes. "I'm sorry. I forgot."

71

Carter's fingers brush against my elbow, and I instantly get goose bumps. "It's okay. Maybe tomorrow."

"Who's that?" Liv points to the dark green Tacoma parked ahead. There's a man with dark glasses inside the truck. "He looks like a cop."

"He is." Carter faces her. "That's Victor. He's T.J.'s soccer coach, too. He says if I keep practicing I can get on the team next year." Carter waves at Victor, and Victor nods.

"If he's a cop, then where's his uniform?" Liv asks.

"I dunno," Carter says. "Maybe he's off, geez."

"Is he picking you up?" I feel a drop of rain hit my forehead.

"Not me. T.J."

"Is T.J.'s mom okay with that?" Another drop, then another. I look up at the sky.

"What do you mean? Why wouldn't she be?" Carter puts his hood up.

"My mom told me never to take a ride from strangers." I feel stupid as soon as I say it.

Carter bumps into me, playfully, which causes me to knock into Liv, who isn't amused by the domino effect. "But I just told you, he's not a stranger. He's a cop and a soccer coach. He does junior lifeguard training in the summer."

As we come alongside the passenger side of the car, I smile at Victor, who's facing us, but I can't tell if he's looking at me. He smiles back, a picture-day smile, and I hear the passenger door unlock from the inside.

"See you guys tomorrow," T.J. mutters.

When T.J. opens the door, I steal a glance at Victor. He's smiling at us still; maybe it's the glasses, but he doesn't look friendly.

"Bye." Liv grabs my wrist and tries to steer me along, but I stop, waiting for Carter. The rain has stopped for now, but the clouds tell me we'll be drenched by the time we get home.

Victor rolls down the passenger seat window and tilts his head to the side as T.J. climbs in. "How are you, Carter?" The sun comes out from behind a cloud, and the shadow disappears from Victor's face. He's younger than I originally thought, so he looks a little nicer.

"Pretty good."

"Have you been practicing your dribbling like we talked about last week?"

"Yeah," Carter says. "I'm starting to get better at running too."

"That's great." His white teeth glow. "Do you want a ride?"

"Come on, let's go." Liv grabs him by the arm; her voice is high-pitched, shaky, but also loud. This is the voice she reserves for Mr. Huckabee and other bossy grown-ups.

"All right." Victor laughs. "Carter's off with the ladies again. I get it. Take care, kids."

Carter shakes off Liv's grasp, smiles at me, and turns to face Victor. "See you Thursday, Vic. Bye, T.J."

"Bye." I wave.

There's silence between us until the truck passes. We watch as Victor goes straight instead of turning on my street.

"He passed it," I say.

"I know." Carter looks at me. "They're going to Vic's house; he lives just down the road, off White Feather I think."

"Oh," I say. "Have you ever been there?"

"No." He shakes his head. "But I'd like to."

"Why? Is he your boyfriend?" Liv snaps.

Carter shoves her. "Shut up. He has a pool table. I wouldn't expect *you* to understand."

"I didn't know he lived so close," I say, but it comes out as a whisper next to Carter's laughter. Liv isn't laughing, but I can tell she's just messing with him, pretending to be mad when she isn't, like always. He's smiling as he picks her up and throws her over his shoulder. She giggles, yells out, and waves her legs up and down until he puts her on her feet. She chases him down the road until I can't see them anymore.

The rain finally comes, hard, about a week later. It lasts all morning and through the afternoon. Instead of watching *The Miracle Worker* in language arts, I watch the rain; it beats the pavement, leaving puddles of oil and water, flooding the gutters with sound. Liv falls asleep during the movie, as soon as Hellen Keller stops smacking Ann Sullivan in the face, and I have to nudge her with my pencil eraser to wake her up.

The rain stops halfway through seventh period. On our way to the bus loop, I carry Liv across a puddle because she's wearing flip-flops. Rain is normal during fall in Florida, sure, but not normal enough for Liv's dad to check out what she's wearing or give her an umbrella, I guess.

When we reach the bus, I nod at Dotty, who's smoking nearby. She's cupping her hand over the cigarette, like she's trying to hide it, but everybody can tell. She smells like an ashtray. She's wearing her white bus driver shirt with nametag, khaki shorts, and navy-blue rain boots that sort of match the wormy veins on her knees and thighs. "Good afternoon, girls," she says.

"Hey, Dotty." We climb the stairs.

My soaking wet sneakers leave soggy footprints behind. Liv slips, bumping into me, and we collide like dead fish in a cooler. "Whoa, watch it," she says, even though it was her fault, and we find the nearest empty seat. I see T.J. sitting alone a few seats behind, and I raise my hand to wave. We lock eyes, but he turns away. My face is hot. What did I ever do to him?

Carter smiles as he moves past me minutes later; his blonde hair is dripping wet, his white shirt sticking to his chest. That feeling creeps up again in my belly—more intense this time, like right before I ride the Bomb Bay at Wet n Wild.

It's pouring sideways by the time we follow the other buses out of the loop. Someone nearby has left the window open and the cold water flings in.

Dotty's voice is on the intercom in seconds. "Hey, you, back there. You, new kid I just met this morning." She's waving one arm, pointing in the mirror. "Redhead. Yes, you. Push that window closed; you're giving everyone a shower in here."

The bus turns into our neighborhood, trudging through standing water, and it groans. Liv grabs a sweatshirt from inside her bag. She also takes off her flip-flops, and I zip up my rain jacket. I'm happy Mom made me pack the jacket this morning, even though we fought about it.

The bus stops. Liv leaps off, dodging puddles. "Aw, my dad's gonna be pissed if I get worms from this water again." she steps through dark water, clutching the plastic thongs of her polka dot flip flops.

I walk around the front of the bus and Carter and T.J. follow. The Tacoma is there again, windshield wipers flapping. Victor gets out, and the door slams. Carter's right after all: he is a cop. He's got the green uniform, the badge, the belt, and the mean, annoying stare. But I wonder why he doesn't have a cop car like my neighbor down the street, the one with the red and blue flashing lights on top and the panhandle on the side. I don't remember ever seeing a cop car on White Feather, but I don't say anything.

"Carter, it's raining pretty hard. Would you like a ride?" Victor's wearing the sunglasses again and I wonder why, considering the rain he just mentioned. They look cheap for cop's glasses, like they came from the $10 rack at The Kangaroo.

"Yeah." he looks up at the sky and then at me. "Sure, I'll take a ride. Wanna come?"

Liv grabs my hand. "We're good, thanks," she says, even though Victor didn't ask.

"See you later," I say.

"See ya." Carter smiles. T.J. is already in the front seat.

Liv tells me not to turn around until they pass and I don't. My red jean shorts are soaked now. The place where my thighs touch is raw.

"I don't care if that guy's a cop." She shivers. "He gives me the creeps."

I know something's wrong when I get on the bus. Liv is already there, which is never the case when she's in ISS. She has her sweatshirt on, the gray one she stole from Disney World on our sixth-grade field trip, with the hood pulled tight over her head. Her cheeks are red. I know she's been crying.

I join her quietly, as if she's sleeping, because I don't want to bother

her. But the silence feels heavy. "You forgot your language arts homework again," I say, finally. As soon as it comes out, I wish I hadn't said anything. Her eyes are half-filled with tears now. "I'm sorry." I grab her hand.

"It's okay." She squeezes back. "I did good for a while, right?" She chews on the drawstring connected to her hood, and the plastic crunches between her teeth like seashells under sneakers.

"You could have copied," I say, but it sounds like *I told you so.*

She looks up at me, and I feel farther away. "I did the work, Mary."

"Then, what happened? I watched Mr. Huckabee pull you out of class and you didn't come back, so—"

"All this time I've been lying. To him. I hadn't been doing the worksheets until last month when he threatened me about Pathways. I did it last night like I have been, you know; I wanted Dad to be proud of me because report cards are coming out. I wanted him to look at me for once like he's glad I didn't leave him too, like he notices I'm still here. But I forgot it. It's probably still on the coffee table where I was working. The worksheet was on appositives. I remember, and I told Mr. Huckabee, but he didn't care."

I nod. There's a lump in my throat the size of a peach. "He didn't let you explain?"

"No. I even told him he could quiz me."

"I'm sorry, Liv."

"I'm kicked out." She sounds like she wants to blow it off, but I know she can't. "The only reason I'm on this stupid bus is because nobody could get a hold of my dad at work."

"You can come over to my house until he gets home."

Dotty fires up the engine.

"Yeah." She sits up. "I mean it's not like I have any homework." She lets out a short laugh, and I laugh too.

Carter and T.J. step onto the bus, swiftly. They're both dressed in gym clothes, carrying soccer cleats. Carter tells T.J. to slide into the seat next to us and he does. The aisle separates us, but Carter and I are only feet apart.

Tanesha and Sterling are at it again as we pull out of the bus loop and onto 100. *Slide, baby, one, two, three, four.* I think about asking if we can join them, but I don't. *One, two, three, four.* Instead, I ask Liv if she wants to play Truth or Dare.

"Now?" she asks.

"Why not? It's your last day on the bus. Let's make it count." I smile, showing my teeth. She smiles too. *One, two, three, four.*

"Can we play?" Carter's voice is excited.

I shrug. "Sure."

"I don't want to play." T.J. plugs his headphones into his CD player.

"Yeah, whatever, T.J. I'm first," Liv says.

"Okay." I pause. "Truth or Dare?"

"No, Dumbass," she says. "I want to ask first, not go first. You go first. Truth or Dare?"

I'm afraid of what she'll ask me if I say "truth." "Dare," I say softly.

Liv's grin is pencil-thin. "I dare you to," she pauses for suspense, "to kiss T.J. On the lips."

I let out a nervous laugh. "T.J. just said he didn't want to play."

"So?"

"*So,*" I say. "He doesn't have to play."

"Ask him, Carter. Ask him if he wants to kiss Mary."

Carter taps T.J. and T.J. pulls off his headphones. "What?" he whispers.

Carter whispers something to T.J. and then points at me. T.J. shakes his head.

"Says no," Carter says. "He doesn't want to play."

"Aw, come on," Liv says. "T.J., don't be a baby!" She makes puckering sounds with her lips and points to me.

T.J.'s eyes narrow. He looks at Carter and then puts his headphones over his ears.

Liv stands while the bus is moving and steps over me, so she's halfway on my lap and halfway in the aisle. She leans over Carter and nudges T.J.'s shoulder, pushing his head too close to the window. "Come *on,* T.J., you suck. Can't you speak for yourself or does your *boyfriend* have to do the talking?"

"Hey, shut up!" Carter shoves her away. "God, you're a real bitch. Leave him alone."

Liv stands in the aisle, holding onto our seat with both hands, until Dotty yells *Down!* and she steps over me and sits quickly.

"Yeah, leave him alone," I say. "He doesn't have to play if he doesn't want to."

"*Fine*, then. Mary, I dare you to kiss Carter on the lips."

My face is red-hot. I look at Liv to make sure I heard her correctly. "What?"

Liv elbows me in the ribs. "I dare you to kiss Carter on the lips."

Dotty turns into the neighborhood, and we shift to the left.

Carter's cheeks are pink. "Okay," I say. Dotty stops the bus and two kids near the front trot off. Carter turns in his seat, facing me now, his mouth open a little. I want to tell him it's my first kiss for some reason. Instead, I turn and lean close to him; our lips almost touch. But Dotty starts driving and Carter and I bang foreheads, hard.

Liv cackles, clapping her hands.

"Ouch." My hands come to my head. I wonder if Dotty was watching us and did it on purpose. Carter is massaging his head too, and I don't think he wants to try again. My heart is pounding so hard I think it'll jump out of my chest and run out the door.

"That might be the funniest thing I've seen. Ever." Liv is still cackling.

"Shut up." My head throbs. I'm tired of her making me feel like a joke, and I'm sick of her telling me what to do. I don't want her to come to my house—not today, not ever. I don't even care if she's expelled. "Shut up," I say again, louder. Even T.J. is laughing.

But she doesn't shut up even when T.J. shuts up and Carter tells her to stop. She just keeps laughing, her voice making the tiny hairs in my ears stand up. People are starting to stare at us and Tanesha and Sterling have stopped playing.

"You're so dumb, Mary," she says. "You should have seen your face!"

"My turn," I say. "Liv, you're up."

"Truth."

"Tell us the truth. Why did your mom really leave?"

Liv stops laughing. She punches me, quick and hard in the eye, and then hits me again. All I taste is blood in my mouth. I'm pushed into the aisle by Liv, and Carter tries to grab me. I fall into an empty seat nearby and she's on me, knee in my belly. Her fists are pummeling me, and I'm crying, trying to breathe. Liv is pulled away by the time Dotty stops the bus. Carter's holding Liv, the back of her shirt ripped in half. "I hate you," she screams. It is all I hear that day and every day after that.

When I jump off the bus, my mom's red Subaru is parked in front of Victor's Tacoma. I wish I was walking behind Liv, in her shadow, but I haven't seen her since my mom went to her house and yelled at her dad and she started going to Pathways. It's been two weeks, the longest we've ever gone without talking. Victor is standing outside his truck, and he's not wearing his uniform like he usually is; he's leaning against the front bumper. My mom steps out of her car.

"Hey kids," she says. "I got off work early. Want a ride, boys?" I'm embarrassed she's here. She never gets off early.

"Come on." I look at Carter and T.J., and T.J. freezes. "Come on," I say again as I open the passenger side door.

"The boys have a ride." Victor's voice is cold.

"Excuse me," Mom says. "Who are you?"

"I'm a Flagler County police officer, ma'am. I've been giving T.J. rides since last fall. This is the first time I've seen you here."

"You're a police officer?" She looks him up and down. "Where's your cruiser—in the shop?" Her eyes meet mine and then move to Carter and T.J. "And your uniform? Come on, boys. Get in the car."

Carter and T.J. move quickly. T.J. is looking at Victor, into whatever eyes he has hidden behind the glasses.

"Ma'am," Victor says. "These boys are in my custody. I have been asked by their parents to take care of them after school. If you force them into your vehicle, I'm going to have to call back-up."

Mom sniffs. "Call back-up? Go ahead. I've known these boys for years. This is the first time I've ever seen you."

"Th-thanks, Victor," T.J. says, and my mom's eyes shift to him again. T.J. only stutters in math class. "I-I'll just ride with Mary and Mrs. Cosgrove today."

I place my hands into my sweatshirt pockets and feel the beaded friendship bracelet inside. The last of the rain brought a cold snap, just in time for Christmas, and the palms of my hands are cool and dry.

I'm thinking of Victor the way I always do when I walk in the neighborhood, which isn't often. My mom doesn't trust the bus, so she or my dad usually take me to school. She doesn't trust the police anymore either, even though the newspaper said Victor was never a cop. I had to show her the bracelet and beg her to let me walk to Liv's house today. I promised to call when I got there and also not to fight.

I try to keep my eyes fixed on the stop sign ahead, but I just can't. I glance at T.J.'s house, and I can see a Christmas tree blinking in the front window. There's a shadow sitting in the plastic chair on the front porch. I squint and look closer; it's T.J. His head is down, and I can't tell if he's avoiding me again. When my feet stop, I'm in his driveway, just barely. "Hey, T.J."

"Merry Christmas. Did you get lots of presents?"

"Yeah." I look down at my new Adidas sneakers.

"I got some new games and so did my brother. You should come over sometime. We can play SSX Tricky like we talked about."

"Sure." I pretend to be excited. My mom would never allow it now. I try to swallow. The peach-sized lump is back in my throat. "I'm going over to Liv's house, so I'll see you later."

"Hope you don't get beat up."

"Thanks."

I push the doorbell and remember I'm wearing the purple nail polish Liv bought me for my twelfth birthday. When Liv's dad answers, he has his cell phone pressed to his ear, like normal. He looks behind me, probably looking for my parents, and then waves me inside. The tree's lights are blinking in the dark, cluttered living room.

"Hold on," he says to the phone. "Olivia, come downstairs, please. You have a visitor." He smiles at me and then goes into the kitchen. I can't tell if he's smiling because he's sorry she beat me up or if he's happy I came over two months later. I smile back.

Liv's footsteps thump down the stairs. She's wearing the Disney sweatshirt and blue flannel pajama bottoms she probably got for Christmas. When she sees me, she scowls. "What do *you* want?" She folds her arms across her chest and sits on the stairs.

"Merry Christmas." I join her. "These are new."

"Yeah." She tugs at the pants. "My grandma."

I pull the bracelet out of my pocket and hand it to her. "I made this for you."

She looks at me, confused, and then takes it. "But I punched you."

"A lot," I say. "But I deserved it. I never should have said that about your mom, not in front of everyone."

"You're right." She nods. "Especially since I got Carter to kiss you and all."

"Almost. I'm still waiting for the re-do." We giggle for a second and then fall silent.

I clip the baby blue and purple bracelet to Liv's wrist. I know she'll probably never apologize, but I forgive her anyway. I can tell we both feel like crying. "Friends?"

"Friends."

It's almost dark when we reach his house on White Feather. The sky looks like cotton candy. Soon, there will be nothing to light our way. Even though we've never been there, it's easy to spot which one is Victor's. The lawn is overgrown with weeds, and there's a for-sale sign staked into the ground as well as graffiti on the front of the house. Whenever the neighbor kids found out about him and he went away, they tagged the house. With mean stuff, too. All that's left of Victor is a couple of decorative rocks and an aloe plant on the front porch. It's the only plant I know of that can survive so long without water.

I grab Liv's hand like I have since we were little and let out a sigh. It's the only sound I can come up with. She squeezes back, our wrists touching.

"Let's go up there." She points at the house.

"What?"

She drops my hand. "Come on."

"But—"

"For T.J." She leads the way—from the driveway to the sidewalk to the front door. It smells like piss at the entrance. "Do you smell that?" She covers her nose.

"How could I not?"

"Gross." We stand there in silence and look at the words on the door, and what's written above the front window. Liv picks up a rock.

"What are you doing?" I ask.

"What does it look like I'm doing?"

"You can't."

"Why not?"

"You'll get in trouble."

"Look at this place, Mary. Forget it."

I pick up a rock too. It's heavier than I expect—some kind of stone, like coquina, from the beach. We walk to the front window, and I look around to make sure nobody is watching.

"Ready?" she asks.

"For T.J."

She throws first and the rock comes apart in chunks when it bounces off the side of the house. She hasn't hit the window. "Go. My aim sucks."

I throw the rock like I would a softball from third base. When the window breaks and I hear the shatter, I also hear the neighbors in the house next door. I hear voices. A few lights come on.

"Let's get out of here," Liv says. We run through the lawn, and our sneakers hit the pavement. Liv giggles. "You're so badass."

My heart beats quickly. I'm faster than Liv, so I grab her hand again when she starts to fall behind—that way we can stay together. Every time I look over my shoulder, I can see we're alone, but I keep running. I keep running even when Liv wants to stop because somehow it feels like we're still being chased.

Daphne: The Aspen Version

Erica Soon Olsen

In ancient Greece Daphne flees Apollo and is changed into a laurel tree. In Colorado, in the Uncompahgre National Forest, she becomes an aspen, taking root on the steep north-facing slopes below Lone Cone, looking toward Mount Wilson and El Diente. It happens in August, bow-hunting season.

*

Safe inside the cool, damp sheath of bark, she hears him crashing around in the forest, shouting her name.

*

The new girl is the subject of gossip in the grove. The other aspens don't like her. Personal insults are their specialty. They seem to think they know all about her. They refer to her as *that slut*.

I only came up here with him because I wanted to go hunting, she defends herself.

You're not one of us, says the big aspen, the one closest to her.

You're not one of us, the saplings echo.

Apparently *aspen* means something like *bitch*.

Please shut up, she quakes back in her new aspen voice. She tries not to let them get under her skin. Bark. Whatever.

She gives them names: That aspen is Amber. That one is Megan. That one is Gwyneth.

Why couldn't she've turned into a ponderosa or a spruce? The spruce trees seem more mature, dark and thoughtful. They live just a few hundred feet higher up the slope—if only she'd run up there.

Winter brings relief, a frosty silence.

Time passes. Daphne grows tall—tall and straight. She thinks less often about her mother and her father and her dog and her sister in the house on Summit Street in Norwood. She stops caring what Gwyneth and the other aspens say. She can live with this enchantment. She's the nymph of the Uncompahgre. She's the prettiest aspen. In May her crown is the brightest green, in September a glorious reddish gold. When it rains, her wet bark gleams. Sudden aspen decline doesn't affect her—beetles don't burrow under her bark. For all these reasons and more, she's hated in the grove.

She loves being in the forest though. She loves being the forest.

Sooner or later every kind of animal comes into their grove: moose, bear, elk, fox, lynx, porcupine.

*

Everything is fine until the timber sale.

He's looking for you, says Amber.

We heard he's a logger now, the saplings say. They can gloat—for now, they're safe.

Here she stands rooted, rooted deep. All this time she's been growing taller and taller, attractively tall and straight in a way that is most attractive to loggers. She can hear the trucks grinding up the narrow roads. She thinks of all the trucks she's seen all her life, loaded down with aspen whose destiny is to be sawn into wallboard or shaved into excelsior at the mill down in Mancos.

One day a stranger comes and marks them with blue paint.

When the crew arrives at their harvest unit, she finds out that it's true about Apollo. He's driving a half-ton Dodge Ram pickup, which he parks on the road downslope. He listens to KKXK Colorado Country from Montrose. Through the newly thinned-out grove that stands between her and the road, she can see sunlight flashing off metal.

He hikes up the slope with his chain saw, trailing the smell of gasoline. The other aspens hiss: *Take her, not us.*

She hopes the wind won't blow, making her leaves attractively quake, drawing attention to her slim, tall, attractive trunk. She's totally recognizable, she realizes. This is fate: The color of her roots. Her split ends, which he hated—he was always telling her to use a different conditioner. Plus there's this one weird part of her trunk that looks a little too much like human flesh and not enough like tree bark.

Sh-sh-she's here. She's here.

*

The tree hits the ground. "Holy shit," he says. He's a little stoned, he can't make sense of what he's seeing. There seems to be a girl there, a ragged, wild-eyed, skinny girl with leaves in her hair. Jesus Christ, did he almost kill someone? Is he going to lose his job? Is she a hippy backpacker? Is she anti-logging? Was she raised by wolves? Are there wolves in Colorado? What's with the trees—they seem kind of angry? What's with this tree in particular, which he's pretty sure toppled without the chain saw actually cutting into it?

The girl opens her mouth. She says, "I thought you were someone else."

Holding the still-running chainsaw, he watches her flit away into the thickest part of the grove, which is dense with aspen sprouts and saplings. What the fuck just happened? "I watched her flit away," he says later. Those are his exact words. They're not the right words. What are the right words? He's not the kind of guy who'd use a word like *flit*. Evanesce?

Who did she think he was?

*

Her ears hurt. Everything is loud—saws, engines, radios, squirrels, trees, human voices.

86

She walks down out of the mountains, walks another mile down the Beef Trail to the Dolores-Norwood Road, and then she walks the hot, shadeless highway into town. She's sixteen and a virgin in Norwood, with a disappearance she can't explain and a scab on her leg that looks like bark.

That's the nature of disenchantment, of being yourself.

Reapers

Jeffrey Byrem

It's a Florida winter, 1986, and I've been out here on the sidewalks of Ocean Court chummin' for shark, on and off, for the last three years, and like as happens most nights, I got me one. Mercedes, new money, wife somewhere thinking he's hanging with his buds. Clarence used to chum for sharks. Stunk the water with chopped trash fish. Sharks couldn't resist the smell of it, like the shark in the Mercedes can't resist me. Huge hunks of meat on nasty hooks dragged behind a thirty—foot deadrise. Clarence would let them hit the meat, then draw it closer, close enough to loose his harpoon into the biggest of them. This one's big, got deep pockets, the one in the Mercedes. I flash my breast, and he bites hard.

When Clarence's harpoon hit, there was thrashing. Under the surface, the shark in the Mercedes is thrashing, scared of getting caught, but he won't leave the bait. Sometimes they get away. Sometimes, but most times I get what I'm after, just like Clarence got what he was after. No one suspected, no one would have believed. I did what almost every working girl on this street did when they had to choose. Faced with live death at the hands of fathers, brothers, uncles, stepfathers like Clarence, we all ran. The bitch is, none of us thought we'd be giving every Clarence who wanted it what we had run away from, but that's what we did, what we do. The first Clarences taught us well. We knew what to expect from the ones that followed, knew how stupid they were, how focused on their pricks, how easily baited and harpooned.

One of them, maybe more than one of them, infected me, but I thought I was dead anyway and didn't worry about it at first. Nothing could kill what was already dead, but thinking that brought me back to life, such as it was, and what it was made me sick to death. That's when I started thinking of them as Clarences, not Johns, crazy sharks with their own harpoons, cold—blooded killing machines that deserved to die, an eye for an eye, tooth for a tooth.

The Mercedes turned around. He's cruising my side of the street, window down on the passenger side. He stops, leans over. I give him a fuck—me smile before he says anything, and he bites harder. In ten minutes, he's on me in the back of the Mercedes, talking shit he thinks is turning me on. No rubber, I tell him. I tell him I'm clean and want to feel him inside me. He's so gone he doesn't care, doesn't know that when his harpoon strikes deep in me, he's a dead man; doesn't know why I'm laughing my ass off, calling him Clarence, asking him, ain't paybacks a bitch?

When you don't care it's hard as hell to be careful. Damn if I wasn't shaking with the itch that makes me work, blinds me to getting busted. Bastard didn't look like a cop. Looked like one more shark, too chicken shit at a bar to sidle up to some meat lonely as him, him looking to get laid and for free, but fuck, that was my Jones being hungry, wanting a bite of what takes the hunger away.

This cell is no better, no worse, than others I've seen. Corners enough to make a cube, metal walls, cold and white, a bunk along the wall, bright lights twenty—four—seven, and a din, a muffled noise like the old diesel in Clarence's deadrise, never—ending; sound that disappears because it's always there.

Down in the cabin the diesel drowned my protests, swallowed them in that never—ending racket. It was crowded there, the bulk of him filling the space, leaving little room for me in a death chamber of suffocating man smell—a stench of sweat, diesel oil and fish scale—crowded like this cell, three of us in this six-by-six space.

Mary, I know from a short vacation at the women's prison, so we're cool. It's the mammoth hunk of chocolate flesh knocked out on the bunk that's making this place crowded. Don't know her name, but I do know she's someone I'm not going to cross. Sliced the throat of some bitch who stole one lousy crack vial from her, and now Mary and I are leaning against the

89

clammy wall of the cell because neither of us is going to ask her to share. Share. Didn't have to go to kindergarten to learn it. Clarence taught me what it means to share.

Three of his friends thought fishing and a case or two of brew would be a good way to waste a day. Clarence told them he'd be sharing something special with them, and that something was me. At fourteen I knew the drill, knew how to let go the chopped fish, not all at once, so it'd drag out behind the deadrise a long ways, knew how to send who I was to some secret place inside my head a long ways from what I had to do after I finished chummin'. What I did after was a different kind of chummin' with Clarence's buds. I need to find that secret place again, forget this cold, white tomb.

There's a commotion in the walkway by the phone. Some Biscayne bitch, maybe seventeen, asking the matron, do you know who I am? We get to make a call every few hours. Mary says when the matron told the kid her time was up, the little rich puke took offense. I got no one to call, at least no one who could do anything to get me out of here. Patience. In a few hours, I'll be arraigned and maybe have enough cash to post bail. I was patient chummin' that day on the deadrise, no one to bail me out, acting like I liked it, thinking maybe they'd go gentler on me if I did, maybe some place in my head actually wanting to think they wanted me because I was sexy.

Mary tells me to come see this, so I stick my face in thetiny hole in the door and see the matron, all puffed—up like atoad, spitting out fuck bombs on that little, high—brow, Biscayne twit. The girl is so shocked she's bawling, and I can't help laughing. Serves her right, the little rich bitch. Can't believe I'm thinking about toads and how they swell up when you catch them. Clarence told me it was how they kept from being

90

swallowed by snakes. He told me this right before he asked me if I wanted to see how the toad in his pocket swelled up, and that was right before I had to show him I could do what some snake couldn't. That was the first time. I was stupid, I guess, probably scared shitless; I don't remember, but that was the beginning. Clarence's fucking toad.

Don't know how many times I've been in rehab, one miracle two—week cure after another. Seems like I haven't lived enough years to be rehabbed so often. Know the twelve steps by heart, learned them a long time ago, but when I feel like I feel right now, they don't mean shit to a tree. Can't sleep, puking left and right, nervous as hell. Could've been this miserable in County Jail, but rehabs are cleaner and got well—meaning people who try to help. Some, maybe most, have been what I am, so they know. They want me to kick it, but what's the point? I got no reason to. The judge said jail or rehab. Like I said, rehab is cleaner, and this bullshit is hell no matter where I'd have to deal with it. Not sure I'm going to go the two weeks this time. Hell, I'm not sure I'm going to make it through tonight. No lock down so they can't make me stay. They'll plead and tell me it'll mean jail time. They have to know once I'm on the street nobody will come looking; cops have too many other fish to fry.

Impulsive with a personality disorder, that's what's on my file. Least ways it was the one time I got to see it. Wasn't always that way. Used to be a sweet little girl, but I put that thought away soon as it comes up. Don't want that sweet little girl knowing she ended up with a personality disorder and impulsive to boot.

It was that day chummin' for Clarence and his buds that I learned impulsive, I guess because I couldn't take it. It must've been hours I was down there, must've looked like hell, my skin all sweat and dirt from them, slap marks on the side of my face. No one never been there would ever think some filthy, naked teenager would turn on anybody, but it didn't matter to Clarence's buds.

With my life being what it is, I've seen it since, but it was the first time I understood what they were doing to me wasn't about whatever it is most folks think sex is, which I wouldn't know but from watching Oprah the time I got inland to a shelter during a hurricane that didn't amount to much.

This woman on Oprah talked about being intimate, which I never really got exactly. It's like doing something forbidden, I guess, something fun that you got to keep secret with somebody special, what Mom called nasty, but she'd say it with a little smile. That day was about none of that. It was all about being a big man, especially for one of Clarence's buds. He kept coming below, three, four times compared to the other ones. I'd watch that pencil dick of his get longer and longer each time he smacked me.

It wasn't about me turning him on, or even him wanting to fuck me. It was about wanting to shame me, wanting to make me feel small so he could feel big, I suppose. Can't imagine him shaking that pencil dick at no decent woman because they'd laugh at him, least ways that's what I figured as I lay there waiting for the next one.

Billy is always good for a fix. Haven't seen him for a while, and today he's looking bad. The disease has about worked its way through him, nothing but skin and bones, but he can still get it up. I like how he moans and holds me when he's coming, almost like a little boy might hug his mom, but that has to be a fucked—up thing for me to think.

Two hours ago, I told the night counselor to fuck off and walked out of rehab. I was so wound it was hard letting Billy do me first. Other times he'd give me the stuff and I'd owe him. He was cool with it, never minded waiting until I was between Clarences. Tonight, he gave me a double bag after, and when I said goodbye, he looked at me like he knew what I was up to, gave me a hug and a little kiss on the cheek, kind of sweet like. Maybe the two of us could have been a couple had things been different, way different, but I can't think about that. Having trouble getting a vein. The needle is filthy, but it don't matter. It's the only good thing about having the virus: no bullshit worrying about finding clean needles.

It was between Clarence's buds that something happened in my head. Guess I got angry, or maybe I was afraid one more time would kill me. Didn't know then I was already dead. Fool Clarence never figured me to fight, never put two and two together, never put one angry, scared, naked fourteen—year—old together with the double—barreled twelve—gauge, mounted and loaded on the grimy bulkhead, ready to slam punkin balls into the soft skull of a too—big shark.

Pencil Dick was first to go. He was pie—eyed when he came below and didn't even see the shotgun until right before I made him a girl. Jesus. There was blood everywhere, and screaming, not just from Pencil Dick but from the others too. We were way offshore and weren't no one to hear. Clarence came running below and was the second one to go. It was the last I seen his face because I got rid of it. I'd seen him load the gun before, and I knew where the shells were, so while the other two were plotting some scheme in the pilot house, I put two more shells in the shotgun and climbed out the forward hatch.

Must've been some sight to them, me standing there naked in the summer—bright sun holding the shotgun. I didn't make them wait. The last thing to do was to make it all disappear. Weren't too hard. Drove the deadrise to a quiet and deep river Clarence showed me many times. Good place to put an end to it, I thought, given the channel was damned deep at that spot, and it being the spot I learned about Clarence's toad. Two shotgun shells blew a big hole in the bilge.

Wasn't long before I was on the bank watching the short mast on the pilothouse go under.

Stuffed those bastards into the shark hold and jammed the hatch. Somebody might've found them one day, but I never heard and don't care. I like to think of them rotting down there while I'm rotting up here. It was what I wanted to happen, what I wanted to be strong enough to do from the first time I swallowed that toad: to blast the cooks and faces that still haunt me. Turns out, I never could make it all disappear. Thought it'd feel good, doing what I did, but I was fourteen, and everything that happened was a secret. Like I said, no one would have believed.

Clarence always made me wash up before Mom came home. Told me he would tell her what I did, that she would hate me for it, for being a slut. Told me he'd have to kill me if I told. I didn't want Mom to hate me, and I didn't want to die. Like I said, that day on the boat was when I learned impulsive. I had no plan but to run until I was too tired to run, and then I'd run again in no special direction. Ran until I found heroin could make the secrets disappear, even if only for a while. I'm running to it one last time.

The rush don't feel like it did those first times, the times that seared a sensation into my brain like nothing I've known before or since, but the pain does go away, is going away, like me. We reap what we sow. I remember that from church when I was a little girl with pinafores and Mary Jane's and a life sowed with happiness. Love thy neighbor. Do good to those who persecute you. I'm remembering all them things I learned when I was little and believed, wanted to believe, what grownups told me.

When I was a kid, we reap what we sow sounded right to me. If I'm a good girl, good things will happen to me. Thought I understood it, but it doesn't sound right anymore, doesn't fit with what I learned, what I

94

know. I've reaped way too many rows Clarence sowed, and because of it, too many other Clarences are reaping rows I sowed. Should feel even but it don't. Should be glad of it, all those rows, all those soon-to-be-dying Clarences, but it don't. There's so much hurt in all that sowing it breaks my back with the weight of it, leaves me barely enough strength to sow this one last row, this one last row that nobody else will have to reap.

There's so much hurt in all that it breaks my back with the weight of it, leaves me barely strength to sow this one last row, else will have to reap this one last row that sowing enough nobody else will have to reap.

Reading *Herzog*

Michael Simpson

A naturally timid man, James Rogenstadt's approach to life had always been cautious and orderly. Nevertheless, in his mid-thirties, his first and only marriage fell apart. His ex-wife-to-be, her name was Sarah, had been briefly married before. Her dream had always been to buy a house, something her first husband hadn't been able to provide. Within six months of their wedding day, they acquired a modest three-bedroom house, and one of the spare rooms became Rogenstadt's reading room and a make-shift library for his large collection of books.

After their divorce, the memory that stayed with him the longest was the day he came home from teaching to discover the house empty of furniture and Sarah gone. On the drive home, he had been dreading another argument, another episode of plate throwing or, worse, the sharp pinpoints of quiet hate in her eyes as she walked around the house trying not to look at him.

When Rogenstadt opened the door that autumn afternoon, the first thing that struck him was the smell of gasoline. As he absorbed the stark emptiness of the living room and dining room, he walked toward the back and the spare room that contained the makeshift utility shelves that held his books. What he saw generated a confused mixture of despair and relief. The shelves empty, but his books were still there, heaped in the middle of the room, beside them a can of gasoline and a box of matches. Propped up on the still of the only window in the room was a small white envelope.

Rogenstadt didn't open the envelope. Instead, for the next two hours, as the afternoon slipped through evening into night, he pulled books off the pile, checking each to see if any gasoline had been spilled on it or any pages were torn out, and slowly put them back on the shelves. It was a tedious process, but it helped him control the inner turmoil that he was afraid might burst his lungs. All his books were dry, all the pages intact.

When he was finished, Rogenstadt leaned against the wall under the window, the smell of gasoline strong in the air, turning the box of matches around and around in his hands. She didn't even leave me a chair to sit on, he told himself, and that thought almost brought him to tears. The envelope was on the floor beside him. It hadn't been sealed. When he read the note, he could hear her voice as clearly as if she had been in the room with him.

"I could have burned your books, but I didn't. I could have burned the house down, but I didn't. Because ultimately it wasn't worth it. I loved you, and to the degree I hated you there was still love there. But ultimately, you aren't worth loving, so you're not worth hating either. Here are all your books, a useless heap. There's not enough in you worth burning. Nothing in you to love or hate. Nothing worth the trouble."

When Rogenstadt neared his fortieth birthday, the administration of the community college where he worked offered him the position of coordinator for the English composition classes. He turned it down.

"No, no. I love teaching too much," he said. "I wouldn't be good at anything else."

Even as he said it—as he looked calmly into the department head's stern, powdered, matriarchal face—he knew he no longer loved teaching as much as he once had. Like many things pursued too intensely, he decided, teaching had lost its savor. He still loved it, but there seemed to be a numbness at the core. He found himself more in sympathy with his students and their struggles and less able to get excited about the texts he'd taught so many times. Slowly but surely, the word spread among the students that he was an "easy A." He grew a little absent minded. Occasionally he would look up from a passage he was reading to the class and stare in silence for a few seconds, seemingly lost in contemplation of all the different faces before him.

As Rogenstadt's love for teaching faded, he became more and more efficient in the "administration" side of his job. It began with his student papers. He filed them by semester and got rid of a file exactly six months after the class was over. That gave any student who questioned what he had done in class, he reasoned, sufficient time to contact him. Six months after the class: zap, the papers were gone. He was even more ruthless with the memos and reminders he found in his mailbox. Student tutoring, computer classes, surveys: all went into the wastebasket. When he got a scanner for his office computer, he didn't keep any papers around; he just scanned them into the computer. Gone. All the paper seagulls that had hovered around the bureaucratic garbage tug were gone.

Then he tackled the textbooks. What books did he really need? Slowly, his office shelf contained only the texts from which he taught—the Norton Anthologies for his survey classes, the current readers for his composition classes, a grammar handbook. With the years, Rogenstadt reduced his office to the austerity of a monk's cell—a small white room with a desk, a phone, a computer, a scanner, and a printer.

In his apartment things were different. Rogenstadt was determined to make his apartment, however humble, a small world of order and harmony. He didn't care how shabby it looked from the outside, but inside he wanted to make it a comfortable refuge from the world's chaos. As decoration he allowed himself a large imitation oil painting of Van Gogh's "Sunflowers" and a photograph, framed and under glass, he had taken in the Appalachian Mountains of large snowflakes falling on a damp country road. And, of course, there were all the books he owned.

He had long since replaced the original metal utility shelves with solid white floor-to-ceiling bookshelves. He accumulated books more gradually now, sometimes re-arranging them as he went. He had sections devoted to American novels, British novels, European novels, miscellaneous other novels (Japanese, Spanish, Italian). He had sections devoted to philosophy and history and science. A section of poetry and religion. Each book with the date he had read it marked in the upper right corner of the title page.

Ever since college, when he took his first literature class and bought his own copies of the novels, Rogenstadt loved buying books almost as much as reading them. He told himself he bought books because he underlined in them; and, it was true, he would often go back to review what he had underlined. Having experimented with various forms—highlighters, red ink, using a ruler under a pencil—he finally settled on a simple pencil, very sharp, and relied on the straightness and firmness of his hand.

But the deeper truth was that he loved books because they were solid and self-contained and always readily available on their shelves.

Rogenstadt bought most of his books at Craighorn's, the official off-campus bookstore, a large brick warehouse in downtown Covehill. It was a cavern of books. There were ladders you climbed to reach the top shelves and narrow aisles lined with books that led to hidden rooms, second stories, and annexes—all of them equally filled with books. It wasn't like the stores in malls, where all the books were brand new. Here were used books, ancient books that threatened to fall apart if you opened them too quickly. Here were musty-smelling books and corners of the warehouse where it seemed no one had ever been. He envied the manager's assistants—skinny, hyperactive young men with disheveled hair and clothes that seemed spun from the same fabric as the manager's faded white shirt as they rushed through the maze searching for a book a customer had requested.

All his purchases, from Craighorn's bookstore and from the other small bookstores he had visited on his vacations, had created a huge backlog of books Rogenstadt hadn't read. After his separation from Sarah, he pulled those books off his shelves and arranged them together. They occupied four shelves, and it was a long time before he could make himself count them. He loved owning books, but he grew to feel it was cheating to own books he hadn't read. There were exceptions, of course. Reference books, picture books. He didn't require himself to read those. But the others!

As the years passed, Rogenstadt constantly reminded himself: if you buy books, you must find the time to read them. Gradually, he even got rid of the pile of books by his bedside, forcing himself to keep only one book there.

The large number of unread books, however, was a major challenge of a different order, but eventually the number of unread books could fit on a single shelf. Rogenstadt mockingly congratulated himself. As the number of unread books decreased, another difficulty arose: he was left with books he didn't want to read.

For some reason, Rogenstadt couldn't get rid of those books, sell them or give them away to Goodwill. He was determined to make his way through them.

So he compromised. He established a rule: he could buy new books, but only if he read them immediately. Once he had read a newly acquired book, he would go back to that shelf of unread books and ask himself if he had the strength to read one.

A crucial new element in Rogenstadt's life in his forties was Vera Mensing. For all intents and purposes, she was his second wife even though they lived in separate apartments across town. Over the years, he routinely "visited" her once or twice each week and usually, though not always, stayed over on the weekends. Vera was the secretary of the Dean of Arts and Sciences where Rogenstadt worked. She had wild, dark, unruly hair, a plump figure, an independent manner and a broad sense of humor mixed with a certain level-headed compassion for human failure.

They first had sex in Vera's apartment after a day trip to the mountains.

"I can't stay," he said as he untangled himself from her and sat up on the side of the bed. "I'll see you next weekend, but I can't stay."

"All right," she said. She had propped herself up on the bed, her breasts awkward and casual before him. For a moment Rogenstadt thought of all the pin-ups and pornographic photos he had seen as a teenager. The women with arched backs, offering their breasts with perfect symmetry. The studied, provocative stares. The stomachs sucked in. But Vera was simply there, sleepy, trusting. No posing. This is intimacy, he thought.

The next weekend, when they had dinner, she said, "I understand how it is."

At first Rogenstadt wasn't sure what she meant. The statement was so all inclusive.

"I understand why you can't spend the night," she explained. "I've been married too. It's not like we're going to have children."

Rogenstadt just blinked and looked down at his half-eaten meal.

"Maybe at some point you'll spend the night. And that doesn't mean you moving in with me, or my moving in with you. I like having a place of my own." Vera said. "I just want you to know what we have is okay as long as you promise to tell me if you ever lose interest. Do you promise?"

"I promise."

Those words had been their marriage vows.

When he left that night, they hugged, and he avoided her gaze but held her hand tightly.

"Call me when you get back to your apartment," she said. I just want to be sure you made it. You're so tired."

He called her on the phone that first night, and it became part of their routine for him to call her whenever he got to his apartment. There were times when there was nothing to say other than "I made it," but he always called.

After several months, he began staying overnight on the weekends, but they each still kept their separate places. Vera said she preferred it that way. "I would get on your nerves," she said, "and you would definitely get on mine."

Over the years Rogenstadt's relationship with Vera had become as comfortable as a familiar robe. He did very little talking, was reluctant to talk. But he knew to ask questions: about her friends at work, about her father, her brother. There were always anecdotes to relate. On his end he complained about and puzzled over his students and balanced his complaints by telling her what he was reading, giving her, what he essentially gave to everyone, lectures on his favorite books.

One afternoon Rogenstadt once again confronted his shelf of unread books. There were six left. He glanced over the titles: *The Conduct of Inquiry, Food in History, The Oxford History of Music, World of Our Fathers, Herzog*, a translation of Aristotle's *Poetics*. He had separated the fiction from non-fiction, and *Herzog* was only novel left. Aristotle's *Poetics* was a possibility because it was short. But he decided he couldn't deal with non-fiction that day.

Rogenstadt pulled *Herzog* from the shelf. He took the book back to his bedroom, propped up his pillows, swung the table lamp over his bed and opened the book. He leafed through a few pages and discovered at least a third of it had bits of red underlining. He must have gotten the book at a reduced price because of the underlining. He went to the title page.

In red letters at the top of the page was the signature "Sarah Klasky."

Rogenstadt stopped. He didn't do anything dramatic—didn't throw the book down or clutch it fiercely in his hands; his heart didn't suddenly start pounding. He simply closed the book and brought his hand with the book to his side on the bed. His first reflex was to get it out of his sight. He felt somehow tricked. Sarah had been completely out of his life, and now—as a simple signature—she was back. He tried to remember the last time he had thought about her, and he couldn't.

He lifted the book and looked at it. It was foolish to be at the mercy of a woman after so many years. That simply seeing her signature a book could make him uneasy. He forced himself to be conscious of the room around him. Near the side of his bed, where he had his desk with his PC on it, a window looked out on a flat common area of grass in his apartment complex. There was a single young tree not much higher than the first story of the building. The boys in the complex often played football in the field—leaving their bicycles under the tree like oversized pets. Sometimes girls stood on the sidewalk with their bikes, watching the boys play. This was the present. Sarah was the past—the slightest echo from a distant past, less than the softest breath of a whisper.

Klasky was her maiden name. She must have read the book when she was very young, even before her first marriage. Rogenstadt opened the book again to glance at the publication date. 1964. Assuming she bought it fairly new, she probably got it in college, a good ten years before they met. It was somehow reassuring: the Sarah who had read the book was much younger than the Sarah he had married.

Rogenstadt opened the book to the title page again. As an experiment, he moved his finger across the red signature. What was he expecting, he thought to himself. To hear voices? To feel heat radiating from the letters? Besides, the woman—the young girl, really—who had put her signature on the page was not the Sarah he had known. The young woman who had struggled through the book—he assumed she had struggled; the red marking stopped a third of the way through—knew nothing of him, had no feelings for him. Somehow, that made it safer. There was no animosity toward him in the woman who had read those pages. What then, really, did he have to fear?

He tried to remember if Sarah had ever told him anything about her years in college. She had been unhappy. But that was not unusual. It was hard to find any time in her life when she wasn't unhappy. There was too much urgency in her, too many contradictions, for her to be happy. The signs were all there, the disaster waiting to happen. Why hadn't he seen it?

Sarah was in college in the late sixties early seventies—the same time that Rogenstadt was in graduate school. Had *Herzog* been assigned for a class? It didn't seem like something she would have picked on her own. When she met Rogenstadt, Sarah's reading habits were still unformed. One of the things that had first delighted him was how she looked to him for suggestions on what to read. He tried to guess her interests. "Try *Pilgrim at Tinker Creek*, I think you'll like it."

When they were married, a Unitarian minister performed the ceremony in the townhouse they were renting. It was in the afternoon. Rogenstadt's father, brother and sister came up from Cary. Rain poured down heavily. Sarah's parents came, driving the four hours from Halleysville. Sarah had offered to let them stay in the spare bedroom, but they insisted on renting a hotel room. Her father would have driven back that night, but her mother insisted he was not to drive back in the dark, especially in the rain.

As Rogenstadt held the book, absent-mindedly resting it on his chest, his mind caught glimpses of that day. A large arrangement of flowers behind the minister. They had made up their own vows. Rogenstadt struggled to remember what they had said. Sarah's father said something about it being a mistake not to get the "obey" part in, especially where her vows were concerned.

It pained Rogenstadt that, as much as he tried, he couldn't get a physical sense of her. Even when he tried to imagine her face, a face he had seen thousands of times every day for six years, he couldn't remember. There were no photographs; he'd gotten rid of them.

Rogenstadt tried to remember the moment he had proposed to her. Had there even been a clear proposal? Or was it something that had just been assumed after they had moved in together?

Sarah had underlined most of the first sentence in *Herzog*: "IF I am out of my mind, it's all right with me." She had used a red felt-tip pen—something Rogenstadt avoided because the ink bled through the page. As he read, Rogenstadt ignored the red underlining as much as he could, but at times it was impossible. "Why did she underline that? How stupid. And yet she could miss this." Here he would underline in pencil the relevant passage.

In her reading, Sarah alternated between underlining, putting a line down the side of the page, bracketing a sentence or phrase. Rogenstadt couldn't see any method in it. But Sarah had always rebelled against method. In the last year of their marriage—before the bitter never-ending argument began—Sarah began putting the stamps on envelopes upside down. It was an experiment. Let's see if we can get a different perspective on paying bills if we stick the stamps on upside down.

"IF I am out of my mind, it's all right with me." Rogenstadt didn't always like Bellow's mixture of philosophy and Chicago-Jewish slang—it sometimes seemed artificial, the dialogue a little stiff. These weren't real people talking; these were character types going through the motions, making certain points.

He also couldn't help but see his resemblance to Herzog—a meek academic type with failed marriages. The second to a wild woman,

Madeleine, who left him for a friend. Did Sarah have a friend waiting for her, helping her? He never knew.

Rogenstadt kept drifting back to the phrase Sarah had underlined: "If I am out of my mind." He remembered her medication, her various psychologists and her psychiatrist. He never knew exactly what medication she was on. Different doctors tried different things. Lithium, for a while. "I feel like I'm walking around with cotton in my head," she complained. With other medication it was as if the world had filled up with water and she were walking in slow motion at the bottom of a lake. The doctors kept experimenting with the dosage, trying to get it right.

Rogenstadt shuddered as he remembered her struggles. To be at war with your own mind. To not trust your emotions in the most elemental way. Is this fear real? Is there really something out there to be afraid of? Will this anger destroy me? Will it take me over? Am I really happy? The never-ending complexity of it made him vaguely nauseous.

Schizophrenia. Manic-depressive. Bi-polar. The doctors debated it endlessly. But to Rogenstadt it seemed that Sarah would be seized by a frenzy. She would start spinning and couldn't stop until she crashed into something. Often, he felt, it was his job to be what she crashed into. "I'm not asking you to save me," she shouted at him in one of her fits of anger. "I'm just asking you to stop me. I can save myself, I can handle myself, if there's just someone who cares enough and is strong enough to stop me."

The truth was, he couldn't stop her. He was too intimidated by her hatred, a hatred so powerfully endless.

He was tempted to put the book away, chose another one. But then he decided he couldn't allow her to intimidate him anymore. It was ridiculous. He picked up the book, settled back into the pillow and began to read.

In the years they were married, Rogenstadt had detected a pattern in Sarah's emotional life. It was a predictable cycle—though she would reject the notion there was anything predictable about her. The cycles lasted roughly a year and a half. At the beginning of a cycle (which could almost be seen as the end of the previous cycle), Sarah was curiously content. She saw things clearly; she played her piano, laughed. Was timid and sincere in her tenderness toward him, was full of plans meekly offered.

This was a time of hope, when projects were started. It was during one of these periods that they bought their house. During this part of the cycle, Sarah added a glow to Rogenstadt's world, a glow he freely admitted he could never have added himself. She fixed dinners for him—took pains with the lasagna, enjoyed his enjoyment of it. But there was always, even during this phase, the danger of her getting exhausted, making herself sick. She would be radiant but sniffling with a cold. She would be attentive, they would sit curled up in front of the TV, but she would fall asleep. And he would have to wake her up to get her to bed.

Toward the end of this phase, she would get restless. Things weren't happening fast enough. She knew she should be happy, but she wasn't. She didn't blame him, didn't question his love. This was the time she usually changed her doctors, complained about the medication. If she was tired, if she was susceptible to colds, it was because of the medication. It wasn't working right. It left her vulnerable. This was the time when she sometimes experimented on her own with the dosage. After all, she said, she better than anyone knew what the effect was. She was better able to judge how much she should take and when.

But those experiments inevitably lead to confusion. A panic attack—"I just couldn't make the left-hand turn. I had to go around three blocks because I couldn't make that turn against traffic." A drinking bout that got out of control. The hangover the next morning. The inability to deal with work. Though she was unusually compulsive and thorough in her work (she investigated fraud cases for an insurance company). When the panic attacks came at work, she had to steady herself in the stall of the women's room. Then the questioning began. Had she reduced the dosage too much? Had the drinking thrown everything out of balance? She knew she shouldn't drink, but she couldn't help herself sometimes. It helped her to relax; it helped her to forget. It was necessary. She could find the balance again between the medication and the drinking. She had just temporarily lost the balance.

Several days after starting *Herzog*, Rogenstadt mentioned it to Vera. "I'm not sure I like it," he told her.

"That's Saul Bellow, isn't it? Haven't you read some of his other books?"

"*The Adventures of Augie March. Henderson the Rain King.*"

"If you don't like it, why are you reading it?"

"It's from my shelf of unread books."

Vera knew about his shelf of unread books and just shook her head.

"I've had it for quite a while," he continued. "The pages are even slightly brown. It was printed when quality paperbacks were only a dollar ninety-five."

"That *is* old."

"The main character kind of reminds me of myself."

"I'll definitely have to read it then."

"I don't know if I'd recommend that."

He knew Vera could tell he was flustered and that she was savoring the moment.

"Let me think about it," she said. "You finish it first, then I'll try. If I find anything diabolical, I promise not to tell you."

Rogenstadt came back to *Herzog* the following weekend. He did not read for long, his reading slowed by the sporadic influx of his memories. Each of Sarah's red markings seemed to generate echoes in his mind, like a cannon fired somewhere in a distant, hidden valley.

After three weeks, he finally got past her last marking. This time—strangely enough, in slender black ink—she had underlined several lines from one of Herzog's unsent letters.

Have to go back. Not able to stand kindness at this time. Feeling, heart, everything in strange condition. Unfinished business. Bless you both. And much happiness.

Her last words to me, he thought. But immediately he knew he was wrong. She had read it in college, long before she had met him. How could the underlining be addressed to him? The Sarah who had read the book was someone he didn't know and who didn't know him. He was imagining things, seeing things that weren't there. Making connections where there weren't any.

Rogenstadt was a sound sleeper; he rarely remembered his dreams. But over the weeks he had been reading *Herzog* he would remember fragments of dreams that included Sarah. She would be standing by the house they had bought or walking beside him down a heavily overgrown path. There was a sense of late afternoon and rain.

One night he woke in the middle of the dream and it stayed with him for several hours. He was walking in the mud. Then he was climbing up a steep hill. But when he looked down, the hill seemed to be made of books covered in mud. But the books were moving under him, and he was afraid to look down. He thought he saw people's faces on the covers, but he didn't recognize them, they were so covered with mud and distorted.

It was raining, and the rain made the hill treacherous and he stumbled. Then he saw what he thought was a child crouching on the side of the hill, a girl it seemed, and he thought, "Where are her parents? How could they leave her out here like this?"

But then he saw that it was Sarah, her hair dark and tangled from the rain. She was crouching on her knees and making motions with her hands. Then he was beside her, reaching down, when he saw what she was doing—constantly striking matches against a box. She turned and looked up at him, snarling. "Why can't I do this? What are you making me do?"

Rogenstadt finished *Herzog* one Saturday morning just before he and Vera were taking their annual drive through the mountains. He packed his suitcase, took a few minutes to re-read the last pages, and carefully recorded the date on the title page.

He called Vera.

"I'm heading out in a few minutes. Just finished *Herzog*. Do you want me to bring it over?"

"No, I'll get my own copy. Don't dawdle. Remember we need to get to Henry's before twelve."

"Vera ..." he started.

"Yes?"

"I've been having dreams about Sarah. I can't get over the feeling that I failed her."

"Oh, you're such a noodle. You read too much and you think too much. Get on over here, before I really put the fear of God into you by telling you how much I love you."

Just before he left, Rogenstadt glanced at the unread books left on his shelf. "Only six more to go," he thought, and then he put *Herzog* in the section of American novels between *Henderson the Rain King* and *Humbolt's Gift*.

Iris with Mermaids

Deborah Johnstone

"The mermaids watch over Iris and me." It's one of the only coherent sentences in the entire journal. Illegible scrawls and half obscured cryptic symbols cover yellowed pages. My mother's fragmented notes appear before me even when I close her journal and shove it to the back of my closet. The journal is a talisman I believe, something I can't discard for fear of the consequences.

I am five. I watch my mother's opaque shadow pitch back and forth in the darkened bedroom. I've seen and heard it all before. This is how it's always been—the sound of rustling sheets and constricted moans, muffled whispers and the dull slap of flesh on flesh. Our small, dark bedroom sits beside the kitchen on the second floor of a dilapidated Victorian house in Toronto. Cold, lightless halls, peeling wallpaper, mice, and smells of transient men are familiar. We share the house with boarders. Sometimes my mother drinks with the men but she never sleeps with them; they don't make enough money. She draws a line when it comes to that. Her preference is for adulterers and criminals—men who have access to plenty of cash but few morals.

"Don't ever depend on any goddamn man for anything, they're useless. Learn to do things for yourself. Don't do what I did, depend on some fucking man." She stirs my oatmeal with a wooden spoon, the same spoon she uses to dispense my beatings. Her wavy, jet-black hair is pinned up in a metal clip, but sections stray and waffle erratically as if trying to escape her head. Her bright orange cotton sundress whirls around her slender hips as she rants, seemingly caught up in the fury. It's winter and freezing in the house, but she needs to look a certain way. She has to be vain. Her looks are currency. They allow us to eat. I remember a stranger once telling me my mother was exotic, as if that validated his actions. He pressed a twenty-dollar bill into my hand as he left and disappeared down the stairs into the street. It was as though my existence was legitimized by his gesture, as if I'd been determined worthy by virtue of the fact that I was her daughter with the same Mohawk cheekbones and hazel eyes. No one guessed my mother was Indian. She took great pains to stay out of the sun. The façade was perfect. I watched her draw perfectly arched brows and apply Revlon Red lipstick each day. She would sew herself perfectly fitted dresses and jackets made from Vogue patterns and customer's remnants—silk, wool, chiffon, *bouclé*, fabric she could never afford to buy for herself. She had one pair of black patent, high heel shoes that carried her into the bowels of seedy clubs and bars and guaranteed her a score.

"Don't speak and stay in the kitchen when I come home with someone." It was an easy command to follow—to remain invisible. The repercussions for breaking silence were severe. "Get out!" She screamed once when I entered the bedroom, tired and angry that I couldn't get into the bed we normally shared. "Get out and stay out until I tell you!" When I refuse, she beats me until I can't breathe. As she screams, the stranger watches, blank, without judgment, waiting for her to finish and for me to leave. I glare at him through bleary red eyes. Each strike of my mother's hand brings me closer to the floor and I have to strain my neck to continue to hold his gaze. I want him to understand what he's done. I want him to see that this is his fault. His eye twitches and his fleshy, white torso shifts uncomfortably in our bed. At first, I think he might try to restrain her, but I could see his hesitation, his inability to make a decision that in the end wouldn't benefit him. Sometimes, in the early morning before dawn, I'd stand just outside the bedroom door to see the men's faces as they leave. I wanted to stare them down. I wanted to tell them that I hated their smells and even after they left, their stench remained. Some would acknowledge me with a grunt but most of the men were startled; they had no idea a child was in the house. I never said a word.

I am six. I hear extra footsteps stumble into the house with my mother near dawn. I crawl out of our bed and go to the kitchen with a blanket and sleep on the floor. The linoleum is freezing in the winter and I wake up cold and stiff. I can barely move. The next night, I refuse to sleep in the bed I share with my mother after a strange man has been in it the night before.

"It's late. Get into bed, goddamn you and go to sleep."

"Someone else was there and I smell them and I'm not sleeping in that bed. I'm not," I yell. She drags me into our bedroom by one of my braids and I scream until my lungs chafe and my face burns. Her arm comes down on my back forcing me to collapse to the floor. I yearn to be free of her. I wish that one day, she will go out and never come back. If I shut my eyes and hold my breath long enough, I'm sure I can will it to happen. "I'm not sleeping there!" I clench my fists so tightly my nails draw small half-moons of blood in my palms. I curl up in a ball on the floor with my knees rammed into my stomach and my face pushed into the cold hardwood. I pant for breath to sustain myself—to continue to scream my dissent. The neighbors call the police. I'm cast as a problem child—sullen, spoiled, unable to comprehend rules. The police are skeptical. The metro police are familiar with The Junction and our boarding house. They know we live in a pit stop for transients.

"We don't want to have to come back here, Mrs. Hill. We don't want to have to call Children's Aid." I wondered why she never let Children's Aid take me away. When I was older, I looked for clues in the journal. Some entries appear in red ink, some in pencil, and others in tailor's chalk. Parts of words are scribbled in dagger-like ribbons. Ideas are broken and torn apart without resolution, without end. I began to think she hid the journal from me in life so that I'd only be able to see it when she was no longer here to explain it.

I am seven.

"Come and try this on, Iris." It's a white cotton dress with pink dots. I never ask her to make me anything because she's always so busy sewing for other people. This is a surprise. I understand it to be a birthday gift. The fabric was left over from a customer's garment—remnants—but enough to make something nice. It's a gesture she makes, I suppose, to mitigate the amount of time she spends ignoring or beating me. I try the dress on, and my mother fastens the buttons in the back and combs my hair as if I'm a doll that can be dressed and redressed until I reflect what she hopes to see. "There, now you look like a little girl." She smiles at me, something she does rarely. I feel a sudden wave of relief, as if we've closed the door on a dark void and she will always be this loving, caring mother. "No climbing trees in the dress—do you hear me?" It was my favorite pastime, next to drawing, and there is a perfect climbing tree behind the garage in the backyard. She'd never made me such a pretty garment and I was actually afraid to sit down anywhere. I felt special, as if I had acquired a new life, as if a sacred space had opened up before me. As a child, I marveled at how she could turn a piece of fabric into a gorgeous dress that billowed around a women's body like ocean waves, or at how she could fit a wool coat so that it made the woman wearing it look more elegant than she could ever hope to be. She needed no pattern. It was all in her head and yet, she never explained to me how her mind conceived of this beauty nor did she speak to me of the rage that so often obliterated everything. I can only think of how beautiful my dress is and how nice it is to have something new, particularly something my mother took the time to make for me. Suddenly, I'm just like all the other children who come home from school knowing that their mothers will always have a nice dinner ready for them, always want to hear what they have to say, or ask them how school went, or tell them they will vacation at Wasaga Beach, or perhaps visit an ocean with mermaids.

A new suitor has spurred her generosity. Lou is a stoic and reserved Jewish man, unlike most of the rogues she associates with but of course, he is married. I understood that my mother occasionally worked for him in some capacity—probably sewing garments. He also owned an old, modest hotel in Peterborough with a busy bar where businessmen, adulterers, and drunks, could be comfortable. On several occasions, I traveled there with Lou and my mother. I take great pleasure in running up and down the halls in my bare feet on a thick, deep blue carpet until I'm ordered to stay in our room while my mother and Lou got off to entertain themselves.

I don't mind the hotel room because the sheets were always clean and smelled nice. I was allowed to bring lots of paper and crayons to draw and time alone was a luxury. Those were the only occasions my mother didn't mind me using my time to draw. On this trip to Peterborough she brought her sewing—a garment for a customer had to be finished. I woke up to find her laying fabric out on the other bed and pinning the pattern pieces to it. She was crying. I remember her cutting out the fabric while silently sobbing but never stopping to take a breath.

"Mama, what's wrong?" It was the only time I ever asked her that question. The only time.

"Go back to sleep."

She wasn't drunk. She normally only sobbed when she was drunk, but this was different. Her sorrow while sober was more devastating. It seemed as if the full weight of all the possibilities in the world she had missed were laid out before her on that hotel bed where tissue was pinned to fabric. Always, something was never finished, never resolved, only more pins and patterns and different points of possibility that veered off into nothingness. For the first time I felt like a burden—as if I'd been dragged along because there was nowhere else to leave me. My mother brought her work to a hotel room in a remote town because she had no choice. She brought me because she had no choice. In that moment, I realized options were something other people had. My mother would always be trapped in some hotel room waiting for someone to pay her. I drew my knees into my chest and pulled the covers over my head. I inhaled the smell of the sheets, their clean fragrance a brief respite offering the possibility of escape. One day, I'd have my own sheets. They would be washed every day. No one would touch them but me. I peeked out from the covers to gauge whether or not my mother's sorrow would change into rage.

"Helena, take this—just take it." Lou entered our room and pressed some money into my mother's hand but for some reason, she didn't want it. It made her angrier. My mother shook him off, partly in fury and partly in anguish. It suddenly occurred to me that since we never had enough money, whatever money she got from men was never enough. It made sense to me that money was the one thing that made a difference and that people who had it were far, far better off than those who didn't. I can't say when I made the connection to the fact that men gave my mother money for sex, but I'm certain it was in that hotel room.

I've come to the end of her journal again and still I can't discard it despite the fact it provides no answers. "I worry for Iris." Words I've never noticed before. Or have I? It's clear she left something of herself on these pages and yet I can't find it. Each anniversary of her death I suffer the same longing—to know my mother. Every year, on July 31 at dawn, I pull the journal from my closet. Amid the silence of night ending I try to find something that will redeem me.

I am eight. I show her what I've drawn in art class. She hates it when I spend my time drawing or painting but it's what I enjoy the most. I'm very proud of this painting because it's extremely difficult to render water realistically. I'd spent days trying to get the waves to look just like real water in an ocean, which incidentally, I'd never seen. I scoured art books in the library and found a painting by Winslow Homer depicting rocks, sky, and ocean. The image is dominated by a pulsating swell of water rising over a rocky shoreline. In the background, a blood red sky fades into sunset. I spend weeks on my painting. I want to recreate a never-ending torrent of collapsing and cresting waves. I want the waves to rush at me when I look at the image and sweep me away. I want to create a world where escape is possible. In the middle of my painting I've drawn two beautiful mermaids reclining on a rock that protrudes from a turbulent ocean. The mermaids' long, wavy blond hair and iridescent fins shimmer in the sunlight. Their large green eyes are like crystals and follow you wherever you move. At any second, they could slip into the ocean and be free of invaders or strangers.

"They don't look realistic. No one has eyes that large." Her pronouncement is nonchalant, cool, as if everything outside of her is incidental. My mother goes back to sewing the hem on a gold brocade

115

skirt. She remains hunched over the fabric as daylight fades and long shadows creep across the kitchen floor, darkening the disintegrating linoleum strewn with straight pins. I look long and hard at my picture and decide that if I draw mermaids with big eyes, eyes so large they can see in the dark and into the future, then it was possible that eyes could be this big. They could exist with exactly those eyes and they could bestow great powers on anyone who befriended them.

I am nine. The silence between us has become a safe haven and I draw it closer and closer to me. It's customary—expected. If nothing is said, then nothing can be known. Silence was better than anger. In school, my silence was interpreted as insolence. And so, it was. It's always best to say nothing—to be invisible. Once more, as dawn touches the dark, I wake and leave my blanket in the kitchen to peer through the crack of the bedroom door. I watch my mother's pearly body shift in fleshy, monotonous rhythm. A tiny shard of moonlight from a narrow window illuminates the split and peeling walls of our bedroom. The illumination falls on the wall over my mother's head where she's taped the picture of my mermaids. Emerald green, cerulean blue, cadmium yellow, and inky black, define the two beautiful creatures perched on a jutting rock in the midst of a quaking ocean. I imagine this is a place I can reach, an ocean not bound to the Earth and if I could reach it, I would be free. I listen to the squirrels running in between the walls of the old house, scurrying up and down and gathering whatever necessities squirrels require for their sustenance. Car horns and ambulance sirens course and ebb in the night. Quickening gasps echo from the bedroom. Suddenly my mother calls to me, "Iris! Iris!" Her words are barely audible. I move closer toward the room listening for her voice. The mermaid's crystal eyes look down at me from their perch as the west wind raises a torrent of malachite green around the rocks. They are beckoning me to join them and their golden hair is capsizing around their heads. I can just make out my mother's arms groping the dark; her legs thump as the sheets upend. The stranger's hulk flits in and out of shadow and moonlight. His arms are straight, and his hands straddle my mother's neck.

"Iris!" My mother's strangled appeal is garbled in the swollen dark as the sea rears up into white pillars. I have been told to remain silent, to not interfere, to remain invisible. I watch and wait. Then nothing. An old oak tree lists toward the house, its rustling leaves quiver in the night wind. Branches scrape the windowpane and cast frenetic shadows over the mermaids. They have left their perch and are swimming toward the horizon. I wonder what will happen to me. If my mother is no longer in this room, if she is no longer here and I'm not bound to her. I hear the surge and release of ocean waves. There is no other sound. I'm safely hidden in silence while my mother's breath slowly dissolves. There they are, the mermaids, their crystal eyes still watching. Faded, but as I remember them, carefully folded and tucked into the final page of her journal.

Sioux Falls, South Dakota

Marisol Cortez

A short-haired Asian-American nurse sits by my bed in the dark of night and holds my hand as I weep, listening deeply as I tell her how I've fucked up my life, reassuring me that I have not. I get my own room, at least, with yellow walls and empty cupboard and drawers. Now the room is dark but I have the impression all these years later that the ceilings are high, with windows up top that open onto a moon ice-cold bright. Is that a false memory, though, inserted retrospectively to paper over the distortions and absences of the benzos—or whatever it was they gave me?

The nurse, though, the sincerity and kindness of the nurse is real. Was real. Real and vivid and clear after all these years.

Back up, though, back up.

It's my first night in the mental hospital, where my parents had no choice but to send me after a desperate flight north to the Canadian border with my sort-of boyfriend in his glittery green 1974 Datsun Z which he's named Hans Solo's Belt Buckle, both of us trying, in the loopy irony of much mental illness, to cope with suicidal feelings by doing crazy stuff that only makes everything worse.

When the cops find us, we've made it as far as Sioux Falls, South Dakota. It's not Canada, but it's respectably close. I am fifteen years old.

Back up, though. I'm confused. I'm sitting before the immense heaviness of the wooden desk, or maybe it is metal, of the admitting administrator doctor who has been prepped for my arrival, who must have prescribed the tranks my mom brought to the juvie holding tank because we would have to fly to get home from Sioux Falls, and she knows how terrified I am of flying. Or, wait—does she? How could she have known, since at that point in my life I've hardly flown? Maybe the doctor just figured I'd need to be tranked in order to be captured? Which—probably I did. But lacking experience with psychoactive medication, I gulp two pills before the plane takes off when one or even half a tab would have done.

I am drugged out of my gourd when we get to the hospital, dizzy when I walk, falling-down tired, layers of heavy blankets piled on the warp and woof of my grasp on consensus reality, bending and melting it. I am crying. I am being asked questions by the doctor behind the desk, but what? And what did I say in response, my words slurred, coming to me from somewhere so far away? Both my parents are there with me now. I am being weighed in hospital gown—80 pounds at last, my goal, I reached it—and my blood pressure taken, first while lying and then standing up. After days of not sleeping not eating not drinking, my pulse is low and I have postural hypotension, meaning my pressure drops when I stand. I am determined sufficiently dangerous to myself and admitted. I am given a meal I don't want to eat: a dry baked potato, heated-up frozen carrots shaped like widgets, boiled potatoes, chocolate cake, Gatorade. I am paranoid—I know they're trying to trick me with those buttery potatoes and chocolate cake, to see how easily I'll be fooled, but I won't fall for it!

At night, before bed, a nurse comes in with a can of vanilla flavored Ensure and says I look *normal, average*, and *thin, but not especially thin*. I burst into tears, unable to believe what I'm hearing. Two years of depression, starvation, binging, razors, shrinks, scales—and I look "normal"? Then what the fuck am I doing here? I flush the Ensure and Gatorade down the toilet.

Incidentally: Sioux Falls is where we would fly in when we visited my grandparents in Minnesota, whenever we flew there rather than driving. We'd fly into Sioux Falls and then drive 90 miles East to Slayton, a small town just over the South Dakota/Minnesota state line. My mom's not from San Antonio; she grew up on a farm in southwestern Minnesota.

Not incidentally: my mother's two older sisters are there in the hotel with us. They've driven in from Minnesota to be with my mom, to support her on her emergency trip to South Dakota to retrieve me

119

from the juvenile detention facility. My dad stayed back in San Antonio, probably to make arrangements with the hospital to admit me as soon as I get back. What other choice do they have? My sort-of boyfriend will stay in the tank until his dad arrives—he's driving up from Texas, not flying—and then father and son will have a nice leisurely trip back in time for Josh to go back to school Monday. Josh is suicidal too, calls me cradling the barrel of his dad's unsecured gun beneath his chin, but there will be no hospital for him.

How terrified and frantic my parents must have been. I can only take their perspective now that I myself am a parent.

But my calm Midwestern aunts are there in the hotel with us in Sioux Falls, where we stay a night before we fly back home to the chaos of Texas. They are gravely worried for me, but their quiet presence is calming for my mom, and for me.

Back up, though.

My memories of the juvenile detention facility—a single reference in a letter from Josh names it as *that Threshold place*—are also fragmentary and disorganized. When we arrive around 3:30am on Friday, May 12, 1995, the first thing they do is take our shoes, probably wisely, to foreclose possibilities for either running off or attempting suicide. They pat us down, ask us to empty our pockets. I pray they won't find the diet pills I've stashed there, over-the-counter speed the only thing that can save me from the relentlessness of my appetite. I keep trying to kill it off, to cut it out of me, but always it returns, worse than ever. I've come almost all the way to Canada to get away from the roiling hunger I carry inside my skin.

On intake they separate me and Josh, boys in one wing and girls in another. They have me shower, handing me new clothes, soap, toothbrush. The next day, cooped up during "school time" in big rooms filled with other lost girls, I start but don't finish letters to Josh and my friend Sarah to pass the time. In these letters I describe the kids as nice, but I don't remember interacting with anyone. Lunch is hot dogs and baked beans, but I don't want to eat because, the night before—after the pat-down and paperwork and shower, when around 4:30am I was finally bade goodnight and led to a couch in the middle of the building where a guy named Dan sat all night keeping watch—I lay in the black silence and, finally at rest after 1,100 miles, felt my stomach begin to churn and quake, a nauseous emptiness rushing over me in waves—outcome of three days of depression, adrenaline, amphetamines, little sleep, less food.

Back up.

When the cops find us we're crawling down a backroad about 2am, around the time the bars let out. They must think we're drunk, we're driving so slowly and suspiciously down this gravely road, but what we're doing is looking for a place to pull over and sleep. Feels much less romantic than it did the night before, beneath the stars in an empty field. The bubble has burst already; the next day we'll turn around and drive home.

At first the cops are going to let us go, but then they decide to run our licenses—somehow we'd thought to bring those, mine a learner's permit because I'm only 15, though Josh has let me drive—and discover we're runaways from Texas. I don't remember riding in the squad car, though surely we must have. We leave Hans Solo's Belt Buckle on the side of the road, to be retrieved by Josh and his dad a few days later, when he gets out of Threshold.

Back up.

It's around midnight. I'm standing in the grassy median of the highway with the car door hanging open, watching Josh's white t-shirt recede into the dark as he bounds off in his black boots. I really think in that moment that he'll leave me there, on the side of the highway in Sioux Falls, and then what will I do? It's because I've finally disgorged my confession that I think we should go back. Anxiety has been brewing in my chest for hours, since Nebraska, as late afternoon cooled to evening and we sank into night, speeding down a narrow highway constricted by construction, taillights and headlights rushing past in an endless, dizzying blur. What if the problem isn't home but *me?* What if we make it to Canada but I'm still suicidal? What if I'm too unstable to get a job and start over, as planned?

It's our second night on the road. The car's been fucking up, engine seizing after two days running hot. And my anxiety grows and grows until finally, when we hit Sioux Falls and miss our exit, I just have to blurt it out. *I think we should go back.* On hearing this, Josh pulls over to the side of Interstate 90, slams to a stop, throws open his door, and storms off into the night. *If you wanna go back, you can go by yourself!* A letter I start to Sarah while at Threshold mentions that I follow him, that we cry together on the side of the highway—but I don't remember any of that. I remember only the shoulder of the interstate median, the hanging-open door, the 18-wheelers thundering past, rattling my heart inside my chest with each passing blast of wind.

Back up, though.

Before the rising panic of late-afternoon Nebraska, Kansas is beautiful. We've come straight shot up the interstate from Texas, but in Kansas we fork off onto a smaller, slower state highway that passes through a number of little towns. Outside one we spy a homemade billboard that warns, yikes: *Unmarked nuclear waste trucks travel these roads. Keep our children safe and radiation free!* With sun shining and wind high and cool, northeastern Kansas is an expanse of rolling green, not at all the grey flatness we expect from movies.

Before that, Wichita is tattered and overcast but also feels warm and inviting, like a favorite armchair battered by coffee stains and cat scratchings. We roll through mid-morning, in time for plain black gas station coffee, sweetened with aspartame, and half a blueberry bagel from home, carefully shredded and eaten scrap by scrap, slowly, to make it last. Wichita is where Josh finds a CD store and sells his discs for 80 bucks in gas money. Now CDs are less than worthless—obsolete, a liability, something to string together in desperation as yard art—but back then a stack of discs could fetch a few bucks.

Back up.

From where we live outside of San Antonio, we drive north and north and north until we force back the creeping onset of early Texas summer and it becomes spring again, miraculously, somewhere where the soil is red clay. On our first night we find some grower's freshly plowed field and eat dinner sitting on the warm hood of the Z, food hastily packed in plastic grocery bags. A giant yellow apple for me and nothing more. When the sun sets it grows cold, something we haven't anticipated or prepared for, and we fold down the seats of Josh's car to form an almost-big-enough bed in the hatchback, clinging together for warmth. We fall asleep for a few fitful hours to psychedelic-era Moody Blues booming on the stereo. The sky is rich with stars, and it is almost like camping out, almost—but there is something in the music, *On the Threshold of a Dream*, my mother's favorite album, that disturbs and almost frightens me. The poetic interludes are just slightly too loud, a maelstrom of dark chords churn beneath the sweetness of melody, the piano builds to an ominous crashing crescendo before receding into the hiss of empty space.

But back up.

That morning I fully intend to go to school. I wake up at 5:45am, I run a mile, I drink two cups of coffee with aspartame for breakfast. But when Josh swings by to pick me up for school, I am heavy with depression. We're late, again. It feels pointless to strive. We make it out the door but halfway there I tell him, *turn around—I do want to go. Let's just go.*

We go back to my house to pack. Some apples, bagels, our wallets, some clothes, my writing notebook, what else? I riffle through the contents of my bottom dresser drawer, where I stash letters and journals and mementos, things precious to me. I write a note of apology to my parents and leave it on the dining room table, explaining that if I don't leave I will die, I will end up taking my life. Not a suicide note but one of survival, ironically. Running away is how I will save my life. The plan is to make it to Canada and … busk? Sell poems on the street? Really?

Back up, one last time.

In the utility room the night before, on the phone with Josh, the idea crept into my head when he said, *You know, I could take you away from all this. Just say the word.* I've spent the evening binge eating until I feel sick, then cutting my arm as punishment, then walking around the neighborhood in the dark trying to figure out what I'm going to do about the spiraling chaos my life has become. Josh has a car, a succession of cars that he drives for awhile before crashing them in error or anger. Three in all by the time we break up for good. He likes cars, likes to work on them in the yard. He reads Tolkien; he listens to Rush. His parents are permissive in a way that agitates my own parents. Me, I like him as a friend but not really as a lover, though I want to. I want to like him more than I do, and I try. I'm willing to try. I want to be in love with him, like he is with me. I am wrecked by the rejection of a previous boy, a best friend I loved intensely but who played me when I told him. Josh is my attempt at annihilating not only my own anguish but also my desire, to give away the *yes* I wanted for myself to someone who asks it of me. To save another from their own desire and despair.

The problem is it doesn't work that way, and it never will. I had to learn that. The problem is he can tell I don't love him like he loves me, though I tell him I do. The problem is that trying to be with him because he wants it and not because I do confuses him, makes him crazy, deepens his own suicidal and self-destructive impulses, which are as intense as mine. He was already cutting himself when we met; I pick it up from him like a cold.

After breaking up, I would blame Josh for our volatile and eventually violent dynamic, and later I would see my role in it and blame myself.

Now I have only compassion for both of us for being what we were: suicidal children.

I couldn't, I say slowly, in response to his offer over the phone. But by the next morning, I'll have changed my mind.

Mental hospitals are blunt instruments for bringing the mania of flight to a full stop all at once, more brick wall than therapeutic process. So when you crash, you crash hard, breaking every bone in your body. But you don't die. You don't die—and that's what they're good for.

Beyond that, they're essentially prisons. And you're so desperate to get out that you will do whatever you need to do to prove that you're better. And maybe you are, but probably you relapse as soon as you're out. Or maybe you get better eventually, but it takes a really, really long time. And you have to decide you want to do it, and you have to do it yourself, for yourself. That's the thing.

Maybe several years later you'll find yourself in graduate school, recoiling in surprise and self-consciousness when a colleague grabs your upper left arm and gasps, *What happened?* You never think about the scars anymore. They're just a part of you now, something you carry on your skin without embarrassment, like a birthmark. It's easy to do if no one says anything, if their eyes slide over in silence, past the surface of your skin. But for someone to ask about it—like that, anyway—opens up the shock of remembering the shame and stigma of being ill, strange, unfit.

But maybe you'll find that experience theorized for the first time in books, read for the first time in classes that place those scars, so long a private matter, within a larger history and politics. Not your fault, the intensity that made them seem like some kind of solution. Not some strangeness to keep secret so as to pass, like you've always assumed you had to do.

Maybe you write a synopsis, a—what did they call it in grad school? A précis?—of Michel Foucault's *Madness and Civilization,* read as part of your disability studies seminar. The book strikes you as profoundly weird, like seeing yourself in the mirror for the first time:

125

Michel Foucault's classic Madness and Civilization: A History of Insanity in the Age of Reason *might be just as aptly subtitled* The Extermination of Madness at the End of the 19th Century. *For Foucault's main argument is that "what we call psychiatric practice is a certain moral tactic contemporary with the end of the 18th century, preserved in the rites of asylum life, and overlaid by the myths of positivism" (276). Through numerous case studies and extensive quotes from prominent figures of the era, Foucault examines how shifts in the role of institutional structures such as the leprosarium, the house of confinement, the hôpital, and the asylum paralleled shifts in European society's understanding of madness. From the 15th century's conception of madness as indistinguishable from indigence and criminality to the 18th and 19th centuries' delivery of madness unto a normative and condemning bourgeois moral order, Foucault documents the process by which institutional structures and practices have inscribed themselves upon the bodies and minds of those considered mad: excommunication, physical abuse, regulation, and judgment have given way, in more recent times, to the creation of that "serene world of mental illness" in which "modern man no longer communicates with the madman" (x).*

Curiously, Foucault leaves off his historical analysis here, at the doorstep of the 20th century. We can only guess that his silence regarding contemporary society echoes the great silence of an Unreason stilled by the totalizing discourse of medicine. After all, he warns us in the preface that "I have not tried to write the history of [psychiatric] language, but rather the archaeology of that silence [which results from such a language]" (xi).

Confronting this strategic silence, I cannot help but wonder about this obstinate absence of the present. To critically address the history of madness, do we not also have to discuss contemporary psychiatric language, given that it continues and has real force in the lives of modern subjects (especially those defined or who self-define as disabled)? The language of unreason may indeed be the unreachable abyss beyond which no Western discourse can venture— but what of the ways, immediate and concrete, in which contemporary society treats and represents those considered mad, insane, crazy, mentally ill? Certainly, for me one of the most surprising aspects of Foucault's text was this subjective disjunct between his history and my experience—two things which, objectively speaking, should be seamless. As a teenager, I ran away from home and subsequently was hospitalized for a time in a psychiatric institution, primary effect of which was to scare me straight, basically: an experience that echoes Foucault's description of the asylum as "an instrument of moral uniformity and of social denunciation" (259) which merely masquerades as modern medicine. Yet reading Foucault, I am left with the sensation that the history he details so painstakingly in no way bears upon the now. It seems a disembodied account of madness, a history discontinuous with present times and present practices—an impression strangely belied by the realization that what I am reading is somehow "our" history, "our" legacy. Not until I have finished the book does it hit me, and then only oddly, in the space of his silence: these things continue, and I have lived them.

I stay in the hospital a week, three nights inpatient followed by four days in outpatient. Intent on getting out, I decide I will eat regular meals if it means I don't have to drink Ensure—I've figured out that if I stick to salads and vegetables and dry potatoes and pickles, I can appear to eat quite a bit while keeping my actual calorie intake low. The nurses still accompany me to the bathroom to make sure I'm not purging, but I don't do that—I have a lifelong phobia of vomiting even more profound than (and just as disabling as) my compulsion to starve. During my time in outpatient, a white van picks me up each morning to take me to the hospital during the day, where I study for my algebra finals, go to group therapy, write letters to my friends, and take a battery of psychological tests, including the famous Rorschach. On my last day, the same white van takes the adolescent wing on an afternoon outing, to a nearby mall where we see a Billy Crystal rom-com—*Forget Paris*, I think? So weird, to think of it now.

Everyone wants me on anti-depressants, but I refuse. All the kids in the hospital are on meds, and their stories of side effects and social control scare me. *They start you on 50 mg,* one girl tells me, *then jack the dosage up*

127

without telling you. She mentions another girl, transferred from Acute to Long Term—where they can detain you indefinitely—just because they want to adjust her medication. I decide I can't let them snare me, that I have to do something, and quick. I had better gain weight fast, while my mind is free. Not too much, but enough.

And then a week is up, and I'm free. I'm nowhere near better but the hospital's not really meant for that, and my parents can't afford it anyway. Years later, I will learn that they paid for that one week with all the college savings they'd carefully put aside for me over the years. Who might I have become if I'd been able to use that money for my education rather than for treatment, if mental illness had not interrupted this intended transmission of economic stability? Who might I have been had I not needed hospitalization? But I did need it, and there is no shame in that.

A few years ago, during another acute episode of mania and depression, I tried to recover all my medical records from my adolescence. All those psychiatric visits, all those tests in the hospital—somewhere, someone must have notes and notes filled with diagnostic codes, analyses, clues into the meaning of the mystery of the intensity at my core. But nothing was retrievable; nothing existed any longer. It felt like returning to one's childhood home only to discover it had burned down years before. Like a library fire, an arson.

Of all the many things I have written about my life, I have never written about running away or the hospital—except obliquely—and I don't really know why.

Sometimes, though, I still think of that nurse sitting beside my bed, holding my hand as I cried. If hospitals were only that, instead of brick walls or carceral spaces—someone to sit beside your bed holding your hand and listening intently, real kindness softening their face—it would make a real difference, I think. It made a real difference.

Sever

K.B. Carle

I hang around for the after.

Aerin sees the scars of the women moving throughout the train station as thin strips of duct tape. The same scars she hides beneath her oversized sweater. She rolls her black socks down to pick at the scabs. The woman at the information desk has strips of duct tape over her hands. Passes a train schedule to an elderly woman who has duct tape forming small X's along her back, disappearing within the green dress she wears. A woman who runs her fingers through the hair of a sleeping man, his head resting on her lap, has duct tape wrapped around her feet, stretching up to her ankles. A mother with duct tape across her mouth escorts her daughter, with duct tape knees, into the bathroom.

Aerin's husband believed everything could be fixed with duct tape. However, the tongue drying out in her pocket needs water from either the fountain outside or the bathroom, Aerin hasn't decided.

As a Reaper, I can't help her decide, not that she would hear my opinion if I spoke it out loud. Another woman waits for her husband who is having a warring conversation between his cellphone and anyone who dares to shake their head at him. This woman, with duct tape around her eyes, sits on the fountain's edge, drags her finger over the water's surface causing minor collisions that no one feels but her.

If Aerin chooses the fountain, she would have to explain the tongue. At least, I think so. Though, I don't know what it's like to have a tongue.

Or to have someone steal it from me.

Aerin grabs her suitcase, feels the weight of her life packed inside. Notices how easily she can spin with it in her grasp, free to release it and injure others. Free to hold everything she has left, everything she could snatch without thinking close to her chest, over her shoulder, in front of her face. For now, she holds the suitcase at her side and walks to the nearest bathroom.

Inside, the mother with the duct tape over her mouth waits outside a bathroom stall. Her cheeks puff when she notices Aerin and, maybe me too. I like to think she's smiling at one or both of us. Aerin doesn't feel the same, grip tightening around the tongue. The mother knocks on the door of the bathroom stall.

"Almost!"

Is it weird to rinse a severed tongue in a public bathroom?

Is it worse to do it in front of a child?

The little girl, instead of doing what humans do in bathrooms, is making toilet paper bows and tying them in her hair. However, toilet paper is a weak material as Aerin discovers in the stall next door, unable to unroll enough sheets to wrap the tongue and slip it into her suitcase between her last minute collection of baggy sweatshirts with chewed off cuffs, a roll of duct tape, and scissors in a Ziploc bag with blood smeared on the inside.

Duct tape can't fix everything.

The girl comes out of the stall at the same time as Aerin, both losers in a war against single ply toilet paper. The little girl soaks what remains of her tissue ribbons with tears and her mother pats her head in a way that moves the girl towards the door. I remove my hood, pat my skull, wonder what a mother's touch feels like.

Aerin kneels in front of the girl before they leave and, for a moment, I think she's going to give the child the tongue as a parting gift. Instead, she angles her suitcase so neither mother or daughter can see inside and pulls out her roll of duct tape.

While she works, Aerin thinks about the husband she left behind on the kitchen floor. How he gazed at her, body lurching from the shock or struggle of trying to gasp for air but having blood seep from his throat at the same time. I missed all the screaming, the angry exchange that probably led to him grabbing her wrist. I phased through the wall just as she grabbed a kitchen knife and, foolishly, I raised my hands. She held it pointed between my rib cage before she turned away, slashing the air between her and her husband until he decided to come closer. Until she decided to keep the knife moving even when an easy flick of the wrist became a jagged pull.

Until she decided she couldn't stop.

Or refused to.

Aerin uses her teeth to tear into the duct tape because they are strong after years of barring her words. Her hands steady because they are the same hands that reached for her husband's wallet when his body stilled. Hands that collected the remains of an unwanted life and threw the pieces into a suitcase. Same hands that used the money she found to buy a ticket to a place she doesn't know but is hours away from him, from this final duct tape solution. Aerin laughs, is surprised by the feel of it expanding her throat. She sticks the duct tape bow on the girl's forehead, which is very unflattering. The girl thinks so too and decides to transform the gift into a bow tie. She thanks Aerin and I think the girl's mother would too if she could.

Once they leave, Aerin places what's left of the duct tape in her suitcase. Turns on the hot water, waits for the steam to appear. She removes the tongue from her pocket, watches the taste buds rise. She exits the bathroom, tongue tucked in her pocket again, counting her steps to her train.

I follow her until I can't, left floating above train tracks.

She never looks back.

Lubbock 1974

Bobby Horecka

If the stars had aligned better, the boy could've been the son of a teacher, a scientist, or a business tycoon. He might've spent his days blowing out birthday candles, playing catch outside with dad, or singing silly songs with mom, full of elaborate gestures. The itsy-bitsy spider, perhaps. Or He's got the whole world. That one about that bridge that kept falling down.

He'd settle for the alphabet song. Johnny Cash. Sabbath. The Doors. The son of son of a sailor. Anything, really. Was it so much to ask?

Other kids did such things. He'd seen it, out in the world, the few times he got to go. But not at this house. Never here. It could've been a fairy tale for all he knew. Make believe. Something in a faraway, near forgotten dream.

He often swipes a grimy paw at his overgrown hair. It is forever falling in his face—pasting to one of his cheeks, poking him in the eye, or crawling up a nostril—always itching something awful. It's a blonde like you rarely see, not so much a color as a *light*. It seems to emit its own luminance, an untamed radiance of tangled muss.

Paired with those ice blue eyes and a devilish perma-grin Kool-Aid stain, he's impossible to forget. Even if he wasn't yet three and already scrawny for his age.

Those cold eyes, that wild flame-like hair.

They burn in your soul, alive and living, as he was, beyond the outer fringe of nightmares out at reality's bitter edge. That fiery hair, those frozen eyes, consuming …

The *fuzzies* came on bouncing, bounding *footses* into his hidey spot, his hole, his safe place, beyond the *owey* pokes that make you bleed. He found it following *bunnies*. They were always outside. Light and *dawk*. Nibble, nibble. *Hawp*, hop, to over *they-yuh*.

Thems eated da gwass. The boy snatches a tuft of winter-burned stems, holds it high. Grass, he meant to say. The man with long dark hair listens intently, looks on in bemused disbelief.

"No thanks," the man says, his voice deep, mellow. "I got my own."

He laughs like a whisper, airy, holds up funnel-shaped hand-rolled, the smoke curling and vanishing. Curling. Swirling. Gone. Curling. Delicate. Swirling threads. *Kitty whiskers*, the boy tried to say once, then vanished and gone.

The man never understands him.

He comes out every day and sits on the wooden steps, smokes his smoke beside the half-opened back door. Twirls of smoke vanish in the cold air. Smells so good to the boy. Not the smoke, but behind that door.

He can't tell him that. He doesn't know how. No one taught him how. But the coffee brewing, butter melting, eggs browning, sizzling bacon: The boy's insides churn each morning, his senses keen.

Like something wild. Half-starved wolf cub. Always the same.

The man never understands.

Often, at night, the boy raced off in the dark. Had to, you see. Got crazy inside. He made the red-dirt yard in seconds flat, dodging minefields of junk, rusted, jagged-edged cans, busted crates spilling broken bottle shards, sharp as razors and hidden by night. Barefoot, of course, but much safer there than he was inside. He spied the secret path deep into the thorny brush. He knew the spot well. He had used it too many times before. They never ever wake up it seems, when darkness gives way to light. They stay up moaning, screaming, fighting is what it sounds like to the boy, and it goes on all night. Don't try and wake them, though, or walk in when there's noise. They get awful mean. They just don't like little boys. Or perhaps they do—too much—that's what sets them off. But it's times like those, when they caught him, he thought he wouldn't make it out. They'd hit with belts and boards and fists, often swinging blind in the dark. Twice they'd connected when they lashed out like that, and twice they'd knocked him out.

The *Preacher*, everybody called him, and with him always that skinny white, white pink-eyed man that everybody called the *Ghost*. They were always trying to hurt. Just last month, the little boy, stuck his finger in a door hinge, a stupid thing to do. Split his finger and his nail, got blood all everywhere. Over the next few weeks, though, it was healing. Until *Preacher* stomped it flat at church. *Ghost* grabbed his head and shoved him to the floor. That wasn't bad, though. Not until *Preacher* took his heel and ground round, mashing it hard into the floor, like he'd seen the *Hunter* do with cigarettes when he was through. He never heard anybody call *Hunter* anything. He scared everybody because he was always mean. He carried a big, bone-handled knife and had taken it to the boy once or twice. It doesn't hurt so bad, getting cut by his knife. Nothing like when they hit him instead. The last time he got hold of him, he turned his whole bed red. But the *Candyman* was hardest of all to read. One minute he'd be almost nice, the next he'll beat you half to death. And he does things, awful things, that hurt so bad. Just know you need to run hard and fast, no matter how hungry you may be, you ever hear him ask *Want some candy, baby boy?*

So, mornings the boy always spent outside. Most days, he was already there anyway. And one day, he tried to catch a bunny. The boy thought he'd finally have a friend. They're always hopping around, nibbling on this, then hopping over there. But whenever he got close, they ran away. Ran away fast. He followed it one day, down its hidden bunny trail, to see where it went. What might be there. Perhaps he'll find bunny houses, or big piles of carrots someplace. He sure could eat a few. Fuzzy warm mommy bunnies. He can go live with them. She might even sing to him. Teach him the words to that bridge song.

The spines on the bushes left him several *owies*. They burned for days and bled and bled. Took several tries to get it right, but he could run full speed and dive like superman, his belly in the dirt. The bunny may have disappeared, no bunny house ever found, but the boy had a new hidey hole.

One even *THEY* wouldn't brave. Not *Preacher* or his *Ghost*. Not *Hunter* nor *Candyman*, even *Maybelle* and *Iris*, too. None of them got to him here, and all of them had tried. *Hunter* even tried to burn it down, with fire and a can of gas. Almost burned down that awful house instead. The boy would have been glad.

Its entrance hidden beneath sprawling boughs, pointy thorns like needles, some long as the boy's hand. Unlike before, too, when he ran out in the night, this time he brought a blanket. Probably not a blanket, really. Probably more like a towel. He wasn't exactly toasty warm now, his breath hanging in white wisps about his face, but it was better than nothing. He nearly froze to death that last time without it, when the snows almost buried his boney hide, inside his secret hidey hole. Still, better than inside. He didn't dare go there. That's the fringe of nightmares ...

Run away, if you can. It only hurts in there.

If only he had something to eat. But each time's the same.

The man with long dark hair never understands.

The man with the long dark hair considers the boy with matted fiery hair. He only appears after he's had his pain pills, dabbed the salve on the wound by his heart that never wants to heal, and lights up on the back stoop. The boy never appears until the pills kick in, until he's smoked half his smoke. Not every time, but often enough. He's not quite sure if he's even real.

Maybe it's the mix of those pills and the smoke. It doesn't help that he's always alone whenever the boy appears. His old lady said it's just a hallucination, a vision, something she read about in a book.

He just doesn't know.

The last time the boy appeared, the man with the long dark hair stuck his hand in the wound by his heart that never wants to heal. The pain was real enough. Even the boy's strange babble seemed real, too. He couldn't make it out, quite yet, but he knew he was close. His old lady, though, cooking breakfast just beyond the door, said she heard nothing, just the man with the long dark hair talking to himself.

So, that's his routine now, every day. Pills. Salve. Grass. The boy doesn't appear every day, but enough. He tries to interpret what it means when the boy appears, if it's omen or luck. He hasn't figured that out either. His old lady says it's just him, starting out the day too fucked up. He'd love to latch onto the boy, bring him inside, dangle him by one of his scrawny arms, show him to the woman beyond the door cooking breakfast. But he can't. His pain is always worse at first light. Plus, for all he knew, his hand might pass straight through. The boy, that is. But at least he'd know if he's real ...

It doesn't help that the boy always looks the same whenever he appears, barefoot and barebacked, heavy diaper he's always hiking up. Covered in grime, always the filth, babbling away beneath his matted fiery hair. It doesn't matter, July hot or fresh fallen snow. When he appears—if he appears—it's always barebacked and barefoot.

So, he keeps his routine. Pills. Salve. Grass. Then he sits, he sits and he waits. Every day. Sometimes the boy appears; others he does not. But it's happened enough, he wonders if today will be the day.

He found his grass in jungles far away, where he got that oozing wound by his heart that never wants to heal. It won't let him work, forever oozing. The medic told him they couldn't get it all out. "Liable to fester a while," he'd said, right before they shipped him home.

Medically discharged, but not because of that wound by his heart. No, according to the papers he had, his brain had gone bad out there in the jungles. There was a mix-up of some sort, that day in the jungle, something they called *friendly fire*. It wasn't the Slopes that shot him and left him for dead. His own sergeant, the crazy bastard, shot him.

The part that truly peeled back the man with the long dark hair was the fact he couldn't get his military award, his Purple Heart. Wounded in battle, he was, right there by his heart. They discharged him at the capital, when all was said and done, him and his bad brain. The first stop he made, down back alley street, was a seedy old pawnshop. He got him his heart, purple and proud, an ornament made for another man's wound. But still he wore it on whatever he had on that day. Some days, there on his stoop as he plays out his routine, he'll have only a blanket draped on his shoulders, like a cape. And always—every time—if you look close and hard, you'll see that gold medallion, it's ribbon purple and white, pinned to the blanket he bled on that night.

He'd left DC for California in a second-hand car, his pills, his salve, his purple heart, and his smoke. When his wheels gave out, just half the way there, he hit the local paymaster, withdrew his combat pay, and decided to stay there. He bought him the little wood-frame house, with the stoop where he now sat, right on the edge of town. Right on the fringe of madness and nightmare, it turned out. His yard was haunted by a small, babbling boy. Or maybe, just maybe, the jungle had indeed clouded his mind.

He wished he knew of some way he could really tell.

Looka! The boy, commanding the attention of the man with long dark hair, hops, circular in the snow. Barefooted, barebacked. Filthy. Just the heavy diaper he has to hike up. He stops hopping. He points, stamping his tiny foot.

Looka, fuzzies house.

The man with the long dark hair and the wound by his heart, shrugs his shoulders.

"I don't understand, little man," he says. "What is it you're trying to say?"

The little boy looks up at the man, whose long dark hair is tied in back to make a tail. Most of it lies on his right shoulder, but falls behind him, strand by strand, each time he shrugs and takes another long drag. He never understands. As the boy kicks his bare foot, he hears another whispery laugh from the top of the stairs, the man with the long dark hair, sitting on his stoop, beside an open back door.

It visibly bothers the boy, that much is clear to the man. It frustrates him, this talking gap. The boy stares at the ground, hikes that heavy diaper again, left-handed, while grimy right bats the tangled sticky bangs from his eyes. Arm twists, pretzels. He rocks the knuckles of that grimy right, back, forth, back, forth. Thinking.

He wants words. So much to say. Doesn't know how.

The boy stops sudden. Frozen, head cocked. Listening. His hands out, fingers spread. Elbows at forty-fives. Angled and frozen. The man with the long dark hair listens. He hears something, too, maybe four or five houses down. The places get progressively worse, the farther down the road. His wood frame house, although not very large, was a palace in comparison to some of those at the end of the road. If it's coming from one of those places, no wonder the little ghost boy seems so scared.

An old screen door opens, the popping thrumming sound of the door spring stretching, the needs-oil creak of a rusted hinge. The sound of someone stepping out, followed by the familiar pop, wood smacking wood when the spring snaps back. A crisp new sound rings out on the cold morning air, the *chingle* of shattering glass. The man with the long dark hair looks down at the little boy. He, still frozen, a tiny statue, unmoving. Well, not entirely unmoving, he appears to be keeping tabs of each new crash of glass.

"Aw man," the man with the long dark hair says. "I didn't know we were—"

The boy silences the man with the long dark hair, popping up his hand like a traffic cop. The boy cocks his head, listening. From the sounds of it, someone was getting rid of a whole box of bottles. But these weren't typical beer bottles. They sounded larger, heavier, like wine bottles, or pop bottles. Surely, they wouldn't dispose of them. Those are worth money, probably a buck or two by now, the man estimates.

The ringing stops. A deep smoker's hack rings out.

"OH-oh," the little boy with matted fiery hair says, not at all loud, but clear and distinct. His sergeant, the one who shot him, had a voice like that.

"I galla go," the boy says, but before he vanishes from sight, the man with long dark hair suddenly perks up, snaps fingers, and points at the boy. "You said you gotta go!"

The boy smiles, mimicked his point. Some other time, maybe, he'd teach him that snap. He looks back to where all the noise had come from, four or five houses down, cautious at first, peeking inch by inch around the corner.

Then wink-quick, seeing it clear, he bolts round the trees and is gone.

The man with the long dark hair sucks at the nubbin, but just as he

138

is about to flick his roach down to the red dirt, a very thin, very pale, very unusual man walks up, slow and quiet, craning his neck this way and that, checking the space between the houses. Something about him, the way he moved—the man with long dark hair couldn't put his finger on it—was just off. Unusual.

The man with long dark hair hardly breathes. The only thing moving, aside from the thin silver line of smoke rising, curling into the sky, is the wounded soldier's eyes. The pale man, rail thin, has a thick navy coat, the kind you'd see on men working the docks. Red corduroy pants, poking out from below the coat, twig thin.

Seeing him, dressed so warmly, only lent credence to the impossibility of the boy. Plus, this fellow pulls the top of his coat tighter, as if, despite all those clothes, he was still cold. There's no way that a baby in diapers and nothing else could possibly be out here. Barefoot and barebacked. Besides, pale as this cat was, he's probably just another backyard premonition. It's why he looks so damn weird. His face, pale as snowfall, could've been whittled from wood for all the expression it held. He'd be impossible to beat at Five Card Stud, face like that.

And very thin. Very pale. Very unusual.

The fellow keeps scanning the ground, this way then that, like a pigeon following an old man round a park, looking for handouts from that bag of popcorn he smells. Would've thought he passed by earlier and dropped his favorite dollar. The man with long dark hair stays statue-still, moving nothing but his eyes, which stay glued on the pale man, who falls flat to the ground, as if his drill sergeant just hollered to give him twenty. He never gets around to the push or the up. Rather, he stays down there a good minute and a half, at least, staring deep in the darkness underneath the house.

Just as the man with the long dark hair decides to ask the dude if he's OK, he rocks on his knee and stands back up, moves on to his house to peer at its underside. Before he does, though, the unusually pale man notices a blue metal five-gallon can there at the foot of the stairs. The man with the long dark hair watches the pale man open it up, remove a combat boot that's inside. The pale man squints his eyes, peering at the boot.

The man with the long dark hair has had enough: "Morning," he says. The pale man jumps. He had no clue the man was there, but it has positively no impact on the color of his cheeks. They're practically clear.

He mumbles something.

"What was that?" asks the man with long dark hair.

Through a significant hair-lip, the pale man speaks: "Have you seen a little boy come by here?"

He's seen him, too. But how? The man with the long dark hair doesn't understand. He rises and steps through the half-open door, closes it behind him, and bolts the lock.

The little boy with fiery matted hair disappeared in the brush long before *Ghost* wandered over. He decides to go exploring, down Bunny Biways, trails running this way and that, all over the ground, like a tangled-up net. Intertwining, Bunny internet.

Then there comes a loud sound, like a bucket of gravel dumped on an old tin roof. The boy goes toward it, having never heard anything like it before. Not knowing what the sound is, he comes up slowly, keeps his cover in the in brush. He lets out a small squeal from his spot in the trees when he sees. *The Fuzzies!* All there in a pile, all playing and biting and—wait a minute—what are they biting?

The boy stands at the edge of the brush, checking for people. He's not sure who here he can trust. He looks as far as he can one way, then spins round the other way, checking, ever so careful. He doesn't want to be found.

It appears the coast is clear.

He doesn't relate the two, what he sees with the noise that he'd heard, but his buddies, the *fuzzies*, are all there.

Someone laid the lid to a trashcan in the middle of the red dirt yard and in its center, piled nice and high, is what looks like a cereal of some sort, the kind that comes with a toy. The *fuzzies* sure seem to like them. And the boy's so hungry ...

"Gots any fo' me?" the boy asks the fuzzy little dogs, all too immersed in their meal to pay much mind to the boy. He walks behind them to the huge serving tray and sits right down in the middle of all his fuzzy friends where he can reach the pile, too. His buddies all round him don't mind in the least. And the boy couldn't be happier. He was surrounded by his little buddies and they had something to eat. The cereal they ate could've sure used some milk because it was awful dry. It didn't have much of a taste either. But this was his first food in a couple of days. Now he could tell the man with long dark hair how his buddies, the *fuzzies*, had found him a feast.

So there, surrounded by eight little mongrel pups, the baby boy and baby dogs form quite a sight, especially when he points his diapered butt up to the sky so he can eat like his friends. For once in his life he looks like the biggest pup in the pack.

And as he swallows kibble, there in the yard, wouldn't you know it? He'd let down his guard.

The boy in the house is looking out the window while his momma warms up some chicken soup for him and his brother from a can. Why the woman bothered with such nonsense like heating it he'd never understand. She stood there stirring, stirring, stirring for like ten minutes. Then it sat on the table for next to forever, so it could cool off enough to eat. What a waste! So, while she stirs, stirs, stirs over the stove, the boy watches as another boy wanders into his yard, plops next to his dogs, and eats their food.

"Momma, there's a baby outside eating with the dogs."

"Sure there is, honey. What's his name?

"I don't know. I was gonna ask you."

"That's nice, honey ... Listen, mamma needs to make a phone call. Why don't you go get your brother so y'all can get going."

She grabs the receiver and dials her number, dial whirling again and again. They wash up like they'd been told. The elder of the two finishes faster, wipes his hands on his pants. When the smaller one comes, he joins his brother, looking out the window.

"Whatcha looking at?"

"A baby."

"Nu-*uh*."

"Uh-*huh*. He was eating their food walla-go," big brother says.

"*Nuh uh!*"

"*Uh huh!*"

"*Mom!*"

If only the stars were better aligned …

Running in Circles

Merrill Gray

"Your mum's a whore!" is all I hear at the other end of the phone. I'm sitting eating cheese and crackers and watching afternoon soaps while rummaging through a keepsake box I promised to clean out before my trip. I'm thinking *who is this idiot?* and *he must have the wrong number.* But I sort of recognize his voice and I turn down the TV. "I don't care," I say back to him. "I don't believe you!"

I hang up and look out the window at my mum mowing the lawn; her beige crochet bikini hangs onto the small fold of skin below her waist. We had to convince her to buy the property a few years back. She was living in low cost housing and had made a midnight move from my abusive dad. This was years before "child support" payments were required; when men ran away from their jobs and the government to avoid paying.

She is just starting to stand on her own after a few years of depression where she lay in bed most days staring at the ceiling. Now she is dating a variety of slime balls.

Around men, it's like she turns into this Barbie doll, all smiles and flirty. Her outfits are perfectly accessorized with glitzy matching shoes and handbag. She's a Geisha without the benefits. It makes me wince; I just don't get my mum's behavior. If I was to ask her, she likely wouldn't have a clue what I was talking about. We never talk about it, but if we did, I would say something like I never want to end up like you. Even though I know that would be mean. Talking about sensitive issues is like spitting in public; not permitted.

I'm twenty years old and have already lived away from home for four years but I'm crashing here for a few months after my first university degree. I'm working two jobs to save enough money to go to France.

July 1978

I pick up a small worn book from the keepsake box, *Becoming a Woman*.

"Becoming a woman takes more than your body; it takes your mind and heart and soul as well." p. 22. *

Gawd, I remember this book. I was about twelve years old when my mum slipped it into my room. This 35 cent copy of "explosive" ideas preached information and knowledge girls needed to learn in order to "control themselves" and grow into the kind of woman the patriarch society expected them to be. Why did I keep it? I watched my mum work two jobs, do all of the housework, raise four children... and then hand her paycheck over to my father. I knew there had to be a better way.

I tuck the small book into my backpack along with Northrup Frye's *The Educated Imagination* given to me by a friend for "light" reading on my trip. He knew I was on a quest for a meaningful life.

I can't bring myself to tell my mum about the phone call. She is living on the edge and I've been living on the thin side of life myself. I have a suspicion that it's the vacuum cleaner sales guy that she dated a few times. He is an alcoholic chain smoking racist. He smells of gin and Brylcreem. The night before my departure, one of my mum's rig pig friends from Ft. Mac takes us out for dinner at a family restaurant and orders a bottle of Mateus to celebrate my trip to France. I don't mention that Mateus is made in Portugal. Run from this madness.

August 1978

"You're not the little girl you used to be. You are a stranger, somebody your mother stores at with wonder—a person who bewilders you." p.13. *

My plan is to hop a one-way flight from NYC to London Heathrow for under a hundred bucks. I fly student standby to Toronto and then on to NYC. My London flight leaves at 2AM and I manage a bit of sleep sprawled across a few uneven seats. A train ride from Heathrow and a few transfers on the tube to Finsbury Park station and I am at my cousin's flat. Finsbury Park post hippie era is a circus of people; "teddyboys" with tattoos and shaved heads, actors, musicians and street people. I'm in London for a few weeks. I explore the British Museum, Westminster Cathedral, Buckingham Palace, and The Savoy. I even catch a popular play with Tom Conti called "Whose life it is anyways?' I am en route to take a job as an "au pair" (nanny) in Nantes, France. I have arranged to work for an acquaintance of a friend who has four children and desperately needs some "childcare" help. Nantes is on the northern west coast of France and during the 18th-century slave trade it was the major port in France for human traffic. I'm running away from a boyfriend back in Canada. Not really running from him, but from his parents who think I'm not good enough for him. After all, my parents are divorced, I'm not Anglican and I'm poor. I also come from a genetic cocktail of psychoses that they don't even know about yet. But in some ways, I don't feel like I'm good enough for him either. We're a bad mix. He is a body builder in love with himself and I'm sure in love with men. I miss him though. I write poetry in my journal about him every day. *My heart never again cut into small bits and lay on the sand to dry.* Run away.

September 1978

"It's more important to develop a good attitude about homemaking than it is to learn how to be the best housekeeper in the world. Sewing a button on for your father isn't, perhaps, as exciting as sewing a button on for a man you're madly in love with—but it will help you to look like the soul of efficiency later if you practice on Dad now." p. 157.*

By the time I'm able to sew on a button, my Dad is history. I watch my mum scrub floors on her hands and knees. Work as a nanny/housekeeper should come easy to me.

The family has an apartment in Nantes and a country home. The country home is an idyllic white stone cottage. Small lizards run the walls both inside and out. The youngest child has a similar French vocabulary to mine, states her request with "Voila!" and then points at objects. The other children can speak a few words of English and between my high school French and their gestures, we get along splendidly. Every morning my job is to make the beds and get breakfast for the children. *Voila, here is your cereal. Manger veuillez. Voila.* The mother inspects my bed making daily, checking to see the sheets are tucked in with a hospital fold. I also learn how to de-lice hair. A wine carafe sits on the table at every meal. Dead animals hang from the ceiling. Flies touch down on all surfaces and swirl in my mind.

I stay at the city home on my own on the weekend. A black wrought iron staircase leads to the second floor apartment. The windows have internal shutters. Mice scratch at the walls so loudly I wonder why the plaster hasn't worn away. My bed is a small foldout cot. I'm in the study making a phone call to Canada overdramatically complaining about my life; *I can't stand being a slave.* My foot up on the old desk, an enormous mouse or is it a rat, runs across the room, pauses half-way, stares right at me, *what they hell are you doing here?* Sleep is sporadic and when the sun allows me to escape to the street for coffee at an outdoor cafe, I'm relieved. I look intently at my French-English translation book. The only English I have heard in the past two months is a Gordon Lightfoot album. *At times I just don't know how you could be anything but beautiful. I think that I was made for you and you were made for me.* I play it over and over again. I know I can't stay here long. Executer d'ici.

October 1978

"Don't delay purchasing your first bra when you need it. Go to a reputable store, one with professional fitters.... a good foundation garment will help create the smooth, trim look that sets a woman's figure to the best advantage." p.19.*

The country home is a short walk to the small town where Jules Verne spent the summers near the banks of the Loire River. I studied utopian literature in university and think of myself as an expert on his life. On one of these walks, my bra is driving me nuts. It's scratchy and old and I just have to take it off. I decide to bury it in French soil. This was long after "burning bras" was a popular women's rights demonstration. I am a decade behind. At the side of the road, in a row of trees, I ceremoniously place my white lace bra in the dirt and cover it up. I stand up and right there in front of me is a boy sitting on a dark horse. Not a white horse. He says something like *well that was sexy* or at least that's how I interpret his French. He distracts me for a few weeks with his blond shag haircut and rugby body, until he tells me his girlfriend is coming home and I need to leave. I also leave the nanny job. I make up some excuse that my Aunt in England is sick and needs me to take care of her.

I just have to see southern France before I head north. I jump on a train and randomly leap off in Biarritz and find a Caravan Camping spot right on the ocean. After a few weeks, I hitch a ride to Calais with two campers I meet on the beach. We squeeze into a yellow Citroen and putt along the highway as cars whiz by. I decide to stop in at the Jersey Islands and then hovercraft back to England. I then take a bus trip to Amsterdam where I groove through shops dancing to English music and eat waffles with too much sugar on them. I watch the movie *Coming Home* about Vietnam War veterans facing difficulties adapting to life back home, starring Jane Fonda and Jon Voight. I visit Ann Frank's house and I feel hollow. I book a flight home to Canada. It's time to leave the continent. Run away fast.

December 1978

"And marriage is wonderful.... it means you belong—heart, soul, spirit, body and breath—to somebody you've chosen to share your life. It means you'll never be as alone anymore, or as afraid." p. 149.*

I land back in Canada in December with plans to stay in British

Columbia for a while. I go out with friends in Vancouver and meet a musician acquaintance of theirs in a bar. He is lanky, has dark curly hair, olive skin and plum shaped eyes and I can't take my eyes off his hands. He has perfectly shaped fingers and when he talks, he waves them like he is swatting mosquitoes. Of course, I instantly fall in lust and follow him everywhere like he's my pied piper. I'm in a trance. He's a draft dodger from southern California and he plays guitar, sings and writes his own music. I can't believe my good fortune. The fact that he's ten years my senior and already been married twice doesn't faze me. I'm enthralled with his stories of playing in a band with Warren Zevon. A few years back I believed another guy who told me he wrote "You've got a friend." The next day, I hear James Taylor singing the exact same song on *Casey Kasem's American Top 40*. I'm still gullible and think I've hit the big time. I run off with him and in an acid induced state we get married in Reno. I wear a cream smock dress; a symbol of the last phase of my hippie days. He wears an unclean creased collared shirt. I phone my Mum to tell her my news.

She says, *are you sure you know what you're doing?* And I say something like *I'm not a child anymore, I'll figure it out.* And I just know it's going to be hard to live down this one moment of madness. Run before it's too late!

February 1979

"You refuse to face that fact that his eyes aren't focused on you anymore, they're roving up and down the street, and they have a wild look in them. Eventually he has to tell you the truth: he wants out." p. 127. *

A few months of me in a cockroach infested apt. in San Diego and him on the road conveniently unavailable by phone at all hours; I pack my bags, jump into my red and white VW Van complete with raspberry print curtains I made myself. I'm off to Santa Cruz. Don't ask me why; I just like the name. I get the phone number of a place where I might stay from one of the other band members. He's in AA, he says reassuringly. I need to find a lawyer and get a divorce. I feel like driving off the road and hitting the nearest pole. I start smoking.

I'm not even a US citizen and I've brought my VW over the border with Canadian plates. So obviously I have to get a job working under the table. I arrive with purple circles under my eyes and crabs living off my body (I've picked up a bad case from the guitar player). The Santa Cruz guy has no idea who I am but let's me stay. I get a job selling flowers in local bars. I pick up my basket of roses in the evening and walk through every bar until I sell them all. I make about ten dollars, but it feeds me for the next day. I am now calling myself Lara. I don't want anyone to find out how stupid I've been. I feel like I at least need to tell my mum. So I call her from a payphone at a gas station. I tell her not to worry, that I've left the cheating musician and am driving up the coast of California. I ask her how she's been and she says *I'm selling vacuum cleaners now; we drive to small towns and cold calls but I'm making good money.* And I just know that she's with that yellow toothed puffy handed liar. I have no money because I've lent the draft dodging musician one thousand dollars. I consider donating plasma, but I hate needles. Drinking coffee and looking cool in small cafes is my new MO. I even wear the beret I bought in France. Run like I've never run before.

April 1979

"A boy is 'aroused' or stirred physically by a great many things; his body was designed that way. He can be stimulated by such indirect things as smell or sight. Even an intangible thing like a dream has the power to arouse his sex organs to physical release. A girl is built differently—it usually takes a good deal of direct physical contact to create in her an urgent need for complete sexual union." p. 133. *

I go to the Santa Cruz poetry festival. A woman is reading her feminist poems. There is a film projector flashing pictures of women's vaginas on the wall behind her. It's like she's wearing a huge floral hat. And I wonder where she finds her models. Most of the people I meet in California are screwed up and in counseling. Back home, no one talks about their problems; especially not to strangers. Down here, the kids my age are either just out of rehab, just run away from home or inherited a fortune. I fit right in.

Of course, the Santa Cruz guy I'm staying with falls in love with me and wants me to marry him. *I'm not even divorced from the last loser yet.* I just can't think about getting into another relationship and so I lie to him and tell him I'll be back in a few months. I leave a few items of clothing in his closet to be convincing. I notice a few bottles of vodka tucked in beside the shoes. Run someplace else.

May 1979

"It's so easy to be wrong, even when you're wild about a member of the opposite sex. Take that marvelous, masterful boy who's so decisive about everything. What if he turns out to be a husband, who'll dominate your every move, crush you under the weight of his personality?" p. 152. *

It takes me three months to get the divorce organized, sell my Van and save some cash. I've lucked out and got a Datsun 510 on trade but still have USA plates and worry about getting back across the border. I drive back to San Diego to get my things from the apt. and surprise surprise, there is my cheating musician serenading another woman. I can tell that she is moonstruck as he sings "I'm just another California boy." *And I wonder what parts of this event my mind will choose to remember when I'm older?* The Datsun is a tiny four cylinder and has no horsepower. On every hill through northern California and Oregon I have to drive on the side of the highway. I sing the Loggins and Messina song "Celebrate Me Home." *Whenever I find myself too all alone, I can make believe I've never gone, I never know where I belong, Sing me home.* I get back into Canada by some miracle. *I have nothing to declare.* They believe me. I can't license the car in Canada though and have to drive it back over the border later and leave it parked at a car lot. The owner promised to mail me a cheque when it sold. I never hear from him. Nor do I hear from the musician or the alcoholic. Run scared.

June 1979

"Before she realizes what is happening, she has no more control, she has reached the point of no return. The mechanism of desire can be triggered unexpectedly. There can always come a moment between a woman and a man when control and judgment are impossible. Whatever the reason for pre-marital sex experience, it always destroys." p.141.*

I'm not back in Canada long before I meet another guy. He's a clean freak which should have been a warning. He's not bad looking, but his eyelashes curl up naturally and it makes him look like a Kewpie doll. Nothing in his life is out of order. He's obsessive; he's also the reason I don't like kissing anymore. After a few weeks I tell him to go away. He won't. I'm staying at a friend's duplex and I see him pull up. I know I've got to get out of there quickly so I run out the back door and hide in the alley. I see him in the house madly going through my stuff. He pauses and reads something. *Shit!*

He sees my head peak out behind the edge of the garage. He's out the back door in a flash and jumps at me like a cougar; pointy teeth glaring. His pursed lips hold back a foamy spew. He waves my diary; looks like he is ready to bash my head in, mutters *you don't know how close I came to liking you.* And that is supposed to lure me in? He throws the diary at me and then grabs my arm in a wrestling move and twists it until I think I hear a snap. Weird guttural moans are somewhere outside my body. *Leave me alone you asshole.* I stare at the fence along the back of the garage; the place where our neighbor killed a rat with a pitch fork. Is this my cenotaph? I'm lost in the white forget- me- not's growing out of the pavement. Run home.

July 1979

"In pursuing these new interests, it is easy to be careless about hurting your parents' feelings. Sometimes a casual conversation that shows them you

*really care about what they think will relax them to revealing a new side of themselves…" p 43.**

I plan for this like I'm a homecoming queen and I'll be in the parade. I phone ahead to give my mum my arrival time. I have visions of a tearful airport greeting, like the kind you see in a movie. Just picture any sappy movie here. My eyes burn because I have not slept in days. The other passengers meet and pick up their bags. I glance over at the exhibit of homemade quilts on the airport walls. I want so badly to attach myself to their stitches; find a place to call home. My tears fall on the petals of my vintage dress bought for this special occasion. My orange toenail polish is too loud for this prairie town. I catch a cab to the townhouse and sit on the stairs waiting.

---

* Williams, M.M., & Kane, I. (1958). *On Becoming a Woman*. Dell Publishing Co. Inc., 750 Third Ave. New York 17, NY.

Under the Grapefruit Tree

Shelbi Carpenter

Tar blistered on the road and popped under Ida's bare, calloused feet. Ida carried her broken flip-flops in her right hand and a paperback copy of *Scary Stories to Tell in the Dark* in the other. Ahead, her brother, Benji, swerved the width of the road on his bike. Around him ribbons of heat twirled.

"Benji!" Ida waved him over with her scrawny tan arm. "Let me ride on your bike."

"You have two feet." He circled her.

"My shoe broke now let me on."

"Walk on the grass."

"No, it's crunchy. That will hurt worse."

"Fine, but you're pedaling. I can't pull your giant body." Ida lifted her lanky, developing body onto his bike. The hot petals burned under her feet. On the horizon, clouds of smoke bulged above the mountains from this year's summer forest fire.

She turned her brown eyes up to the sky and noticed how erroneously perfect the layers of clouds were today. All of them seemed to be the same size and shape with pure white tops protruding up. Their grey bellies sweeping low. Ida was always mesmerized by how many colors and flabby appendages the clouds could grow and still be beautiful. Still be unnoticed by everyone else.

In town, the movie theater let out lazy Sunday moviegoers, and as they passed by, Ida swerved between them before she crossed the street and made a wood-paneled station wagon slam on its breaks. The driver honked its horn.

"Oh, you weren't even going that fast, dumbass." Ida rolled her eyes. She turned down one more street and then pulled up next to the public library. Benji jumped off before Ida stopped and the force almost knocked her over. Her feet hit the ground fast, trying to keep balance, and her calloused skin ripped off a little from the impact. Ida threw the bike on the sidewalk, not bothering to use the bike rack before she took the steps two at a time.

The bell above the door dinged as they pushed into the air-conditioned room. The lady who worked the front desk didn't even bother to look up. She brushed the white powder, that collected near some powdered donuts onto the floor.

"Whoa what a scar!" Benji's eyes grew double their size when he saw the deep, ragged scar along the front desk lady's face.

"Benji! Sorry about that." Ida pushed her brother by the shoulder away from the front desk. "You're not supposed to point out someone's scar, dumbass, especial not someone with a scar like that. She could probably kick your butt." She hit him on the back of the head. Benji darted on a path to the comic books.

"Ida," a girl whispered as she walked down the fiction aisle. Ida turned to see Cassandra in a crop top her grandmother would not approve of, and baggy blue jeans that were rolled up above her Converse. "Where are your shoes?"

"They broke. Did your grandma see you leave in that?"

Cassandra didn't bother to look up from the row of books when she said, "Nope—still waiting for her to croak, so I don't have to hide my real clothes anymore. Her test results come back on Tuesday. Let's pray for cancer."

"Want to come over tonight? The Johnsons are coming over to play poker with my parents. Ida's nose detected the usual lusty, rubbing alcohol scent of Cassandra's cheap perfume.

"There you are!" Cassandra said to a black hardcover book and pulled it off the shelf. "Can't. I got plans!" She pulled out a scrap of paper hidden in the book and waved it in front of Ida's face.

"What is that?"

"A secret."

Ida knew Cassandra wanted to tell her. "Hmm, cool. Well, have fun."

"It's with a guy. An older guy."

"Oh, has grandma arranged your marriage already?"

"Very funny. Fine, I'll go alone."

"Fine, I'll act interested. Where are you going, Cassandra?"

Cassandra looked around. "There is this guy, Charles or Charlie, some crappy name like that really, that get girls modeling jobs in LA. He's found like so many models, and he is having a very exclusive party tonight. This is the address."

"A modeling scout left the address to a party in a book at the Merced Public Library?" Ida pulled a book off the shelf, but she couldn't concentrate on the back cover, so she pretended to read it.

"No, he didn't leave this himself, idiot! Madison left it in here for that hippy-dippy friend of hers, Ruby, but I'm getting it first. Madison was bragging about it in the PE locker room because her cousin is part of his modeling group. This would have been a waste on Ruby anyways her nose is too crooked for her to be beautiful. Come with me!"

"Can't. I have to replace my blinds."

Cassandra sneered. "When I'm famous, I'll be sure to forget about you."

Ida snorted. "But really, I'm being forced to watch my siblings while my parents get drunk off their asses."

"Ida, he found Cindy Crawford! Just come after the kids fall asleep."

"And when baby Sam, wakes up?"

"Benji's like ten—"

"He's seven."

Cassandra crossed her tan arms. "He can take care of it. Just when all the lights are off in my house, we'll meet at my grandma's grapefruit tree."

Ida huffed and looked through the row of books again to find her brother stretched over the counter of the front desk.

"Oh, gosh."

"How did you get it? Was it a knife fight? Can you teach me how to throw knives—"

"So sorry again. Let's go, Benji!" Ida pulled him out of the library by his backpack. She looked down at the book in her hands that she forgot to sign for. She tossed the stolen book into the bushes. "Now we can't go back to the library!" Ida said as Benji picked up his bike.

"Just take it back inside."

"Can't. You've already embarrassed me."

"Ida! I'll see you later tonight!" Cassandra said as she followed them out of the library. She threw her backpack into Ian Carabotta's, a junior at the high school, topless Toyota Celica."

"When'd Cass start hanging out with them? When'd she start wearing things like that? Is she coming over tonight?"

"Do you ever shut up? Come on let's go before that librarian hunts us down."

"You think she'll give me a scar like that?" Benji beamed.

Ida watched Cassandra skirt away in the car, jealous that she was starting this empty summer before ninth grade with upperclassman while Ida was left on a seven-year old's rickety bike.

As Ida pedaled down Main Street, she thought about how Ian's hand was probably on Cassandra's soft thigh. Womanhood had started to boil in Cassandra this summer much like Ida yet more people noticed. Ida felt her friendship with Cassandra starting to wither, and she knew that once summer started to die and give way to short school nights and busy early mornings, Ida would become a relic that Cassandra outgrew. Ida could see three college denial letters sitting on her counter at home. In four years as she worked the cashier at the drug story scanning Xanax for house wives, and Cassandra's face would be plastered on magazines around her.

A toddler shrieked as Ida and Benji walked into the front door of their house. The crying toddler squirmed against the straps of his highchair. Ida absorbed the chaotic liveliness that tumefied from their home. It churned it her mind and crystallized into bitterness.

"Ida! I haven't finished my makeup. Will you feed Sam?" Her mom dropped the kid spoon without waiting for Ida to answer and picked up the mascara she had left on the countertop.

"Where's Dad?" Ida asked and pushed a spoonful of cold corn towards Sam who refused the drippy, pale vegetable.

"He went to go get beer. When you're done feeding Sam, will you get the poker table?" She dropped her mascara and picked up the lit cigarette that was in the ashtray by her blush. "Ida, come here. Are you wearing mascara? Who taught you to put on mascara?"

"Cass's mom."

"When? Sandra hasn't been in town for ages."

Ida shrugged, "I dunno it was the last time she was here. I was ten, I think. I have worn it before."

"That was like four, five years ago?" This was another time Ida's mother made her feel as if she was a shard of glass embedded so deep in the flesh of a foot that the skin had grown over it. If her mom stepped on her foot a certain way, she would feel the shard rubbing against the beef of her foot, but otherwise it was unnoticeable.

Ida's mom rubbed a large brush around her cheek and said, "well it looks good on you. Here." She handed Ida her brush "move it in a circle on your cheekbones. Wonder what Sandra is doing now? Running around and leaving behind her child. That's no way to be a mother." Ida didn't argue, but she fantasized about all the wonderful stories Cass's mom could tell. Ida gave the makeup brush back to her mother. "Beautiful. Blush looks good on you, and maybe we'll get some from Christmas."

Ida pulled the two-year-old out of his highchair. She carried him to the extra room, where they left the toys and TV. She plopped him in his playpen and grabbed the poker table. In the living room, she started to unfold it by a tray of cream cheese salami roll up that sat on the end table welcoming flies. Her mother walked to her room, puffing on her cigarette and smothering herself with hairspray.

"Hairspray is flammable, Mom."

"I still have my eyebrows, don't I?" She yelled from inside her bedroom. "Ida! Why do my favorite jeans have a stain on them?"

Ida muttered under her breath, "because I wore them yesterday."

Her mother walked out of the bedroom in only underwear and a button up. She held the jeans in one hand and her smoking cigarette in the other. "You're not allowed to wear my stuff."

"I wanted to look good."

"You have your own clothes."

"They're all used. I might as well go in a trash bag." She rolled her eyes. "It'll come out." She wasn't sure about that.

"Used is all we can afford. Nothing is ever good enough for you, huh? Get a job and buy your own damn clothes."

"Can't I'm too busy taking care of *your* kids." After two large steps, her mom was standing in front of Ida, and with one small flip of her thin wrist, she slapped Ida. Her long fingers left behind a blotchy red mark on Ida's soft cheek. Ida's limbs went numb with carbonated rage.

"Woah, what's going on?"

"Your daughter's being a smart ass. Wonder where she gets that from?" She walked back to her room, leaving the metallic scent of hairspray as a fingerprint.

"Yes, blame me for the things she says," Her dad said and threw the beer in the fridge. Ida watched her mom, from the doorway of her parent's bedroom, lay on her back, sucking in to fit into her jeans. Her mother could cling to her dying youth as much as she wanted, but her bones were thinning and would fray at the ends. One day the alcohol would become more of a daily activity, and someday Ida's dad would leave for a woman that didn't smell like nail polish remover and infected phlegm. Her mother would need someone to take care of her, to drown out her delusional rants. Ida hoped she wouldn't be here.

Later, Benji and Jeremy Johnson paraded in the back room and were freaking out over Jeremy's new game and watch. The twins walked in last, in oversized t-shirts and no pants. Ida looked through the open door at the parents who snapped open beers and listened to the gargling of vodka mixing with cranberry juice as they chatted about the new boss at work. Ida's mother caught her staring and closed the door.

"Ida, what do you wanna watch?" One of the twins dug through the box of random VCR tapes with no covers.

Ida huffed, "I don't care." She picked up a discarded copy of her mom's *Cosmo* magazine, that she had already looked through a hundred times, and marked the pages of items she wanted. She flipped open to an "Are you Sexy" quiz, that contained scribbled hieroglyphics from the first time she took it. Laughter billowed from behind the closed door. The twins pulled out blankets and covers to make a fort while Sam giggled at his favorite stuffed giraffe from his playpen.

"Do you have dimples?" Ida read to herself and circled an already marked "yes" before she looked out the window of the back door. Cassandra's house was beyond the strawberry fields. The lights were still on at her house. Ida flipped the pages, and Cindy Crawford was staring at her in a flowing ruby red dress. Ida thought about the fast, one-sided deal she made with Cassandra. She knew the address would probably lead them to some open field, making the whole trip a bust. She flipped the page to "How to Act Like a Rich Girl," but as she read it for the third time, her gaze floated over the words and towards Cassandra's house over and over again until the girls had fallen asleep, the boys had taken over the TV to play Nintendo, and the lights were off at Cassandra's house. Ida's bare feet touched the cold floor when the door to the kitchen opened.

"See Nancy I want to make the lower half of the walls wood paneling and then the upper half the same wallpaper in the living room," Ida's mother said to Mrs. Johnson when they stumbled in. They didn't notice that their vodka cranberries splashed on the floor.

"Or paint the top half? Something bright. Bright colors are in, ya know? You'll have to replace the floors, first, you just can't have plyboard as floors." Mrs. Johnson swayed as she spoke. Her purple covered eyelids were heavy with sleep that tried to overtake her. "Oh, Ida look at you. You have changed so much. You've grown so much. Becoming a lady? Yes, you are."

Ida rolled her eyes, "Yes, I have changed a lot from last week when you were drunk."

"Ida, shut up." The moms left the extra room as Ida turned to look at Sam. Sam slept on his stomach, not moving, saliva dripped from his fat, pink lips. Glad she didn't have to deal with an awoken beast.

She slipped on flip-flops that her mother kept by the door for easy retrieval. Outside the crickets talked to the toads and Ida walked along the back of the house. Her parents stood by the window above the kitchen sink, but they were too busy yelling at each other to see their daughter slide past. Through the window, Mrs. Johnson was asleep on the couch. Her makeup smeared, and her glasses crooked. Ida wondered how she slept with all the yelling. The darkness crept around the light streaming through the windows, densed up, swelled between the gnarly trees. Its coarse hand slid down Ida's neck and sent shivers down her body. She looked around at the shadows moving and conjuring in the darkness and debated going back.

A shallow groan shot a short scream out of Ida's lips, and she looked around until her eyes made out Mr. Johnson throwing up over the porch. He was too drunk and concerned about the chunks of cream cheese and salami on his cowboy boots to notice her scream.

With a hand on her chest, Ida caught her breath and walked to the edge of the yard. She slipped between the barbwire fence. She heard strawberries pop and oozed under her shoes as she walked to the grapefruit tree.

Under the grapefruit tree, bells and wind chimes sang in the dark. Dew-damp ribbons reached out and licked Ida's face and neck. She swatted them away with numb hands from nervous adrenaline racing through her arms. She remembered when Cassandra's mom came back, glowing and smelling like lavender, from an extended trip and told them about fairy trees. That evening the girls stuffed their pockets with ribbons, beads, and bells and threw them in the tree, so fairies would come and grant them wishes. The two girls held each other's dirty hands, sweat-caked strands of baby hair caked to their faces, and, with eyes closed, made wishes at the tree. Now she knew it was useless, but she held her breath anyways and silently sent a wish up.

"Cassandra?" Ida whispered. "Cassandra?" Ida's voice wouldn't be anything more than a limp whisper. She walked around the tree and felt the dirt engulfed her feet.

The sudden light and foreign scream happened fast and ended before Ida's body hit the dirt. Cassandra's laugh cracked and squeaked as the yellow, faded beam from her flashlight bounced around the tree branches.

"Very funny. I knew I should have stayed home."

"And done what? Listen to your parents crack each other skulls against the walls? You're fine, now get up."

"Does this party even exist? Or was this just a way to lure me out here and scare the crap out of me? Because, if so, I'm going home," Ida said and watched Cassandra set her flashlight on the ground with the beam faced up so she could see into her backpack.

"It's real, okay. Lighten up and put this on." She tossed a laced black shirt at Ida.

"This is see-through."

"I know. Sexy, right?" Cassandra raised her eyebrows.

"Where did you get this?"

"Found it in an old box of my grandma's 'before she found Christ' clothes."

"It looks like lingerie."

"It is!" Cassandra said, taking off her worn church camp shirt from two years ago.

"Ew! You gave me something you grandma had sex in." Ida threw the shirt into the fairy tree to hang between what was left of a pink ribbon, and a string of faded, yellow beads.

"Gotta look hot for Charles, besides I'm pretty sure all the germs are dead by now," Cassandra said, as she finished changing into a leather crop top, and pulled out a set of keys with WWJD keychain from her backpack. Cassandra swung the keys, letting them chatter, as they walked to the carport and waited for Ida to gawk at her bravery for stealing her grandmother's keys. From the passenger seat, Ida flicked a cross necklace hanging from the review mirror. Cassandra put the keys in the ignition, paused.

"R is for reverse. You want to put it in that first."

"Shut up. I know how to drive. Ian taught me on our date."

"Isn't he dating Katie Fisher? You've been hanging out with him a lot."

"She doesn't put out for him."

Ida turned to the window and rolled her eyes. "And you do? Cass, do you even know what a condom is?"

"Yeah, it's those things your mother doesn't use." A smile slowly grew on Ida's face.

"Dammit, that was a good one," Ida said, unable to think of anything sarcastic to say back.

"There's trail mix in my backpack and a map. You're copilot," Cassandra said as the car's tires slowly crunched over the gravel driveway. The map covered Ida's lap, and the open bag of trail mix sat on Fresno. The chocolate had melted, engulfed the raisins making it hard for Ida to avoid them. She would grab a chunk of chocolate pick out the raisins and throw them back into the bag. Cassandra dug her hand into the bag, and with her knee propped up against the steering wheel, she used both hands to sort through her findings.

"Ida, I swear if you're taking all the good stuff and leaving me only raisins, I'll dump your ass off on the side of the road."

"No, no, that's not at all what I'm doing," Ida said and lifted the bag to peer inside. Cassandra rolled down the window to throw out a handful of raisins.

The wind smacked Ida's face. "Remember when we drove to the beach last summer, and you were upfront with your grandma—"

"And I rolled the window down to spit a lugi!" Cassandra cut her off.

"Yeah, and it came back through the window and landed on my face!"

Cassandra choked on a peanut from laughing too hard. When the saliva drenched peanut flopped onto her lap, their snickers fizzed through the car. Back then, the girls never spent a day apart.

Two hours later, their car stopped in front of a brick mailbox with 2684 on the side. At the end of the driveway was a tall iron fence. The gate opened for anyone. Couples leaked out of a large house in lustrous drips. The girls got out and walked in the grass along the circle driveway packed with glistening convertibles. They passed an elderly man that closed the car door for his wife and caught her headscarf in the door. While the lady adjusted her shoulder pads, Ida noticed how much younger she was than him, that there was no ring on her finger, and how intoxicated they both were. The couple drove on the grass and out the front gate.

Ida and Cassandra walked into the house. They stepped over a puddle of wine spread on the marble floor.

An older woman snatched another lady's short grey bob as she said,

"Look what you did, you toothless whore!" Her empty wine glass swung in her hand.

"Cass, where the heck are we? There are only old people here." Ida said as they walked past a white cake topped with two plastic elderly men. Ida swiped her finger through the frosting. Their bodies wiggled through the crowd to the far wall, made of glass and overlooked the Carmel coast. "I wish it wasn't dark, so we could see the water."

Cassandra's back was towards the windows, too busy looking at the crowd. "I think we are the only people under sixty here."

"Don't worry, I think everyone is too drunk to notice your boobs spilling out," Ida said and gazed at the bundles of saggy arm fat and delicate threaded clothes that packed the room. She felt the acid in her stomach froth from nerves and crossed her arms over the stale NASCAR shirt. She wished she had accepted the lingerie.

"Really? Because that guy over there is drooling at me." Cassandra crossed her arms over her chest to shield her body. She turned around to look out the windows at the porch dimly lit below.

"Yeah, he might be having a stroke though...." Ida's voice trailed off as a mesmerizing brunette, with a long slit in her red dress, walked by. The lady gulped her whiskey and placed the heavy glass in Ida's hand without so much as a second glance. Ida's eyes followed the glamorous scarlet woman to the center of the room where she wrapped her glossy arms around two older men taking pictures. She kissed their wrinkled cheeks branding the men with a shimmering mark, as the camera's light flashed against the guys' puffy faces. The flash illuminated her face, and Ida recognized the soft smile. It was the same smile Cassandra's mom had beamed down at Ida when she told her about the fairy tree. That's Sandra.

The fluffy contrails of the women's sophisticated perfume floated around Ida. She had to be wearing some scent that Ida would never be able to afford. What had she done that transformed her into the poised woman standing in front of her?

A dream unfolded in the flaps of Ida's mind. She could be as beautiful as Cassandra's mom was right now. Diamonds would dangle from Ida's wrist as she carried sparkling flutes of intoxicating carbonated liquids through crowds of the rich and educated. Her apartment would be ages away from Merced and her family. In the mornings she slips out of silk sheets and stands in front of glass windows overlooking Central Park as it snows. A handsome man that smelled like leather and firewood would bring her coffee they brought back from an extended trip to Europe.

A future like that was somewhere in this room with Charles.

"Ida, why would Madison leave an address to a wedding? Maybe it's her grandpa's wedding?"

Ida didn't bother to answer Cassandra, who was picking up a flute of bubbling, clear liquid. Cassandra took a sip and winced. Ida stared at her with a blank face. Didn't Casandra notice her mom? Cassandra picked at the deteriorating strawberry in her flute with a partially painted fingernail.

Ida's feet followed Cassandra's mom. She pushed between the married couple and through swinging kitchen doors. On the other side of the kitchen, Cassandra's mom flowed down a staircase. Ida, a pendulum, swung at the top of the stairs. In the kitchen, behind Ida, cooks tapped spoons against bowls as they stirred oil and vinegar dressing. It sounded like the bells in the fairy tree. Steam rose from pots of boiling noodles and pressed against her clammy skin like the hot, dry Merced air. She felt like she was under the grapefruit tree again, dreaming of her wishes. Her mind swayed back to the scribble that was her mother's life. Then, to the enigma at the bottom of the stairs.

"Ida, what are you doing?" Cassandra's voice shook Ida from the trance.

"I saw your mom. She went downstairs!"

"My mom?" Cassandra's thick brown eyebrows collided together. "Who cares? Let's go find the casting agent."

"Don't you want to talk to her?"

"Why do you care about my mom? She's a crackhead now. Let's go find that guy."

"Your mom was traveling the world. I mean—"

Cassandra chuckled. "You still believe that? That was all a lie. I mean, who was going to tell us that my mom was giving out blowjobs for cocaine? I never even saw her after that day under the tree. She's probably rotting in some ditch right now. I'm going to find Charles so I can come to parties like this all the time, only with people that don't smell like Ben-Gay." Cassandra left, but Ida lingered.

Ida crept down the wood stairs trying to be light on her toes. Her nose met the pudgy smell of weed. Cassandra's mom stood in a row of wine, her diamonds glistening under the dim light. Her bony shoulders and small chest moved up as she took a long deep drag of a joint. There were two younger guys in suits around her. The lady was too young and promising to be Cassandra's mom. Ida should have known that.

"What are you doing?" The lady's moisturized leg shimmered as she strolled over to Ida. "I-I-" Ida swallowed the gritty lump that cultivated in her throat, "I'm looking for Charles."

The lady smiled, grabbed Ida by the chin, tilting her head to each side, and then looked at her breasts. "I'm Charles."

"Charles is a guy's name. He is a modeling agent."

"Charles is my last name, little girl. Why are you here?"

"You found Cindy Crawford, and I wanna be a model."

"Ha, Crawford? My reputation precedes me." The lady turned to smirk at the guys.

"Um, hey, Charles, is it? How many other models have you found?" One of the guys asked, cocking his sharp, square jaw to the side.

"Mostly, actresses." Charles winked.

"Actresses. Really? That's what you call a girl in front of a tripod?"

"Listen girly if you want to be a model, we're leaving for San Fernando in like five minutes. There's a black Cadillac outside waiting on us."

Back in the foyer, Ida saw Cassandra buzz around the party. She stepped up to her but then turned and followed Charles. Ida turned to get one last look at Cassandra. Ida knew what Cassandra's life would fizzle into. Cassandra would drive back, crying. Her mind would be too busy thinking of Ida, to remember to change out of her shirt. When her grandma saw her walk in dressed like Ginger Lynn, Cassandra would be subject to bag searches and chaperoned dates.

She'd spend her post-high school days planted as a grocery store cashier flipping through magazines stocked by her checkout line. She'd walk home kicking stray rocks into the road until she got to the cat-piss-smelling one-bedroom apartment she shared with Ian. Ian would re-heat the boxed mac n cheese they made for last night's dinner while they play scrabble on overdue notices.

The dry years would pass on only distinguishable by ordinary markers like buying a house and bringing home their third and fourth baby girls—a set of twins. Madison Clark and her family would come over for light games and heavy drinking until they spill blood on the floor.

One summer she'll look up from her window at the forest fire in the distance. Ida, a thought that had slipped into her mind throughout the years in drops like a leaky faucet will pour in, and she will think about what would have happened if she had walked down those stairs with Ida. She'd think about her lost friend's mysterious life. That same summer, when a forest fire stretches over the mountains and into the valley. The flames will submerge the fairy tree burning up any ribbons and unanswered wishes.

Willie's Crucifixion*

Rick Campbell

The boy pressed the nail against his father's palm and scraped it toward the wrist. He looked at the fresh line among the old work lines. "Are you sure Daddy? It'll hurt bad."

"I'm sure, boy."

"Ain't it enough to tie your arms up?"

"It ain't right without the nails. Drive it through."

He put the nail in the center of the palm again and probed for the soft spot between the small bones. He sure didn't want to hear any bones snapping like he was breaking chicken wings. At least his daddy was letting him use smaller nails than the 60 penny spikes they'd nailed the cross with. Those would tear a hand in half.

"Come on, hit it."

His arm floated toward the nail like the air was honey. When the hammer hit the sound was flat, funny and far away. The boy opened his eyes and saw blood spurting at him. His stomach turned over. The nail was in the palm, but not deep enough into the wood. He hit it again. It was easier the second time. It rang like nails he remembered—nails in the house, nails in the barn. Daddy bit his lip and his body stiffened. "Are you sure, Daddy," the boy whispered.

Daddy grunted, "the other one."

The boy grabbed another nail. He felt like he knew how to nail a man to a cross now. He ran the nail around the soft center, found his spot, and drove it deep with one shot. He hardly saw the blood and never looked at the nailed man's eyes. If there had been more hands to nail he could have driven them home clean as a carpenter. But he was glad they weren't nailing up the feet. Learning hands was enough for one day.

Daddy groaned a kind of pleased whisper, "Tell your ma now. Go on."

"Do you think she'll come back?"

"She will, boy."

* Winner.

"What if she don't?"

"She's got to. I done nailed my damned self to a cross for her."

The boy couldn't tell whether it was pain or uncertainty that made his daddy sound doubtful. He took off down the road at a trot, but he was worried. He started thinking about what he would tell his mother.

Daddy's hanging on a cross.

How'd he do that?

I nailed him up.

What'd you nail your pa for?

He told me to.

It just didn't sound right and the sheriff might not think so either. Might think he should lock a boy up who drove nails through his father's hands. And why should his ma come home just because his daddy was nailed to a cross? She left because things were bad, no money, no crops. Daddy sitting and staring at the fields. Drinking in the mornings. What was so good about being nailed to a cross? Ma'd probably think it was worse. Crazy. Have to come home and clean his hands and still nothing really changed.

Willie got the idea in church a few months ago. We love Christ, the minister said, because he died on the cross for us. Willie stewed on it awhile and figured if he hung on a cross for a few hours his wife would come back to him. But the boy had his doubts now. Everybody didn't love Christ that much. And besides, what worked once for him wouldn't necessarily work for his daddy.

About that time the boy heard a car coming down the road and he just stuck out his thumb. Like that, quick without thinking, like he just decided to go somewhere because a car came. At least that's how it looked to the man in the car. He looked out from under an old ball cap, hesitated, and then coasted to a stop forty yards down the road. The boy cut through the dust trailing the car and climbed into the front seat.

"Where you headin," the man asked. He didn't really seem to care. It was just something to say.

"I don't know," the boy said," south, I guess. Maybe Florida." The boy hadn't ever been anywhere, but some folks from his county had given up and moved down around Jacksonville. It was sort of a repository for failed farmers and people beaten by the dust and the Depression.

"Leavin home?"

"Yeah."

"Why?"

"Look around," the boy gave a sort of empty wave.

That was enough to let the questions ride in silence. There wasn't much of an argument strangers could make for sticking around. Everything was dusty and about as dead as a living thing could be. When the land and the farms that people work all their lives go fallow, little redeems the loss. A green tree here and there, someone who refuses to give up and paints his barn anyway, these things just point out how bad everything else is. The cripple dragging himself down the sidewalk isn't an inspiration to those going down. He just makes the lucky ones nervous.

The pain in Willie's hands wasn't roaring in his head anymore. There was a dull ache in his outstretched arms. He was glad they'd thought to put the bucket under his feet. If he was hanging free, only his arms to hold him up and only the nails keeping those arms outstretched, things would really be bad now. The bucket and the thought of Elizabeth coming home made being crucified bearable.

By now, Willie thought, the boy should be at her pa's house. This will bring her back. People will talk. Did you hear what Willie Pettigrew did for his woman? Had himself nailed to a cross. Went and damn had himself crucified for her.

He didn't know why it didn't come to him sooner. It must have been the hundredth time he heard the story, but he never really thought about it as a thing a man could do. Of course it did take some getting used to. The thought of hanging on a cross the better part of a day wasn't something an ordinary man looked forward to. But after Willie considered it for a few days, as he looked out over the fields where the weeds had taken over and thought of all the things he had done in the last twenty years on this farm, it started to make sense. He figured it couldn't hurt worse than sticking himself butchering hogs or that winter when the ax had slipped as he was cutting firewood and almost cut his foot off.

Things had never been easy here, and Willie didn't really know of a place where things were easy, except maybe in some rich, glass and steel world immune to drought, bugs and worms. The soil was bad years before he and Elizabeth had married. His father's cotton had leached the life out of the poor dirt. And even when there was a good crop there wasn't enough money to pay off the past year's debt and get ahead. Maybe this would turn things around. Maybe Elizabeth would come home and it would rain. Maybe something would go right.

Willie worried about the boy. Jackson was a little squeamish. Once the cross was built and set up in the garden, it took a couple of hours to talk him into driving the nails. Willie had wanted to get an early start, but they'd fooled around and lost the morning and now the sun was beating down on him and making things worse than he guessed they had to be. At least he remembered to keep his hat on.

Willie wished he could have a nip of whisky, but then he decided it wouldn't look right. If he drank too much it might not hurt enough. It had to hurt; he had to suffer some. What good would it do to be a drunk hanging on a cross? That sounded like some fool thing any bad drunk might get himself into. Maybe not the nails and the hanging part, but the rest wasn't much different than being passed out spread-eagled in the sun.

He wanted Elizabeth to know that he hurt for her. She could clean his hands in good cold water and wipe his face with the folds of her skirt. Nothing would be better right now. Not a full field of cotton shimmering white in the sun. Things could be as good as they first were.

Willie wasn't that superstitious back in the day, but year after year the crops got worse and their luck just died off. Worms, drought, weevils, worms, more drought. They were always low on money. Not enough for seed and fertilizer or another mule. And even if the rains came and things grew, something still went wrong. Rot, more bugs, a bad price from the buyer. All this time, Elizabeth had not born another child, though for years they tried. Then they stopped trying. The doctor said Elizabeth wasn't ever going to have another child. Willie started staring out across the dying rows and putting wrong things together in his head.

The sun was low when Willie admitted something had gone wrong. She should have been here already. This had to work. Most of his life now he had worked this farm for nothing. He had to get something for this. A man shouldn't hang on a cross for nothing.

The man and the boy didn't talk much. The man didn't seem like a talker. He was gray under the ball cap and the skin on his face was dry and brown. The corners of his mouth had tobacco juice working into his stubbled chin. He took his eyes off the road to spit out the window and that was about it. That was fine with Jackson. He was worried and didn't much want to talk about where he was going or why he was leaving. He didn't have many answers anyway.

After they had gone about a half hour down the road, Jackson said that "Plymouth made a good old car. They held up well." But he didn't know if they held together or how long long was. Twenty years? As long as a life? His father had never owned a good car, just junk pickups now rusted and dead. All he really knew was this car was carrying them down the road. That was more than he could say for anything else.

The man didn't have much more to say about his car than he did anything else. So the boy stayed quiet and looked out the window. The man said he was going all the way to near Jessup and that it was a straight shot to Florida from there. That sounded good to Jackson—a different state. He was sure his daddy was going to be mad at him, and he figured the sheriff might want him too, so being in another state wouldn't be a bad idea. Might as well just go to Florida like he said he would.

Outside everything looked pretty much the same—dry, brown, and dusty as home. Jackson was worried about his daddy. He knew it wasn't right to run away. He shouldn't have nailed him to the cross, but when Daddy said to do it, he always did it. This was the first big thing he'd ever crossed his daddy on. Now he was worrying that it might be days before anyone came by the farm and he wondered how long daddy could hang there before it got too bad. He decided he'd have to tell someone.

The sun was almost down when the man said he was pulling into the store to get a Coca-Cola. Jackson followed him. Two mutts on the front porch watched without interest as they walked through the screen door.

The man walked with a stiff left leg, like his hip and back had been fused together. The boy looked around the store. The canned goods mingled with hardware. In the far corner he saw a phone. He decided to call Mr. Owens who ran the general store back home. He figured if he told him, then Owens would get his daddy down some way.

When he went to the phone it was the first time he thought about money. He had less than a dollar. For a moment he got scared and wondered how he was going to make it to Florida and find a place to sleep, but then it just didn't matter. For the first time, right then, he realized that he couldn't go home. He didn't want to run away, but now his old life was over. He had hammered nails through his father's hands and run off without delivering the message to his mother. But also, somehow, he knew that he would have had to leave even if he had gone for his mother. It was over when the first nail went in, over when his father decided to be crucified.

He called Mr. Owens. At first Owens didn't believe it was him. "What are you doing so far away, boy?"

Jackson said "It don't matter where I am or why, but would you go out to the farm and get daddy? He's hangin on a cross and I guess he's in trouble now."

"Hangin on a cross?"

"Just go get him please," Jackson asked again, "and tell Pa I'm not coming home and I don't know where I'm going." Owens promised to ride out to the farm and look, so Jackson hung up.

The storekeeper had heard something about a cross and that the boy wasn't coming home. "So where you bound for?" he asked.

"Florida," Jackson said. He guessed it was really decided now. "I'm 17 and I'm going to Florida to find some work and I ain't going back home. How's that?"

"Well, it ain't my affair."

"No." The boy walked out the door and watched crows whirl over a brown field. The man was leaning against his car. "You call home?"

"Yeah."

"Still going to Florida?"

"Yeah." That's all that was said. He was a good man to leave home with if you didn't want to think about what you were doing and be bothered by someone trying to make you figure out why things happened like they did. The boy just wanted to be done with it now. He wanted Florida to be different than the parched farms he was leaving behind. He wanted a new life even more than his father did. The crucifixion just made it all clear. He knew that Daddy's hanging on a cross wasn't going to change anything but his own life.

When Milton Owens got off the phone, he told his wife what the Pettigrew boy had said. She thought they better call Sheriff Cantrell and let him check it out. What if it turned out Willie was really out there hanging on a cross? What happens next?

Sheriff Cantrell was annoyed at being disturbed after dinner, but he agreed with Owens. "I ain't dealt with a crucifixion before, but drivin nails through a man's hand on purpose must be wrong."

As Cantrell drove over to pick up the Owens, he decided to go out and get Elizabeth Pettigrew at her daddy's farm. Cantrell said, as much to the dust as the Owens, "Willie's been a little crazy ever since Elizabeth left out on him. I don't want too much trouble here."

"Willie's been trouble for longer than that," Mrs. Owens said as they drove out to the Walker's. "I don't know about the boy though. I guess he would nail Willie if Willie said to."

At the Walker farm, Elizabeth Pettigrew said she didn't much care if Willie was hanging on a cross, or just staring at the fields as if he was trying to will the crops to grow. "He's been coming round here with schemes to get me home for months now. I'm not going."

"Now Elizabeth," Sheriff Cantrell coaxed, "I don't mean you have to stay there. I just want you to be with us in case Willie really is hangin' on a cross. Hangin' on a cross is a pretty stubborn thing to do and I don't want no more trouble than I already have." He took her arm and eased her into the car.

As they drove through the dusk Elizabeth stared out the window and said to Mrs. Owens, her voice resigned, "He said I never gave him enough boys to work the farm. Said the land was sick 'cause I was. But more mouths would have just starved us faster. He said I owed him for ruining his life. That's when I left."

It was just after dark when they reached Willie's farm. Cantrell led the way round the back of the house with a lantern and then he stopped short. Willie was hanging in the old garden like a scarecrow Jesus, and in the lantern beam he looked ghostly. Cantrell thought he might be dead, but not yet. H'd been up there for about ten hours and his pain had finally been overcome by fatigue. The light startled him. He jerked his head up and banged it against the cross. He let out a little moan.

"What the hell you doing, Willie?" Cantrell was almost whispering.

Willie couldn't answer because his mouth was stuck and dry. Mrs. Owens went to the well to get a dipper of water. Willie tried to drink it and started coughing.

"Slow," Cantrell said.

Elizabeth stood back outside the lantern's light.

Mr. Owens picked up the hammer the boy had left below the cross and began to pry the nail out of Willie's palm. They hurt more coming out as the nails ripped their holes wider. The cross didn't give up the nails easily.

"For Elizabeth," Willie managed to say.

"It won't work, Willie." Elizabeth was still outside the light and Willie couldn't see her. "I'm done. I don't believe in us anymore."

When the second nail came out Willie sagged, then collapsed, but Owens and Cantrell caught him before he hit the ground. They sat him in the dust and leaned him against the cross. "Where's the boy," he asked.

"He called a while ago," Owens said, looking at the bits of skin and blood on the nail still caught in the claw hammer, "said to tell you he's not coming home and he don't know where he's going."

Cantrell swung the light down near Willie's face. Willie flinched. Cantrell ran the light up the length of the cross. He studied the cross like he was trying to figure what kind of a crime this might be.

Owens walked back to stand by his wife.

"He's the only one, Willie, and he won't come back." Elizabeth knew she was leaving too, but she wasn't going to tell anyone here. She had a sister who worked in a factory in Fayetteville. Now that the boy was gone there was nothing.

Willie was too tired to talk. He just stared at the dirt and pressed his stinging palms against his belly.

"We should clean his hands," Owens said.

Cantrell scuffed his boots in the dead garden. "This gotta be some kind of crime, Willie. I oughta arrest you or the boy. 'Course you made him do it. But a man can't go around havin himself nailed to crosses."

"I think he's got enough trouble, Tom. Let's just get him out of here. Take him to the doctor for now." Owens dropped the hammer in the dust.

Willie kept looking at the bloody holes in his palms. "Do what you have to. If being crucified's a crime, take me. I made the boy nail me up."

They looked around for Elizabeth but she had walked away and was heading for the house.

"Elizabeth, you coming?"

Elizabeth called over her shoulder, "No. Just leave me here. Take care of Willie."

Cantrell held the door and Willie got in the car slowly and quietly. He sat up front, rocking slowly and humming. In his mind he had succeeded. Elizabeth had come back. She was here, in the house, and as the car drove off into the dark, Willie imagined that when he came back to her tomorrow, the house would be clean. The bed sheets changed. Dinner ready. Everyone else figured it wasn't going to go down like that.

Elizabeth knew her path now. She went to the bedroom and picked up her mother's hairbrush and Jackson's baby picture. She'd asked Mrs. Owens to call her father to come get her. She wouldn't sleep in this empty house. In the morning she'd be leaving too.

Jackson was alone now. He stood on the bridge where the highway crossed the Big Satilla River, puzzling about how long the darkness took to fall. He knew he needed a place to sleep, and he was glad for the old barn blanket the man in the car had given him. Somewhere south and east of here the river ran into the sea and all Jackson knew for sure was that he was heading that way too.

The Thing

Lou Morrison

She sat out on the back stoop under a gathering summer storm and remembered how once, a couple years ago, when she was still in high school, she sat out on this same back stoop under a hissing, steel wool November sky and wished her parents had never met. Brown leaves stirred. The million little white houses were shut up against the cold. College basketball games were on TV, parents were getting bleary-eyed on booze, and in all these homes, or so she imagined, kids were curled up in their bedrooms or maybe gone already, walking down a wet highway thinking: I wish none of this had ever come to be.

And on that autumnal day a couple years ago, her dad, now dead from a DUI by which he manslaughtered another, which seemed somehow inevitable all along, was in the den, smashed. Her mom was in the kitchen, smashed, gazing at a stack of yet-frozen TV dinners, watching them glisten and thaw in the dull light. A game was on. If she was lucky they'd get through the evening without somebody freaking out and throwing something.

And she remembered thinking, I wonder what they were like before they met. She'd seen pictures. They looked happy. Her dad the young tough guy, handsome, stocky, football jersey, a cocky grin but eyes a little shy. All that meanness and alcoholism hidden in shy eyes. A farm boy whose farm was no more. And there was a picture of her mom, a picture taken thirty miles from where her dad's picture was taken, maybe even on the same day. They had not yet met. She's smiling shyly in a pretty dress by the gazebo in the park of her small Iowa town. She'd never smoked a cigarette by then, never had a drink, never even been kissed. Everybody born in that town lived and died there, except for one or two who went out and made a small stitch in the fabric of the world as we know it.

Just around the time her brain had developed enough to know irony, to get a laugh out of art not intended to be pretty, to stand sideways in a mirror and scowl at the profile of her body, to dread what was coming to the world and to her life, Alison could also see it all fade into another kind of nothingness and anguish. Then she met Jeremy and forgot all about that.

She met Jeremy at work. They worked in a real estate-and-loan company. It was all plywood boxes, like an abandoned movie set out in the industrial park. Jeremy made cold calls, Alison in-put data and so on. Once, Jeremy, still a stranger, chatted her up in a way that was welcome to her, but surprising. Alison considered herself to be overweight. Apparently a lot of guys did, too. She felt they did. But he asked her to lunch and they ate sandwiches at the Schlotzky's down the empty block.

"Pretty fancy," she said.

He smirked at that and looked out the window. She noticed a tattoo on the back of his hand, but did not peer at it, so didn't see what it was.

"Do you come here a lot?" she asked as they waited for the sandwiches.

"No," he said, scanning the parking lot. "You?"

"No. I usually bring my lunch," she said.

He smirked at that and began tapping his knuckles on the table rock style, bouncing his shoulders rock-star-like as he scanned the traffic outside the windows, lips puckered like Mick Jagger as he did the churning cymbal sound softly, his head down like a lizard's, a natural ellipsis for him. She glanced at the tattoo again. It was a heart. Perhaps he was in a band. He did have a cowlick and a smooth, bouncy rock way. He wore a leather jacket. As far as she knew he was sort of in her own predicament, a bit of a pill that no one could handle so they tossed you into one of those business pens making money for somebody else. Him, he hadn't finished high school either. And now he was twenty-four, making cold calls. (He looks like he should be on the phones, he is so handsome, she thought, at home at night, sillily.) Asking me out to lunch.

"Are you in a band?"

"What?" He laughed and laughed some more. "No, I'm not in a band." Sort of snidely but finding mostly humor in it. "Why?" he scoffed. She began to feel embarrassed. Her cheeks turned hot as she leveled on him with her eyes. He rested his hands on hers and said, "Maybe *we* should start a band," and she turned redder.

"What should we call it?" she managed.

"How about ..." He thought a bit, squinting and scowling out the window. "How about 'Jeremy and Alison'?" and as she swooned, he laughed and took his hands away, and then she felt hurt again.

Their sandwiches were called out to them by the guy through the microphone.

It was hard, their relationship. He lived with his mom and grandmother and her breathing machine in a tiny apartment and she lived with her mom. Neither of them had a car in any case. They managed one way or another for a while, hanging out at her place when her mom was at work or getting a motel room from time to time. She felt a part of the world now she had a boyfriend.

Then one day he called her up and asked her to move up to Waterloo with him. Said he'd got a job and a place of his own there. Told her where to meet him the next morning. And so that afternoon she sat out on the back stoop under a crackling cumulus sky, harbinger of summer storm, remembering the time she'd wished her parents had never met.

The next morning she left the house as usual for work, her mom in her dressing gown in the kitchen, as always, having a smoke and a piece of buttered toast watching the little kitchen TV at the end of the Formica table. She was white, and soft as a ball of dough. She was like an unwrapped mummy. After dad's death, life seemed to stymy her. It even palsied her, slightly. Alison put her hand on her mom's shoulder for a moment. Her mom's shoulder felt like a pancake draped over a coat hanger under scratchy lace and Alison withdrew her hand to go through the breakfast motions. Since she was running off with Jeremy today, these motions were especially wooden. Not that her mom noticed.

"I'm going up to Waterloo for a few days," Alison said.

Her mom looked from the TV to her.

"The company's sending me."

"Okay baby. Be careful." Then looked back to the TV.

She walked down to the corner as usual to catch the bus but turned right and walked an unfamiliar block thinking of her widowed mother sitting there, hapless. She had sisters in town, in any case, who would look in on her. When she sat down on a bench and cried hard like an ape become human, someone outside her—an anthropologist, maybe—might have remarked it. "Young woman, crying on a bench." She recovered and walked toward the place they had agreed and there he was, standing by some car she had never seen.

"Where'd you get this car, anyway?" she called over the busted muffler as they sped away.

"I borrowed it."

"That was nice of 'em."

Soon, unable to contain himself, he crowed, "I stole it, dude!"

Someone, a suspicious neighbor, had been watching Jeremy there by the car playing with a knife, the boy and the car both strangers on that street. Then they saw this sort of heavy-set girl approach, talk to the young man, like she knew him, and off they drove.

This would be the final trace of Alison in that town, an image in someone's mind that would fade in the on-going bath of data that is life, its sit-coms and weather reports.

Jeremy had spent two years in Anamosa for possession with intent to distribute methamphetamine, on top of a sheet of outstanding warrants for not always the most petty of crimes. He'd admitted enough to her in dribs and drabs through their relationship.

In defiance of his parole he carried a knife on him, a Buck knife he practiced whipping out quick-draw style over and over. He was always afraid he'd slice his thumb off in the process, and sometimes the knife, half-open, slipped out of his nervous hand and clattered across the floor. He got to successfully dragging the knife out of his pocket and, Taxi Driver style, flipping the blade open with a heavy snap in two seconds eight out of ten times. Then he'd hit the bars and bowling alley looking for his friends. Also in defiance of his parole.

Moving up to Waterloo without telling anybody was definitely in defiance of his parole, and maybe taking this gal along was in defiance of something, too, but he had not had open skies or a human relationship in a long time, and he was not going to let anything stop him from pursuing the nirvana.

They got to Waterloo just in time for the rain. It was coming down like streaks of ink by the time they found where they were going, the home of a friend of Jeremy's who had asked Jeremy to house-sit for him for a while, feed his dogs, whatever.

Jeremy ditched the car a couple blocks away and they ran back to the house through the rain.

Two big, underfed Dobermans, panting steam, watched through the rain from out of their doghouses as Jeremy and Alison came through the gate. She shied from their robotic regard. She feared walking by them, and this fear they seemed to note, which made her fear them more, etc.

The place had a fugitive air to it. Whoever lived here had no compunctions about leaving dirty dishes and empty forties all over the place. There was a poster on the wall of a famous wrestler, with lightning bolts and bloody lettering on it to emphasize the wrestler's ferociousness, and probably to imply the ferociousness of his fan, too. She'd been a crack-ho for a semester in high school and she knew people who lived like this.

"Where *is* your friend?" she asked.

"Uh. He's in Afghanistan. Top secret."

"Oh, wow."

"Naw. He's got some legal problems he's dealin' wif."

"Oh."

"He's on the scram, baby, and we got his crib 'til he get back which might be a lo-ong time."

"Oh." She glanced around.

"You and me can play house, baby, see?"

He wrapped her up in his arms and she tasted the tobacco in his mouth.

By that time of evening, as a rainy night fell on Des Moines and Waterloo both, the last trace of her in Des Moines had almost completely faded into television images of a tenement fire in Southeast Asia.

The rain did not let up over a matter of days and it seemed like the earth was being tilted into the river, now as wide to the south as a lake, and having cleaned the dank, dark place up, Alison stood at the window watching it. Jeremy paced, snapping his knife open, over and over with grave concentration, though not necessarily on the knife.

He had resolved to move the miserable dogs into the cellar, where at least they would be dry, and he even tossed blankets down for them, and made sure they were fed and he cleaned up after them. When he led them from the outside through the house to the cellar and they pulled fiercely at the chains she half-hid behind a doorframe.

Sometimes when it wasn't raining so hard, they walked around outside and he squinted and beaked his lips and pulled his collars up hoping to get cozy there like he didn't know what rain was, and she bore a small umbrella. They walked amidst a jungle of downed trees, the incredible white flash of a downed power line somewhere, a block away, beyond houses, flashing like a giant acetylene torch against the sides of buildings. He going, "Oh, dude."

When she said, "I knew this was going to happen," he decided he might as well get them out together.

So he stole another car, changed the plates and picked her up, headed west. He had left the dogs behind, up inside the house, with a large mixing bowl full of dry food. "They'll manage," he'd told her. "We can't take them with us." She didn't like the idea of leaving the dogs alone like that to the flood but on the other hand she had never really liked the dogs. So she said nothing of the dogs and tried to forget about them.

Over the Rockies and down on a desert some days down the road they saw a billboard that said, "World of Mystery. Are You Ready For," in hideously scrawled letters, "The Thing?"

"Oh let's don't stop there. I've seen the Thing," he said behind the wheel.

Exhausted with alcohol and heat, her heart wasn't in it when she finally drawled, "What is it then."

"Aw, it's just this thing," he said vaguely, losing interest. "I don't know."

At which point she, too, lost interest.

In L.A. they got a motel room in what seemed to be the downtown of the city, but which was in fact miles away from that. It was the heart or thick of something. He went out to get them some microwaved burros, and while he was gone, she gave herself a pregnancy test she had bought on the sly, flushed the results away just as he was coming through the door calling out "L.A. man! Spooky out there."

They ate the burros with the TV on, same TV programming they had in Iowa, and they had the same mannerism watching it as they ate: mostly quiet and spooning and chewing and swallowing. She imagined she'd also carried the Other inside her from as far as Iowa. So in the end it was like they hadn't really come that far at all.

He cleaned up the refuse and wandered around the room flicking his knife. He dropped it once. As he paced flicking it open, he talked about what kind of work he could get out here.

"That's good thinking," she said. "We can't stay in this motel room forever."

"Forever hell. We just got here."

"Besides, I'm pregnant."

"Bullshit. That's a good one." He continued the knife-play.

"I mean it, make of it what you will. I did a test just now. You wanna see it?"

"*Hell* no," he said, as if she had offered to show him the very fetus. She just looked back at him with a gravity that said if she could show him the very fetus, if that were possible, she would. So it was an open and shut case, from where she sat.

He paused, hand on the back of the blade as he folded it shut. The blade fell to with a snap and he disappeared the knife into his pocket. "Well no shit," he said in a way that did not necessarily give her any cheer.

"Yeah."

"Whoa." He sat down on the bed, across the room from her. "Well now." Then he said nothing more, and she let him just think, and watched the TV, jiggling her foot.

"Whattya wanna do about it?" he said.

"I don't know," she said to her knee.

Later, he said he had to go out for a while.

"You coming back?"

He looked defiantly around the room like his buddies were smirking at him.

"Of course I'm coming back."

She thought ruefully about that as he opened the door and looked out, left and right, in a cautious manner.

"I'll just be at that bar next door," he said back to her and shut the door.

Around ten she left the room to look for him. Pink neon women were dancing over a place called Sammy's World Famous something. Loud music thumped through its door, but she felt it was empty, except for maybe Jeremy.

She was drawn to the illumined white pool. She took off her shoes and sat at the edge of the pool and dangled her legs in the water. A thousand bugs drifted over the surface at an immeasurably slow pace. The world was full of laughter and screaming and traffic sounds and sirens. She could not see the sky.

The fence clanged. Jeremy sat beside her on the concrete his knees drawn up to his chest. He gripped his knees and looked at the pool. They looked at the surface of the pool a long time. Finally, he said, "Bugs."

She looked from the bugs to him. His breathing was shallow and quick. He seemed exhausted, or not altogether there, as he looked emptily at the bugs. She put her hand on his.

He looked at her a long moment. It was then she noticed the fresh swelling under his eye, like he'd been roughed-up. He swallowed, committed to speak. His lips began to move. Suddenly the pool lights went out and for a moment she was startled and sat motionless and listened to sirens and voices in the white darkness.

Then he said, "They took my knife."

They left L.A. the next morning. It took hours just to get beyond the grip of the city, then for hours they drove by the towns scattered off into the desert beyond the city, some of them turned toward it, and later, farther into the desert, those turned inward. By the time they'd gotten that far, Alison knew the whole story. About how Jeremy had not only got his ass kicked in an alley where he himself was lurking, but how they had taken his knife from him. So it sounded pitifully like defeat when he said they might as well head back to Iowa. The flood was about over, the rain anyway, he said, as if that fact were his only friend in the world, as if they were living in the nineteenth century. And his refuge, the dogs. He said he should look in on the dogs. Said his friend would be mad if he got back and his living room floor was covered in dog shit and dog carcasses. And then he said he might as well go back and get his cold-calling job back. His P.O. probably didn't even know he had even left Des Moines, probably. He went on and on. She didn't hear and she didn't speak. She was thinking about something else and lost interest for a while.

Late in the day, he let her drive. In the passenger seat he began nipping on the pint of Southern Comfort he'd stashed there.

185

On a long lonely stretch of highway late in the afternoon the Thing billboard whispered past.

"Are *you* ready for The Thing?" she teased.

He ignored her. He seemed despondent.

"Hey Jeremy."

"What."

"Tell me about the Thing again."

"No."

"Aw come on. What *is* the Thing?"

He shut his eyes. He took a blind hit off the bottle, held it up for her, eyes still closed against the world. She declined it. She eased off the highway onto the exit. With the bottle at his lips he said, "What's up?"

"I want to see the Thing," she said.

She turned right at the gravel road at the end of the exit. A semi was approaching with a plume of grey dust behind it.

He lay his head back. He snapped his tongue, impatient, staring at the ceiling of the car. The semi approached and she gripped the wheel as it growled and gasped heavily past them, kicking up gravel.

The Museum of the Weird and Wonderful was an attached series of run-down tin and adobe buildings, non-descript from the outside and which might have contained farm equipment or an abattoir. Only a scattering of haphazard words and images hand-painted directly on the adobe walls suggested it was a road-side attraction and that people were welcome there. "Curios," "Food and drink," "Cactus candy," "Chili dogs," "Gifts." The array of words painted at joyful angles on the adobe wall looked to her like art not intended to be pretty, but she didn't laugh this time. The world was not so hard to figure out.

The remarkable feature of the complex was a fat, square tower rising some forty feet above the heart of the structures, with an enclosed viewing platform at the top. The adobe facing of the tower was crowded in lettering like a spooky side show at the carnival, the name of the place—"World of Mystery"—and a challenge: "See Five States."

They both looked at the moribund place silently. There were no other cars in the gravel lot, and there was no sign of life.

"Maybe it's closed," she said, the only voice in that desert.

"Must be," he said numbly.

"Let's check it out."

She got out of the car and went toward the door. It wasn't until her hand was on the aluminum grip of the screen door and she jerked her elbow impatiently in a girlish pantomime for him to hurry up, that he climbed with petulant torpidity out of the car. Through tortured stations he finally made it to the porch with her. As another semi groaned past on the gravel road behind him he glanced at it and said, as if he were a retired trucker himself, "Beatin' the scales," which was ground over by the downshifting shuff of the semi.

"Jeremy?" She touched his elbow. He pulled away and scanned the landscape in an unfocussed way. He glanced at her between eye flutters.

"It's all right. I'm just drunk." He sniffed it off. He fluttered his eyes sadly toward her. The one was blackened and flesh-heavy now. "Let's go." He took the initiative and opened the door.

A large woman in a muumuu, her eyes like dollops of oil behind her thick round glasses, appeared from a back room at the sound of the bell. She looked suspiciously at them, as if her business did not in fact entail tourists stopping by for a refreshment and a look-see.

"Yes?" she sang, an easily annoyed soprano. They could hear a television in the room behind the counter she had emerged from. Something gruesome was happening on *Inside Edition*.

"We'd like to see the museum," Alison said. A sign on the register indicated three dollars for adults, children under twelve free.

"Yes?" The woman said, again, struggling her mass toward the register, eyeing them. "Six dollars."

Alison paid and they entered the museum.

The first chamber of the museum was a large, dark space crowded with antique machines and amusements—old automatic coin banks, stereoscopes, pinball machines and velocipedes, none of which actually functioned, none of which, according to the signs, were to be touched.

"But where's the thing? What *is* the thing?" she asked him, gripping his arm and leaning toward him.

"I don't know," he said, peering into a machine. "Maybe you pick the thing you want to be the thing."

He followed her into the next chamber. There were stuffed two-headed pigs and snakes, and a two-headed calf. There was a five-legged cat. It seemed all-too predictable in a place like this.

"What's so wonderful about this?" she asked. He hung back.

The walls of the next narrow room were covered with old photographs, brown daguerreotypes on cracked porcelain plates hung on the cracked, whitewashed adobe wall. Many of the images were ordinary enough, except for the eccentricity of the now-ancient culture they disclosed. Tweed suits and bowler hats, those bicycles with the huge front wheel, proud couples. Photos of barn raisings and a fair with a balloon, a photo of a train collision, photos of Indian chiefs, photos of buffalo scattered over the plains, photos of hunters displaying their spoor.

"Jeremy?" she called, finally, but not loud enough, she knew. It was barely an urgent whisper. She walked through to the coffee shop. She sat down and ran her hand over her moist forehead. She felt weak. An enormous girl brought her a menu. The girl's eyes swam hugely and without coherent aim in her thick glasses. She seemed to have split off the woman at the front.

Alison asked for a Coke and the girl went away. Alison went to the ladies room and vomited. This relieved her. She flushed it away and folded the seat down and sat for a few endorphin-merry minutes.

The Coke was on the table when she returned on still-unsteady legs. The girl was at a table across the room from her, trying to locate her exactly over a *Star* magazine.

She sipped her Coke slowly. When you're pregnant, she thought, you get sick sometimes. Everything goes funny for a while. A pregnant woman should not visit the World of Mystery.

A young man came to the doorway of the coffee shop and looked at Alison. He was a scarecrow and his eyes were large and glassy and sleepy and he had an Adam's apple like a peaked stone in his long throat. They had each other in their eyes, this family. Alison watched his Adam's apple slide slowly up his trachea like a snail, then drop, like a medical film of the invisible parts of the body, working sleepy. The fat girl laughed.

He glanced at his sister then left. Another semi ground down the road outside. "Beatin' the scales," Alison thought. She looked at the plastic clock on the wall and worked on the Coke. Dusk had come.

She paid for the Coke and walked through the museum without looking and went out to the empty, stolen car. She realized she had the keys. She walked around the building to the back. Rusted machines were scattered in the high grass. A satellite dish was bolted down near the building. Three rabbits in a chicken wire cage looked at her. She called "Jeremy" once, sharply. The fields whispered back, a long, cold, clean, empty voice. She clinched her fists and she could feel her hands. The rabbits, chewing sheets of cabbage, watched her.

She went back into the building. As she headed back into the museum the woman came in from her TV room.

"Have you seen my friend?"

The woman in the muumuu looked through her thick glasses unhappily and sang with a perplexed, and aggravating lilt, "Nooo."

Alison continued into the museum.

"We're closing in five minutes," the woman called after her.

Alison carried on. She didn't gather any of it.

The thin young man was amongst the aberrant stuffed animals. He was dusting. She looked at the two-headed calf. One head, two glass eyes, looked at her. One head looked at a bottle of hearts, the thick wrap of tissues, sheets of blue veins branching, branching, the very heart of blood itself. Deeper than her belly, somewhere in the seventh heaven of tissues there was a cell splitting madly toward Moment, toward an everywhere and forever of bliss that would last for nine earth months and then, with legs, arms, head, heart, called by time, join her with a scream among people, at the bottom of buildings, under the stars and the Moon and move with her for a lifetime through the noise. She put her hand on the tight fur on one of the calf's heads.

"Have you seen my friend? A man?"

189

Still looking at his work the young man cleared his throat and said, "Maybe he's in the tower."

"How do I get there?"

"It's two dollars."

She reached for her purse.

He looked over his shoulder at her. "It's almost closing time."

She lay two dollars down under the two-headed calf and turned into the hall and followed the signs to the wooden stairs that coiled up, around, the top of the tower choked out of view by the tight spiral.

The old wooden steps squealed with each step. At each landing she saw the empty world through a dirty window. She saw the car down there. She saw a string of headlights fading off into the distance on the freeway a mile or more across the prairie. A planet was out, one bright dot in the sky. It's going to be a long climb, she thought. He'll be up there, looking at five states. He'll say, Oh, *there* you are. She'll say, Let's go, Jeremy.

When she gained the top of the tower she went down on her knees and sat up there in the fading light, saw the sun sinking beyond the black empty hills.

"We're closing, miss," the young man's voice called from below.

She leaned her head against the wood. I haven't got my money's worth, she said. No one in all the world could hear her.

"Hello, we're closing."

She heard footsteps below begin the climb. Two or three steps, then they stopped. There was an uneasy silence.

She looked out the window at space. I've been to the world of mystery, she said. This is what she would tell her child. I saw the thing. I went up to the tower from where you could see five states. But when I got up there it was dark, and it was closing time.

"But what was the Thing, Momma?"

She would look at her child and wonder and finally say, "You pick the thing you want to be the thing."

190

The Anchor Song

Maurice Carlos Ruffin

Santa Claus got a hole where his eye go. Jerron suck his teeth like *that's just girl's luck*, but I quiet myself the same as if I was at the bottom of a pool, counting how long I been under.

I shoot Santa again. In the belt buckle this time. I never touched a gun before this morning. Jerron neither. When Jerron shot, he only popped Santa's shoulder, but I done killed Santa twice dead. Guess I'm a natural, me.

"One more time," I say. The Santa cutout flap against the fence behind this empty garage.

Jerron give me a look. We don't know how many bullets left in the pea shooter 'cause we don't know how it open. Well, Jerron probably know, but he don't liked fooling with it if he don't have to. Back home everybody got a dozen guns and a million bullets to shoot. All we got is this one pea shooter even though it feel like the whole world coming for us.

"Go head, then, girl," Jerron say.

I aim. Jerron's hand almost swallows the pea shooter when he hold it, but it's the right size for me. A fist I can throw across a room. I need to hit Santa in the mouth this time. No more *ho ho ho*. The pea shooter ain't loud, and it go *bap* like a screen door smacking shut. I miss.

We in a field, the middle of fiddle and boots country. I ain't never been this far from New Orleans and all these hick white people scare the shit out of me, but not as much as Daddy do. Down the road the way we come from there ain't no cars. Just a stretch of silence.

I stuff the pea shooter in my coat. Jerron get in the pickup with Babycake, who coughing. The gun ain't ours, and the pickup almost out of gas. The pickup ain't ours neither. It belong to Daddy. Just like the gun. But Babycake ours, belongs to me and Jerron. Babycake our little nugget, crying like how I feel inside. I know she don't need no diaper. Jerron just changed her. Jerron press his nose on her face and snort like a pig. Babycake laugh. Maybe she nervous. Lord knows me too, Babycake. Jerron touch his fingers soft on my cheek where Daddy bruised me this morning.

It didn't have go down how it did. Daddy wasn't supposed to be awake before sunup. Daddy wasn't supposed to find us in my room, packing in the dark. He come in shouting. Knocked Mama's picture off the dresser, shattering glass. Knocked me down, too, and hit my face on the garbage can, but I ain't break.

Now, Jerron a big ole boy, but Daddy a big ole man. And Daddy hate him some Jerron on account of me getting pregnant by him. Daddy said before if he catch Jarron's punk ass around again, he kill him. Jerron was around again.

Daddy went for Jerron, and they scrummed like pit bull dogs. Jerron pointed that pea shooter at Daddy.

"You gonna shoot me over this little ho, son?" Daddy asked, yanking on my dress collar.

Jerron wasn't about to shoot. He scared of things. One time a bottle cap-sized spider crawled on my Disney Princess bedspread while we was eating shrimp po-boys. Jerron saw it and fell on the floor. I grabbed that spider in my hand and let him out the window. Then, I helped Jerron up from the floor—heavy as he is—but he didn't want to eat no more po-boy that night even though he been known to swallow down two big po-boys without barely breathing. He was shamed. That's why Jerron need me—to keep him from staying down. I got him to eat his fill that night. I bet I did.

In my room this morning when Jerron pointed that gun, Daddy pulled a blade and went at Jerron. I heard that screen door *bap*. Daddy fell down holding his hand. Said I better not come back. Said Jerron dead when he catch him.

I'm driving. I ain't old enough to drive. Jerron is, but I drive steadier than him and them policemen less likely to pull us over with me behind the wheel, we figure. We saw a brother face down on the side of the highway a ways back, five policemen's cars for just one dude. Babycake in Jerron lap *coo-coo*-ing the way she do. She okay, but my breath come

192

out in cloud puffs. Can't turn on the heater though 'cause the air it blow stink worse than dog dookie.

We wasn't leaving just to leave. Babycake been sick. She only been here a few months, but the clinic doctor say she got bad blood, and it's going to take her from us. I reach over and tickle her stomach. She wiggle her arms. She ain't supposed to leave yet. That's why Babycake need me—to make sure she don't float back to heaven.

We don't have no money for the special doctor Jerron's auntie in Houston know, but what kind of special doctor going to say no to Babycake? He'll help. Daddy said I'm stupid for believing so, but that doctor will help.

I always try to feed Babycake good food, mashed up peaches and pears, but she hardly never eat. I wonder if Daddy back home is still fuming or did he go to the hospital and die? Before I met Jerron, I ran away a couple of times, but Daddy always found me. Jerron and Babycake and me forever. I ain't going home. Not never no more.

There's nothing in the rearview but a yellow strip that run all the way back home. Jerron undo the clip from the pea shooter. A bullet fall out.

"Don't shoot yourself, boy," I say.

"I got this," he say.

He shove it back in and close the pea shooter. I ask how many bullets left. He say two.

We ride downhill. I pull into a gas station. A canal run alongside us with steam creeping off the dirty water. Jerron say he love me, and I say the same back. He take Babycake to the bathroom for changing and leave the pea shooter on the seat. Jerron a wizard with a diaper, change one as easy as I can blink. I'm no good, usually get mess all over everything.

Outside the station, a hooptie pull up and almost hit the pickup I'm inside. Jerron come out the station carrying Babycake in the crook of his arm. Daddy hop out, two men in work overalls with him. They yell at Jerron. Jerron yell back. Babycake cry. People in the station watch us from behind glass like we fish in a 'quarium. I climb down from the pickup and point the pea shooter at Daddy.

"You got some nerve threatening me," he say. "I'm going to beat you with that gun when I get you, ho."

"Don't call me that," I say. I tell Jerron go. He look at me like *no way you for real*. Daddy start toward me. I can't let him keep Babycake from help, and I can't let him kill Jerron. My hands shake. I shoot for the hooptie tire. I don't miss.

Daddy stops shy. The two men in overalls jump behind the car.

I shoot Daddy in the mouth, so he never call me ho again, but that's just me hoping. I can't shoot Daddy. He still my Daddy, and his face crumpled like he fixing to cry, something I ain't never seen. But I can't leave. Daddy follow wherever I go.

I tell Jerron to take off, and he look at me like *baby, you know I ain't leaving you*. I give Jerron the face I always do when I mean something serious, a look like I'm slapping him with my eyes. Jerron crank the pickup and smoke cough out the tailpipe.

Daddy stare at me. I'm still pointing at him. Babycake and Jerron rise up the hill like a bubble out of water. I pitch the pea shooter in the canal, and it sink faster than I can count.

After We're Gone

Brett Riley

The end of the world happened fast. One morning, almost everyone died, but only for two hours. One hundred and twenty minutes of dynamite nerves and electric fear, of screaming and crying and making half-baked plans, and then they all stood up and brushed the dust from their clothes. Back to school, work, bed, like nothing had happened.

Ms. Hodge's trigonometry class seemed like it lasted seven hours after her skin turned green and started oozing off. Her dress stuck to her body in wet patches, and her hair fell out, and when she wrote on the board, her skin mixed with the chalk dust, which got all over everything. She tracked that crap everywhere while she droned on and on about sines and cosines. It really ruined spaghetti-and-meat-sauce day.

Well, for me. It didn't bother the other kids. They were all dead, too.

Jimmy Jones and his family lived in this shack without central air, so he looked and smelled worse than everybody else, which was also true before he died. One day, he raised his hand to answer a question, and his right arm fell off. The hand landed on my shoe. Ms. Hodge told him to keep his stuff on his own desk.

Everybody was coming apart.

In the cafeteria, the dead kids smacked their blue lips and black tongues, talking about the usual crap—crushes and homework and sports, mostly football, even though during one game, D.J. Rose got tackled so hard his head popped off and rolled into the backfield. Both teams jumped on it, thinking he had fumbled, while his body stood up and wandered away. The coach sent somebody after it. After that, D.J.'s body carried his head to class and set it on his desk, and Ms. Hodge didn't even blink. Like, ever.

There were seventeen other living people in town. We talked to other Survivors on the Internet and argued about tactics. Most of us agreed we should meet and build a community somewhere, but nobody could decide on a location. Plus, we got scammed. This guy on our forum, Alexis from New York, fell in love with another Survivor online. One day, I saw them on one of those TV shows about fake relationships. Alexis learned his new soulmate was a rotting fat dude from Racine, Wisconsin.

Wendy Glass lived, though. She was in the tenth grade, same as me. We were the only surviving kids in town, so we became best friends, but I hoped for more. I'd always liked her. Now I stood a much better chance. Maybe we'd fall in love on the road to the new community, just like in the movies.

There are three major theories about why everybody died, and if you miss the discourse from Internet article comments sections, just pop onto the Survivors' Forum and question one of the hypotheses. It doesn't matter which one. You'll get torn apart. Figuratively speaking.

The first theory is called Extraterrestrial Causation, a general term covering two related but competing ideas: one, that in the freak meteor shower the night before the Event, some space rocks got through the atmosphere and released an airborne toxin. I'm pretty sure somebody swiped that concept from *Night of the Living Dead*. Then there's idea two, that aliens did it, how and why depending on whom you ask. If this two-pronged theory makes no sense to you, congratulations. You've got a brain. Even the diehard EC folks can't explain how a few rocks falling in Puget Sound could affect the whole planet overnight or why we've seen no evidence of an alien presence.

The second theory, mostly popular with extreme right-wing survivors—terrorists. Which terrorists, and why, and how? Anybody's guess. Evangelical Christians blame radical Muslims, who blame the West. Russians blame Chechen rebels, or America, depending on the day. A few fundamentalist splinter groups say it's the Rapture, but if that's true, how come nobody went to heaven?

We call the third theory Government SNAFU. Somebody—usually America or Russia or China, though some blame various Middle Eastern countries, and one doofus swears it was Switzerland—somebody's chemical warfare experiments went haywire and broke containment. If you can figure out the logistics, you're smarter than me and everybody on the Forum. What's the delivery system—Santa Claus?

All these theories, no proof.

The explanation I like best? The Wendy Glass Theory. One night, she and I sat in the Wal-Mart parking lot, sipping canned Coke and talking about where we should rebuild the world. I spent maybe ten minutes griping about the three theories before Wendy interrupted me.

It doesn't matter how it started, she said. Everybody died. Then they came back. And now we've gotta deal with it. Hey, you wanna go to Baton Rouge this weekend and see that new Wes Anderson movie?

She was right. It doesn't matter. Plus, she asked me out, so silver linings, right?

The Walking Dead, George A. Romero, that guy who rewrote *Pride and Prejudice*—they all got it wrong. Survivors didn't form roving bands of murderous scavengers. Nobody built walls around their towns. The government didn't collapse, and the military didn't betray civilians, and we didn't return to an agrarian barter economy. The dead don't eat people. Not brains, not flesh, not even something weird, like toenail clippings. They scarf their Double Whoppers with cheese and their vegan pizzas and their green smoothies that smell like wet seaweed, just like before. Edgar Wright got close at the end of *Shaun of the Dead*, when his shamblers gather shopping carts and play video games, but the real-world dead still think and talk and fly airplanes and watch bad movies.

Santa Clarita Diet might be the best example of what life's really like, except that most of the world is Drew Barrymore, and they decay a lot faster, and nothing's funny.

To be fair, some of the legends are true. You can re-kill the dead by destroying their brains, and we all come back after we die, even Survivors. The world discovered those facts right here in Gonzales, Louisiana, when two Survivors made a suicide pact. One guy blew his brains out. He fell over in the street and never moved again. The other dude shot himself in the heart. He fell over, too, and lay there until the reanimated cops and paramedics and coroner took him away. They say he woke up in the morgue, rolled off the table, looked around, and said, Well, damn.

Ms. Hodge stopped coming to school. Our substitute, Mr. Manning, was twenty years older and more decomposed. His veins looked full of ink. His teeth were broken. Maybe his air conditioner was broken. Temperature and climate seem to matter. Survivors from Nevada and North Dakota reported different effects than we saw in humid south Louisiana. Of course, whatever brought the dead back works a little differently for everybody. Some kids looked pretty much the same except for their milky eyes, but I figured one day they'd have to bring Jimmy Jones to school in a bucket.

Wendy came over one day. We went to my room and listened to The Pretty Reckless and Garbage. I wonder if Taylor Momsen and Shirley Manson lived. If not, I bet their voices have gone to hell. I've never seen a dead person playing guitar. The strings would probably cut them to the bone.

Mom made gumbo, but she flaked into it, so I didn't eat any. I made a couple of grilled cheese sandwiches. Wendy and I ate in my room. I didn't know what to say. She looks like Taylor Momsen with less eye makeup and bigger boobs. My dream girl. But how do you say that with your dead Mom making skinflake soup down the hall and your dead Dad working the night shift at Angola Federal Penitentiary? Plus, Wendy never even noticed me until every other kid in town died.

My parents have sex every night, she said as she finished her sandwich. I can hear em. I never could before, but now they won't stop, and they're loud, and I just wanna run away. Like, yesterday.

Run to where, though? I said. Last night, Willie from Stillwater, Oklahoma, argued for Kansas. I guess he likes tornadoes or whatever.

I thought it was down to Key West, Manhattan, or the Irish countryside.

Three days ago, yeah. Now everybody's fightin again.

Cheese globs stuck to Wendy's plate, like the black gunk that oozes from the dead once they decompose enough. It never dries. People slip in it. Rot overwhelmed Wendy and me all the time. The sights, the smell, the sound of people squishing in their own juices when they walked, the boogery feel when they touched you. You could even taste death, like a film of mold over everything.

Wendy set her plate on the floor and stretched out on my bed. I sat next to her, cross-legged. She stared at my ceiling for a long time while I listened to Mom humming *She's Not There* in the kitchen.

Then Wendy said, Come here.

What?

Snuggle. We both need some human touch.

I wouldn't have been more surprised if she had asked me to cut out my own liver and wear it as a hat. Wendy, I—

Hush. You're sweet. We're here, together. So just hold me, okay?

I had dreamed about hearing those words for years. Maybe all it takes for you to get what you want is the end of the world. I lay next to Wendy and draped my arm around her. And when she turned and kissed me, I had never felt so alive.

When the dead rose, they caused all sorts of moral dilemmas. Take Angola. A lot of those guys were serving life without parole or counting their days on Death Row. When they died and came back, nobody knew what to do. Then some lawyer argued their deaths meant their sentences had been served, and a judge agreed, so the state let them go. Serial killers and mass rapists and first-degree murderers walked, while tax evaders and car thieves and weed dealers stayed put. What a system, right?

Of course, if you had gotten more than one consecutive life sentence, you were still totally hosed.

When pregnant women reanimated, their babies didn't. Nobody knows why. When they wanted those lifeless fetuses removed, right-wingers threw a fit. *We're all dead now, so how can you treat those precious babies any differently than the rest of us?* It didn't matter that they would never be born, that they would rot right out of those wombs and splat on the ground like bird crap.

Nobody, not even the radicals, said much about the soul—whether they move on to whatever's next or if they're still here. When a reporter asked the Pope about it, the Pontiff's lower jaw fell off and shattered on the pavement.

Philosophy, metaphysics—we're in uncharted territory. It's tough to orient yourself when everybody's Lazarus and you can't find Jesus anywhere.

I couldn't even mourn my parents because they still asked me how school went and made me take out the trash. I cried for a week after the Event, mostly from confusion and knowing I didn't belong in Gonzales anymore. I couldn't hang out with my friends because they were disintegrating. It's the kind of thing you can't help but notice. I only felt like my old self around Wendy Glass. Other Survivors treated me like an equal, but that made me feel like a fraud. I was just a kid. What could I offer—mad skills at *Dark Souls* or *Resident Evil?* Nobody plays those games anymore. They seem insensitive.

One night, I went to Wendy's house. Her dad, a welder with blackened cheeks and greenish skin like Ms. Hodge's, let me in. Mrs. Glass had gone for drinks with her friends.

Can the dead get drunk?

Wendy took me to her room and closed the door. Her parents didn't care what she did anymore. She opened her laptop and put on some music.

I deleted any band with the word *dead* in their name, she said. The Grateful Dead. The Dead Kennedys. The Dead Milkmen. Hollywood Undead. And You Will Know Us by the Trail of Dead. Et cetera.

She put the songs on shuffle. Every other one featured somebody that died a long time ago—Jim Morrison, Kurt Cobain, Keith Moon, Jimi Hendrix, Jon Bonham, Randy Rhoads. Even if they had lived, chances are they'd be dead now. Of all the musicians to survive the Event, the one that surprised nobody was Keith Richards, though some of the walking corpses look better than him.

When Marvin Gaye's *Sexual Healing* played, Wendy kissed me. A good thing, because I still couldn't make the first move. She tasted like strawberries and smelled like honeysuckle. I closed my eyes and imagined us in a meadow full of tall grass and yellow flowers. When she touched my crotch, I slipped my hand under her shirt and prayed I could undo her bra.

Having sex with Wendy Glass surprised me more than the Event itself. I had loved her so long that she had come to seem more like a movie star than a classmate. Now I had touched her, been inside her, the finest dream in my sixteen-year-old brain come to life.

Not that she loved me back. She liked me, probably felt some kind of affection, maybe even attraction, but love? No. I still hope she will someday, but I can't lie to myself. Mass death teaches you to look hard facts in the eye.

When I got home, Dad sat in his recliner, watching an LSU game. On the couch, Mom read a sticky copy of *Love in the Time of Cholera*.

Dad paused the game and sniffed. You had sex with Wendy, he said. My man. He raised his fist for a bump. One of his knucklebones poked out. I left him hanging.

Good for y'all, Mom gargled. Her vocal chords were deteriorating, or maybe her lungs.

Y'all okay with this? I said. I'm sixteen.

Your babies will save the world, Mom said. Unless you're shootin blanks.

God, Mom.

The Event, the dead rising, the decomposition, and yet that conversation horrified me more than anything.

It's up to you kids to keep things goin, Dad said. After we're gone.

Right, I said. I'm goin to bed.

I trotted down the hall and into my room and locked the door behind me.

Ms. Hodge fell down her porch steps and broke both hips. That alone wouldn't have stopped her from working, since the dead don't feel pain, but before she could crawl back in her house, somebody's German Shepherd ran up, smelled her, and clamped down on her right forearm, ripping it off at the elbow. The dog was last seen heading into the woods with the arm, which kept trying to poke it in the eyes, Three Stooges-style. Ms. Hodge was right-handed, so she couldn't write on the board anymore.

Jimmy Jones showed up with his lower jaw and throat torn away. Somebody asked him what happened, but his tongue just flapped on his chest like a living necktie.

Everybody at school knew about Wendy and me. Even after hot showers and lots of soap, deodorant, Wendy's perfume, they smelled us. The guys congratulated me, like I had won a race or whatever. The girls surrounded Wendy, demanding details. Sooner or later, they all asked us the same question: *you pregnant?*

None of your business, I said to Belinda, a moldering junior Goth girl whose dark eyeliner and lipstick seemed redundant now. She wore a shroud, and nobody even Snapchatted it.

It's everybody's business, she said. Nothin's more important than kids. For after we're gone.

Yeah, right, I said. I bet you eat babies.

She looked at me like I was the walking corpse with one cheekbone exposed. What's wrong with you? She stormed off.

I met Wendy after school. The dead strolled by, giving us thumbs-up signs and applauding. Everyone had watched me all day, like they had just noticed I was still alive.

This is the first minute I've had without half a dozen of em hangin on me like I'm an antique and they're ten pounds of bubble wrap, Wendy said.

Right? I said. And this baby probably doesn't even exist.

God. Yesterday, I was a person. Today, I'm a wanderin womb.

Like we're Adam and Eve or some crap.

Jimmy Jones oozed by, dropping pieces of himself. Crows perched all over him, pecking away, though for some parts, they really needed a straw. They had eaten his tongue and eyes. He walked into somebody's car, and they flew off, squawking. When Jimmy stumbled away, he left a black smear on the chassis.

Wendy shivered. Ugh.

I kind of hurt Belinda Wiseau's feelings, I said.

How?

I told her she probably ate babies.

Jesus Christ. Why would you say that?

Well, they eat people in the movies. And I wanted her to leave me alone.

And that's where you went with it?

I didn't know what to make of this development. I figured Wendy would laugh, but she looked terrified.

It was just a bad joke, I said.

Belinda walked by, drinking a Big Red. She waved at Wendy and smiled. Her reddened teeth looked like she had just eaten a fat newborn. Wendy retched, so I waved back. Belinda stuck out her gross tongue.

Let's get outta here, Wendy said.

You wanna go to Cracker Barrel? I hear the cooks wear, like, HazMat suits.

No. I mean let's leave town. Get away from all this.

They're everywhere. Besides, we still ain't decided on where to meet.

We can check the forums anywhere. Let's go to Canada. Or New York. Anywhere but here.

The weather had gotten colder as Halloween approached. Up north, snow had already fallen. Some roads would be impassible. We didn't have passports. We could get all the way up there just in time for the Survivors to pick Florida, or California, or France. I started to protest.

Then Wendy lay her knuckles on my cheek. I could have looked into her eyes until I floated away.

Okay, I said.

Nobody knows if the dead poop. They eat ravioli and Sloppy Joes like the rest of us, but nobody's seen them taking a dump. Maybe they do it in secret, like Great White sharks mating. Or maybe the food teleports to the same place where socks lost in the dryer go. Survivors debate it on dedicated message boards.

The Hollywood dead still make movies and TV shows. I guess they'll stop once the actors fall to pieces. The dead don't dance because they tend to fly apart. Sports are winding down for the same reason. World culture erodes by inches. Soon it will be gone, except what Survivors carry with them. That's one reason I'm writing this. I had planned to be an author—major in creative writing at LSU, get my MFA, write novels. Now, I'm more like a historian. Maybe one day I'll still get the chance to be the next Stephen King—who's still alive, by the way. I don't know if that's ironic or predictable. He keeps lobbying for Survivors to gather in Maine. Like we'd ever live there after reading his books.

We decided to leave on Halloween. It seemed like as good a target date as any. Plus, the dead were excited, like they belonged to a grand tradition they hadn't understood before. Trees groaned and slouched under the weight of plastic skeletons and other cheap junk. Every yard held six or eight tombstones, cardboard and Styrofoam and hard plastic, along with inflatable characters from movies that had nothing to do with the holiday. I went to Wal-Mart one day and found the costume section ransacked. Corpses dressing as Disney princesses or vampires. Maybe the outfits and masks let them forget for a while. Even high school kids talked about Halloween like it was prom.

We didn't tell the other Gonzales Survivors about our plan. We hadn't known them long enough to tie our lives to theirs. We didn't hoard any supplies—no guns or batteries, no canned food, no bottled water. Why bother, with every Target and grocery store still open? We just packed our go-bags and swiped money from our parents. Either they didn't notice or they didn't care.

Dad turned black and goopy from working in Angola, with its stinking death-house air. Mom, who stayed inside most of the time, looked more like jerky. I wanted to miss them, but they had been gone for weeks. These dead versions lacked something I can only term a genuine self. Living with them felt like driving by the burned-down shell of your childhood home.

I wasn't even sure they'd miss me. Do the dead love?

I said goodbye to them around seven on Halloween night. I had hidden my go-bag in the shrubs outside. Soon, Wendy would pick me up in her car. We planned to drive through Arkansas and Missouri and all the way to Canada. My parents believed I'd be home in a few hours. They also believed Wendy was pregnant. Mom had already bought a crib. For all I knew, they could smell the zygote.

As I left, Dad watched the news and sloughed onto his chair. Mom dumped candy into a plastic pumpkin. We didn't even say goodbye. I closed the door, grabbed my bag, and ran down the driveway. Wendy sat in her two-year-old Mazda. The dead meandered along the sidewalks, the kids ringing doorbells and gurgling *Trick or Treat.* I got in the car. As we drove, werewolves and pirates and prisoners and superheroes carried plastic pumpkins like Mom's, paper sacks, garbage bags. Adults stumbled along behind, dragging their feet, their skin runny or desiccated, half their skeletons showing, faces without noses. Some voices had degenerated into grunts and moans.

I saw Jimmy Jones, Wendy said, white-knuckling the wheel. He's a spine and maybe half a head on legs. His arms look like old tree branches.

God.

I don't think He's in town.

We stopped at the notoriously long red light on Main. I dug out my iPod and plugged it in and found a grunge playlist. Nirvana, Pearl Jam, Soundgarden.

Using only her left arm, a woman in an orange-and-black catsuit and a tiger mask pushed her wheelchair down the sidewalk. She stopped at the corner and looked at us.

Wendy glanced at her and shuddered. Shoo, Richard Parker.

The woman took off her mask. One of her cheeks came with it.

Ms. Hodge.

She bumped off the curb and into the right-hand lane and up to my window and tapped on the glass with her paw. Where y'all headed? she asked, sounding like a deaf person speaking underwater.

Don't tell her, Wendy said, staring straight ahead. Our parents will come after us.

I heard that, Ms. Hodge said.

Scat, cat, I said, making a go-away gesture.

Y'all can't leave, she said. This town needs that baby. For after we're gone.

We don't even know if there *is* a baby, I said.

It's a girl, Ms. Hodge said.

Stop talkin to her, Wendy whispered.

Get outta the car, Ms. Hodge said. She pounded on the glass.

No way, I said.

Get out, she cried, and punched through the window.

Wendy screamed as glass shards fell into my lap. Ms. Hodge grabbed my shirt and tugged. Despite her condition, only my seatbelt held me in place. The smell nearly made me barf. She turned her face to the sky and moaned, long and deep and loud as a foghorn.

The dead on the sidewalk paused, turned, watched us. Then they shuffled our way, returning Ms. Hodge's moan like wolves talking across a forest. Storefronts opened. More dead poured out and headed straight for us.

Oh my God, I said.

Wendy floored it.

The car shot forward, blowing through the still-red light. I felt a jerk. Ms. Hodge's hand still clutched my shirt. The whole arm had torn loose, the ball of bone that should have nestled in the shoulder's socket dangling out the broken window. I pried her fingers loose and tossed it out.

The dead were everywhere, shuffling or running after us, arms outstretched, all of them moaning in a great awful chorus. Some stepped in front of the car. Wendy knocked them aside, across the hood and over the windshield, underneath us. Some were torn in half. The rest fell in behind us, choking the street, bloated and rotten and fragile and slow. We zoomed away, corpses filling our rearview mirrors until we took the I-10 North onramp, their voices like a hand reaching for us, but we drove and drove and didn't stop until we needed gas somewhere in Arkansas.

Long after we reached Canada, I still expected the population of Gonzales, Louisiana, to crest a hill one day. Our abandoned dead. Legs worn to nubs, whole chunks of them lost to decay and animals but still coming, coming, coming, as inevitable as love.

Xmas, Jamaica Plain

Melanie Rae Thon

I'm your worst fear.

But not the worst thing that can happen.

I lived in your house half the night. I'm the broken window in your little boy's bedroom. I'm the flooded tiles in the bathroom where the water flowed and flowed.

I'm the tattoo in the hollow of Emile's pelvis, five butterflies spreading blue wings to rise out of his scar.

I'm dark hands slipping through all your pale woman underthings; dirty fingers fondling a strand of pearls, your throat, a white bird carved of stone. I'm the body you feel wearing your fox coat.

I think I had a sister once. She keeps talking in my head. She won't let go. My sister Clare said: Take the jewelry; it's yours.

My heart's in my hands: what I touch, I love; what I love, I own.

Snow that night, and nobody seemed surprised so I figured it must be winter. Later I remembered it was Christmas, or it had been, the day before. I was with Emile who wanted to be Emilia. We'd started downtown, Boston. Now it was Jamaica Plain, three miles south. Home for the holidays, Emile said, some private joke. He'd been working the block around the Greyhound Station all night wearing nothing but a white scarf and black turtleneck, tight jeans. Man wants to see before he buys, Emile said. He meant the ones in long cars cruising, looking for fragile boys with female faces.

Emile was sixteen, he thought.

Getting old.

He'd made sixty-four dollars: three tricks with cash, plus some pills—a bonus for good work, blues and greens—he didn't know what. Nobody'd offered to take him home, which is all he wanted, a warm bed, some sleep, eggs in the morning, the smell of butter, hunks of bread torn off the loaf.

Crashing, both of us, ragged from days of speed and crack, no substitute for the smooth high of pure cocaine, but all we could afford. Now, enough cash between us at last. I had another twenty-five from the man who said he was in the circus once, who called himself the Jungle Creep—on top of me he made that sound. Before he unlocked the door, he'd said: Are you a real girl? I looked at his plates, New Jersey—that's why he didn't know the lines, didn't know the boys as girls stay away from the Zone unless they want their faces crushed. He wanted me to prove it first. Some bad luck once, I guess. I said: It's fucking freezing. I'm real. Open the frigging door or go.

Now it was too late to score, too cold, nobody on the street but Emile and me, the wind, so we walked, we kept walking. I had a green parka, somebody else's empty wallet in the pocket—I couldn't remember who or where—the coat stolen weeks ago and still mine, a miracle out here. We shared, trading it off. I loved Emile. I mean, it hurt my skin to see his cold.

Emile had a plan. It had to be Jamaica Plain, home—enough hands as dark as mine, enough faces as brown as Emile's—not like Brookline where we'd have to turn ourselves inside out. Jamaica Plain where there were pretty painted houses next to shacks, where the sound of bursting glass wouldn't be that loud.

Listen, we needed to sleep, to eat, that's all. So thirsty even my veins felt dry, flattened out. Hungry somewhere in my head, but my stomach shrunken to a knot so small I thought it might be gone. I remembered the man, maybe last week, before the snow, leaning against the statue of starved horses, twisted metal at the edge of the Common. He had a knife, long enough for gutting fish. Dressed in camouflage but not hiding. He stared at his thumb, licked it clean and cut deep to watch the bright blood bubble out. He stuck it in his mouth to drink, hungry, and I swore I'd never get that low. But nights later I dreamed him beside me. Raw and dizzy, I woke, offering my whole hand, begging him to cut it off.

We walked around your block three times. We were patient now. Numb. No car up your drive, and your porch light blazing, left to burn all night, we thought. Your house glowed, yellow even in the dark, paint so shiny it looked wet, and Emile said he lived somewhere like this once, when he was still a boy all the time, hair cropped short, before lipstick and mascara, when his cheeks weren't blushed, before his mother caught him, and his father locked him out.

In this house Emile found your red dress, your silk stockings. He was happy, I swear.

So why did he end up on the floor?

I'm not going to tell you; I don't know.

First, the rock wrapped in Emile's scarf, glass splintering in the cold, and we climbed into the safe body of your house. Later we saw this was a child's room, your only one. We found the tiny cowboy boots in the closet, black like Emile's, but small, so small. I tried the little bed. It was soft enough but too short. In every room your blue-eyed boy floated on the wall. Emile wanted to take him down. Emile said: He scares me. Emile said your little boy's too pretty, his blond curls too long. Emile said: Some night the wrong person's going to take him home.

Emile's not saying anything now, but if you touched his mouth you'd know. Like a blind person reading lips, you'd feel everything he needed to tell.

We stood in the cold light of the open refrigerator, drinking milk from the carton, eating pecan pie with our hands, squirting whipped cream into our mouths. You don't know how it hurt us to eat this way, our shriveled stomachs stretching; you don't know why we couldn't stop. We took the praline ice cream to your bed, one of those tiny containers, sweet and sickening, bits of candy frozen hard. We fell asleep, and it melted, so we drank it, thick with your brandy, watching bodies writhe on the TV, no sound: flames and ambulances all night; children leaping; a girl in mud under a car, eight men lifting; a skier crashing into a wall—we never knew who was saved and who was not. Talking heads spit the news again and again—there was no reason to listen—tomorrow exactly the same things would happen, and still everyone would forget.

There were other houses after yours, places I went alone, but there were none before and none like this. When I want to feel love I remember the dark thrill of it, the bright sound of glass, the sudden size and weight of my own heart in my own chest, how I knew it now, how it was real to me in my body, separate from lungs and liver and ribs, how it made the color of my blood surge against the back of my eyes, how nothing mattered anymore because I believed in this, my own heart, its will to live.

No lights, no alarm. We waited outside. Fifteen seconds. Years collapsed. We were scared of you, who you might be inside, terrified lady with a gun, some fool with bad aim and dumb luck. The boost to the window, Emile lifting me, then I was there, in you, I swear, the smell that particular, that strong, almost a taste in your boy's room, his sweet milky breath under my tongue. Heat left low, but to us warm as a body, humid, hot.

My skin's cracked now, hands that cold, but I think of them plunged deep in your drawer, down in all your soft underbelly underclothes, slipping through all your jumbled silky womanthings.

I pulled them out and out.

I'm your worst fear. I touched everything in your house: all the presents just unwrapped: cashmere sweater, rocking horse, velvet pouch. I lay on your bed, smoking cigarettes, wrapped in your fur coat. How many foxes? I tried to count.

But it was Emile who wore the red dress, who left it crumpled on the floor.

Thin as he is, he couldn't zip the back—he's a boy, after all—he has those shoulders, those soon-to-be-a-man bones. He swore trying to squash his boy feet into the matching heels; then he sobbed. I had to tell him he had lovely feet, and he did, elegant, long—those golden toes. I found him a pair of stockings, one size fits all.

I wore your husband's pinstriped jacket. I pretended all the gifts were mine to offer. I pulled the pearls from their violet pouch.

We danced.

We slid across the polished wooden floor of your living room, spun in the white lights of the twinkling tree. And again, I tell you, I swear I felt the exact size and shape of things inside me, heart and kidney, my sweet left lung. All the angels hanging from the branches opened their glass mouths, stunned.

He was more woman than you, his thick hair wound tight and pinned. Watch this, he said, chignon.

I'm not lying. He transformed himself in front of your mirror, gold eyeshadow, faint blush. He was beautiful. He could have fooled anyone. Your husband would have paid a hundred dollars to feel Emile's mouth kiss all the places you won't touch.

Later the red dress lay like a wet rag on the floor. Later the stockings snagged, the strand of pearls snapped, and the beads rolled. Later Emile was all boy naked on the bathroom floor.

I'm the one who got away, the one you don't know; I'm the long hairs you find under your pillow, nested in your drain, tangled in your brush. You think I might come back. You dream me dark always. I could be any dirty girl on the street, or the one on the bus, black lips, just-shaved head. You see her through mud-spattered glass, quick, blurred. You want me dead—it's come to this—killed, but not by your clean hands. You pray for accidents instead, me high and spacy, stepping off the curb, a car that comes too fast. You dream some twisted night road and me walking, some poor drunk weaving his way home. He won't even know what he's struck. In the morning he'll touch the headlight I smashed, the fender I splattered, dirt or blood. In the light he'll see my body rising, half-remembered, snow that whirls to a shape then blows apart. Only you will know for sure, the morning news, another unidentified girl dead, hit and run, her killer never found.

I wonder if you'll rest then, or if every sound will be glass, every pair of hands, mine, reaching for your sleeping son.

How can I explain?

We didn't come for him.

I'm your worst fear. Slivers of window embedded in carpet. Sharp and invisible. You can follow my muddy footprints through your house, but if you follow them backward they always lead here: to this room, to his bed.

If you could see my hands, not the ones you imagine, but my real hands, they'd be reaching for Emile's body. If you looked at Emile's feet, if you touched them you could feel us dancing.

This is all I want.

After we danced, we lay so close on your bed I dreamed we were twins, joined forever this way, two arms, three legs, two heads.

But I woke in my body alone.

Outside snow fell like pieces of broken light.

I already knew what had happened. But I didn't want to know.

I heard him in the bathroom.

I mean, I heard the water flow and flow.

I told myself he was washing you away, your perfume, your lavender oil scent. Becoming himself. Tomorrow we'd go.

I tried to watch the TV, the silent man in front of the map, the endless night news. But there it was, my heart again, throbbing in my fingertips.

I couldn't stand it—the snow outside; the sound of water; your little boy's head propped on the dresser, drifting on the wall; the man in the corner of the room, trapped in the flickering box: his silent mouth wouldn't stop.

I pounded on the bathroom door. I said :Goddamn it, Emile—you're clean enough. I said I had a bad feeling about this place. I said I felt you coming home.

But Emile, he didn't say a word. There was only water, that one sound, and I saw it seeping under the door, leaking into the white carpet. Still, I told lies to myself. I said: Shit, Emile—what's going on? I pushed the door. I had to shove hard, squeeze inside, because Emile was there, you know, exactly where you found him, face down on the floor. I turned him over, saw the lips smeared red, felt the water flow.

I breathed into him, beat his chest. It was too late, God, I know, his face pressed to the floor all this time, his face in the water, Emile dead even before he drowned, your bottle of Valium empty in the sink, the foil of your cold capsules punched through, two dozen gone—this is what did it: your brandy, your Valium, your safe little pills bought in a store. After all the shit we've done—smack popped under the skin, speed laced with strychnine, monkey dust—it comes to this. After all the nights on the streets, all the knives, all the pissed-off Johns, all the fag-hating bullies prowling the Fenway with their bats, luring boys like Emile into the bushes with promises of sex. After all that, this is where it ends: on your clean wet floor.

Above the thunder of the water, Clare said: He doesn't want to live.

Clare stayed very calm. She said: Turn off the water, go.

I kept breathing into him. I watched the butterflies between his bones. No flutter of wings, and Clare said: Look at him. He's dead. Clare said she should know.

She told me what to take and where it was: sapphire ring, ivory elephant, snakeskin belt. She told me what to leave, what was too heavy, the carved bird, white stone. She reminded me: Take off that ridiculous coat.

I knew Clare was right; I thought, Yes, everyone is dead: the silent heads in the TV, the boy on the floor, my father who can't be known. I thought even you might be dead—your husband asleep at the wheel, your little boy asleep in the back, only you awake to see the car split the guard rail and soar.

I saw a snow-filled ravine, your car rolling toward the river of thin ice.

I thought, you never had a chance.

But I felt you.

I believed in you. Your family. I heard you going room to room, saying: Who's been sleeping in my bed?

It took all my will.

I wanted to love you. I wanted you to come home. I wanted you to find me kneeling on your floor. I wanted the wings on Emile's hips to lift him through the skylight. I wanted him to scatter: ash, snow. I wanted the floor dry, the window whole.

I swear, you gave me hope.

Clare knew I was going to do something stupid. Try to clean this up. Call the police to come for Emile. Not get out. She had to tell me everything. She said again: Turn the water off.

In the living room the tree still twinkled, the angels still hung. I remember how amazed I was they hadn't thrown themselves to the floor.

I remember running, the immaculate cold, the air in me, my lungs hard.

I remember thinking: I'm alive, a miracle anyone was. I wondered who had chosen me.

I remember trying to list all the decent things I'd ever done.

I remember walking till it was light, knowing if I slept, I'd freeze. I never wanted so much not to die.

I made promises, I suppose.

In the morning I walked across a bridge, saw a river frozen along the edges, scrambled down. I glided out on it; I walked on water. The snowflakes kept getting bigger and bigger, butterflies that fell apart when they hit the ground, but the sky was mostly clear, and there was sun.

Later, the cold again, wind and clouds. Snow shrank to ice. Small, hard. I saw a car idling, a child in the back, the driver standing on a porch, knocking at a door. Clare said: It's open. She meant the car. She said: Think how fast you can go. She told me I could ditch the baby down the road.

I didn't do it.

Later I stole lots of things, slashed sofas, pissed on floors.

But that day, I passed one thing by; I let one thing go.

When I think about this, the child safe and warm, the mother not wailing, not beating her head on the wall to make herself stop, when I think about the snow that day, wings in the bright sky, I forgive myself for everything else.

The House of Unintelligible Omens

Randall Watson

Such as it was: the mother's long fingers glistening with chicken fat as from some German fairy tale: the patterned splatter of the grease-filled skillet, unattended, stove-top as bright as a hummingbird's throat struck by light—

And the daughter, *Precious Me*, scrutinizing the dinner glasses for water stains, white stars of dried soap, flecks of chocolate—

And the step-father, of course, who nightly mocks her—

Who returns past midnight, drunk, his voice like a mallet, the mother jabbing him with her slender needles:

Roused from sleep, brother and sister, side by side at the top of the stairs, the girl imploring—

Tell them to stop, she whispers, bedspread curled around the wings of her shoulders.

You know the story: every shadow is portentous, every gesture, each fugitive vocalization, is inhabited: the attitude of hyperattention—each breath, each place-setting:

light scarring the stained teaspoon protruding from the cup like a medieval ensign—chairs cantilevered, angular, geometric—the cupboard left ajar—the dachshund's coiled retreat beneath the couch's shadow—

It was as though one studied the texts of an ancient religion for their mystical and prophetic secrets: the dripping faucet like a code, an impossible anagram—books on the shelves: *Maldoror, The Dutchman and The Slave, A Season in Hell*—

To remove oneself. To make an art of absence. To practice it, exploring the numinous particulars of that abstract form—that platonic ideal—

Not that it was willed—except as a reaction is willed, a flailing, the retraction of a threatened limb, an accusation—greed and revenge in a single gesture—

That was how he moved—moved west, away from that whale shaped island—from home—from family—catching rides from salesmen with coatracks hung across the backseats of their orange Eldorados—Power vans with Grateful Dead decals on their bumpers, budddhas glued to the dash—drinking Bali-hi and Boone's Farm and nips of Jack—running state highway 27 through Babylon and Copaigue, Wantaugh, Rockville Centre, Valley Stream, terns and laughing gulls drifting on the offshore winds—till finally—across the high span and the low waters—where was it—Bayonne, Hoboken, Jersey City—the abandoned Greek diner where some curious contractor inspecting the worksite taught him how to throw a knife, to plant it in the thin columns of the peeling, almost roofless foyer, to love the hard, definitive, certain, unwavering sound it made when it struck true—

No. Not that. That is the way the body runs. But when the body runs, it carries what it's learned, fueled by what it thinks it's leaving behind.

This, then: the shelves held distance. They made the moving things still, without stopping, the wall like an immense console of coral and mother of pearl, iridescent, where running from was a running toward, a feeding, the bindings glistening in lamplight, a sheen he could drown in without dying.

And inside each bound and folded world, an answer, a response, a curative and a weapon, respite and escape. A kind of Aurelius without an empire one could rule, but a state one could enter. This was the way, a way, a means, a progression, as familiar as a bay at morning, as varied as the boats skimming the waters, clamdiggers drawing their rakes up from the sand-bed, skiers turning away from shore.

And what did he find?

The sea does not look less beautiful because ships are sometimes wrecked by it ...
and
The unseen is proved by the seen ...
and
I don't want to startle you, but they're going to kill most of us ...
and
The seal's wide spindrift gaze towards paradise ...

No. Not home. Not that. But nonetheless, a return. A return that could refashion, that could lead him, into disappearance and arrival, into imagination, into being, both toward and away, that running boy, his roaring softened, his leafing like the maple's first springtime confetti, fresh, an emergence it was impossible to capture, impossible to contain.

The Fishing Dog

By Bonnie Jo Campbell

At first Gwen thought it was Jake coming downstream in the boat, but it turned out to be his brother Dan. At the noise of the boat engine, the yellow Labrador retriever across the river moved up the lawn toward its house, and a great blue heron who must have been fishing on the other side of the cabin launched itself into flight. Gwen watched it ascend, wishing she'd known the bird was nearby so she could have spied on it. There was another guy with Dan, but she could see he was about half as big as Jake. Maybe they'd brought food. She'd like to eat something besides fish that didn't come out of a can. She reeled in her line and grabbed Dan's prow as he idled alongside the dock.

"What do you think?" yelled Dan over the engine noise.

"You got a new boat, Dan."

He cut the motor. "She's pretty, ain't she? Got a steal on her from a guy getting divorced."

"Where's Jake?" Gwen didn't usually talk to Dan. Usually she stood by while Jake and Dan talked to each other.

"That's what I come to tell you, honey. Jake's in jail."

"For what?"

"For killing a man."

"You're lying."

"I ain't going to lie about a thing like that. Jake didn't mean for it to happen."

"If it's an accident, they'll let him go."

"Except this ain't the first time."

Gwen pointed at the five-gallon fish pail that Dan was lifting off the boat. "Give me that."

"Gwennie, are you crying?" He rested the bucket on the dock and put his arms around her. Dan was fatter than his brother, but he didn't feel all that different close up. Gwen thought of pulling away from him, of running in the woods until she fell into stinging nettles and poison ivy. She thought of smashing her fists into Dan's chest. If she'd had an axe in her hand, she'd have swung it into a tree.

She grabbed the bucket, sloshing water on herself and Dan. Two of the three catfish inside were longer than her forearms. Their seaweedy whiskers brushed against the sides as they slid over one another. "I've been waiting for a catfish," she said, holding her head up to let the tears drain through the backs of her eyes.

"These come from Willow Island," said Dan. He seemed even fatter suddenly, unsure of himself, waiting for a cue from Gwen, who wasn't accustomed to giving cues, especially not to men twice her age.

"Who you got with you?" she asked. The other man made no motions to disembark.

"That's just Charley. He works at the plant with me." Charley was skinny and had no teeth so his lips caved in.

Dan took the fish from the bucket one by one and held each carefully as he nailed its head to the nearest oak; the three tails strained and curled against the bark. The men stood by while Gwen stunned one with the hammer and began tearing off its skin with pliers.

"Tell me all of what happened." Though she knew better, Gwen brushed against the catfish fins and her fingers burned.

"Well, we left the Pub and was at the Tap in Roseville having a few beers, and Jake and this guy he's playing pool with gets to fighting, and Jake knocks him against a wall. But Jake don't seem to notice the guy is passed out so he picks him up and keeps hitting him."

Gwen could imagine Jake, crazy-eyed and drunk beyond talking to, slugging like a slugging machine gone haywire. When he was in that condition, he'd even pick a fight with Dan. Or Gwen if she didn't keep out of his way. Gwen's fingers trailed again across a catfish whisker. The pain was so sharp she was surprised not to see blood on her knuckle.

"Next thing you know, the son-of-a-bitch is dead. Brain hemorrhage or some shit like that. So the cops show up and they figure out right away about the other charge."

"What other charge?" asked Gwen.

"The manslaughter charge."

"What manslaughter charge?"

"Well, whatever the hell they're calling it. Up in the U.P. last winter. Jake must've told you about it. Why do you think he's been out here in the woods since February?"

The trees became thicker and taller around her. She tugged on the second catfish skin, trying not to let it split, but she stung her wrist and made a mess of it.

"Hey, Charley, toss me a beer," said Dan. Gwen looked up to see the can fly through the air. When Dan opened it, foam poured all over his hand. "How you coming there, Gwen?"

She worked slowly with the pliers on this last, smallest one, tugging around the sides evenly, removing the skin in one piece down to the tail. If what Jake had done in the U.P. was an accident, why hadn't he mentioned it to her?

"All the police had on that trouble up north was a description including them spaghetti scars on the back of his hand. It was the same deal, Jake drunk and not knowing when to quit."

"Can I see him?"

"It'd be better if you didn't, honey."

What else hadn't Jake told her about in the last five months? A wife, maybe?

Inside the cabin, Gwen fried the fish the way she would have for Jake, with cornmeal and flour in the last of the bacon grease. About the time they finished eating, Dan turned on his battery-powered fluorescent lantern. Gwen was surprised at how bug-stained the walls were, how ratty the rug looked in the cold light, and how grimy she had let her arms and legs become. She asked Dan to tell her more.

"There ain't nothing more to it."

"Does Jake own this cottage?" she asked.

"Me and Jake own it together. You can stay here as long as you want, Gwennie. Don't you worry your pretty head about that."

Dan and Charley drank beer while Gwen washed dishes with water she lugged in and heated on the propane stove. Gwen, who didn't usually drink, managed to get down three beers before she felt herself nodding off. She awoke with her forehead on the table, with Dan stroking her hair. Dan told Charley he could sleep in the rocking chair on the screen porch and threw him a sleeping bag from the boat. Then he half-carried Gwen into the tiny bedroom with him. She felt obliged, as though refusing to go to bed with him would've been inhospitable.

Early in the morning, she crawled out of bed and heated water for powdered coffee. There wasn't much propane left. When it ran out she'd have to take the boat to Confluence to get the tank filled, which would cost twenty dollars she didn't have. She walked past Charley slumped sideways in the porch chair--he'd have a terrible stiff neck when he woke up. From her dock she watched the green Jeep pull away from the house across the river. This evening when the man got home she could watch his yellow dog hunker down again at the river's edge. Since Jake had gone, she'd seen it catch a fish in its jaws five times.

After more than two weeks without Jake, Gwen had forgotten how a big man generated heat around him; the bedroom had been stifling last night. She'd never meant to sleep with Dan, but she'd let herself forget who he was when he rolled onto her. Guilt pricked her, as sharp as the catfish stingers. If Jake found out, he'd punch her like she was a man, and maybe she deserved it. She pushed those thoughts below the surface. The steam rose off her coffee as mist rose from the water.

Gwen found her siphon hose and sucked gas out of Dan's tank, enough for a trip up to Confluence, two maybe if she rowed back down without the motor. Or maybe she'd take a fishing trip to Willow Island where last time she'd seen a heron carry a little snake up to its tree nest. She rinsed the fuel taste from her mouth with coffee and spat it into the river. Back in the cottage, she lifted three beers out of Dan's cooler and hid them in the kitchen cupboard. Dan called her name, and she stepped into the tiny bedroom. He didn't look as much like Jake as he had yesterday; he looked more like a swollen possum washed up on her river bank.

"Come here, beautiful," he said. She hesitated, but the room was small enough that he was able to reach across, grab her arm, and drag her to the bed. He pulled off her loose jeans without unzipping them and pushed her T-shirt up around her shoulders. She bent her knees and tried to sit up, but he held her down with one hand and ran the other over her breasts and along her stomach. He pushed her knee out to the side and heaved himself onto her, then worked his hand beneath her buttock to tilt her, pushing deeper. He sighed her name in hot breath. She turned her head to look out the window but saw only empty sky. She wondered how she had let this happen. "Oh, Gwennie," he moaned again, and she felt his sickening heat over her face, through her hair, filling the room. She longed to see a heron fly across the sky framed by the window, its neck pressed into a tight S. She needed to feel that prehistoric swoop or hear the monster shriek of an angry male. A flash of bluegray wing and she would survive this.

After Dan rolled off her, he fell asleep. Gwen pulled away from him and picked her clothes up off the floor with shaking hands. In the kitchen she sifted weevils out of the flour for pancakes—she needed to do something measured. Each time she let herself think of Dan lying in her bed, she had to sit and hold her head in her hands. She thought about grabbing the butcher knife with the burned handle and going back in there. She'd feel for a place between two ribs and sink the blade in. When Charley appeared in the kitchen with his gummy smile, holding his neck, she invited him to sit at the table. She opened a beer, poured half of it in her batter, then handed the open can to Charley. His company calmed her stomach. "Are you hungry, Charley?" she asked. "Did you sleep good?"

"You's got a toilet around here?" asked Charley. Gwen directed him to the outhouse.

When Dan and Charley first powered away, Gwen was relieved. But as soon as the boat rounded the bend, she felt lonesome and nauseated. Dan had given her the food from his cooler--cheese, summer sausage, and sleeves of crackers—before pulling away to return to his wife. Later Gwen discovered two twenty-dollar bills on her pillow. She wished Dan had said something like, "Jake wanted me to give you this."

Hours later, after the Jeep returned, the fishing dog appeared in his place on the other side of the river. To lighten the boat for rowing, Gwen pulled off the outboard with shaking hands and placed it carefully on blocks so as not to bend the propeller, then rowed across. She had never touched the dog or seen him up close, but when she called him, he jumped into her boat. Gwen petted his head, which seemed to repel drops of water. "I'll call you King," she whispered, thinking of the big-headed kingfisher bird who lived across the river from her dad's trailer in Snow Pigeon. She didn't consider it stealing when she took the dog to her side and let him out to sniff the water's edge. If he wanted to stay and chase the raccoons up trees, that would be his choice. With a companion like him, Gwen wouldn't mind staying in the woods. But it wasn't long before she heard a man's voice shouting, "Ren-e-gade!" The dog plunged into the water and swam the fifty or so yards to the other side.

A week of heavy rain made Gwen a prisoner in the cottage. When Jake was there, she hadn't minded so much being without a phone or a radio, but now she longed for voices. Back in Snow Pigeon, after years of pleading, she and her sister Paula had finally talked their dad into getting phone service. They'd been working on getting him to buy a television next. But even just bickering with Paula would have been entertainment enough now. The rain banged on the corrugated roof, making the same sound as rain hitting their trailer.

Years ago Gwen's father used to take her fishing; Paula was too fidgety, too noisy, Daddy said. Gwen used to practice sitting stone quiet sometimes so she could be a good girl in the boat. For the last couple years, though, when Daddy came in from work in the evenings, he just brooded and drank. For months before she left, Daddy, quiet in the best of times, hadn't spoken to her except to yell at her, and Paula was mad because Gwen upset Daddy by not staying away from boys. When Jake had started fishing in the river in front, talking sweet while Daddy was still at work, he had seemed like a knight to the rescue. When he asked her to come down the river with him, she'd hardly hesitated. And since she'd left in April, she'd never dared call Daddy or Paula, even to let them know she was alive. Gwen could still feel their anger flowing with the river's current all the way from Snow Pigeon.

The first day the rains let up, Gwen crossed the river. She called the dog to her boat, and he jumped in. But before she could push off, the man who drove the Jeep appeared from behind the shed and stepped knee-deep into the water to grab the prow of her boat. He was thin and probably only a few inches taller than Gwen. "Evening," he said calmly. "Where are you taking my dog?"

"A-cr-cr-cross the river. I just ... I live over there."

"1 know where YOU live, but why are you taking Renegade?" His biceps strained against his bones. Tendons stood out on one side of his neck as Gwen continued rowing in place without speaking. He said, as much to himself as to her, "You're just plain not going to answer me."

Mosquitos lined up on Gwen's legs and arms, and she could feel them settling onto her face and sinking their stingers. She watched two, then three, then five mosquitos land on the man's forehead. His hair fell straight down from a center part; if it were any darker, it wouldn't have been blond. When he let go of her boat with one hand to swat at mosquitos, Gwen was able to break free. The man folded his arms and stood in the water watching her, looking more perplexed than angry as she rowed away. His jeans were soaked up past his knees, and his figure grew smaller as Gwen approached her own side. She parked at her dock, and King jumped out and swam to shallower water to sniff along the muskrat holes and mangled roots. The man across the river disappeared and returned with binoculars and walked the plank onto his oil-barrel float. Twenty minutes later he called, "Ren-e-gade!"

When Gwen motored to Confluence to buy toilet paper and bottle gas, she didn't go near the Pub for fear of seeing Dan. Partway home, just above Willow Island, she cut the engine and floated downstream with the current, rowing only to fix her direction. The miles of dark, empty river belonged to her, but she'd have traded it all for one party, where music played and people danced under lanterns strung tree-to-tree. She'd drift near the bank or near a big island, and the people would motion her over to join them. Instead, she rounded the last bend above her hut and saw a speedboat there. A bright, cold light shone from inside the cabin— Dan's fluorescent lantern. She steered herself toward the opposite bank, soundlessly maneuvering to the downstream side of the fishing snag just below King's house. She watched her cottage until the light went out, and then she lay her head on a faded orange life vest. Over and over, she shrugged away the memory of Dan's hairy belly and crushing weight.

Gwen awoke shivering to barking and pale sunlight. King was licking her face. She pushed her fingers into the dog's fur, but when she saw a man standing over her, she jumped up and threw one foot into the boat. The Jeep driver looked into her face.

"I'm sorry," said Gwen. Her clothes were caked with mud.

"Sorry for what?"

"For taking your dog."

"Don't worry," he said. "Dogs are loyal. You feed them and they come back to you." He nodded toward her cabin. "If you're hiding from this guy, you can come to my house. He's going to see you if you stay here."

She checked the knot holding her boat to the fallen maple, then, unsure what else to do, followed the man along the river path. The dew that coated the weeds and grass would be slow to burn off. Where the poison ivy had climbed to the tops of trees, the triple leaves had already turned autumn red.

The side door opened into a kitchen with white-painted walls, yellow countertops, and a glossy wooden floor. But the baseboards were pulled away, revealing the uneven gap where the wallboards met the floorboards, and the table was piled with newspapers and hooks. "Do you want coffee?" the man asked. "Bathroom's through there if you need it."

She ventured onto a raw plywood floor, into what should have been a living room but contained a rumpled, queen-sized bed. Through the sliding glass door Gwen saw her dilapidated cabin on stilts, stained cottage green, Dan's boat still parked at its dock. The top drawer of a dresser was open a few inches, exposing a cache of pure white bras and underwear. Gwen hadn't seen a woman here since she'd been watching, since Jake had disappeared. She traced her finger along the scalloped lace edge of a bra. When the man appeared in the doorway, Gwen hurriedly shut the drawer.

"Oh, don't worry. She's long gone. I guess she left those for my next girlfriend."

"I'm sorry." A woman who wore those things was probably a great loss.

The man handed Gwen a mug of coffee almost white with cream.

Jake had insisted she learn to drink coffee instant and black. She inhaled the aroma so deeply that she had to touch the dresser to steady herself. She had eaten French fries in Confluence yesterday, but nothing else.

"Do you want to take a shower?" he asked.

"No."

"You can't wear those clothes. Take something of Danielle's."

Gwen looked at the dresser and back at him.

"Why the hell not?" He laughed. "I was going to throw all her clothes in the river, anyway, let them float away with the current. Go ahead and take anything you want."

She took a long draw of the coffee, which tasted so good she didn't want to swallow. It didn't surprise Gwen that the man would want to take care of her; after Daddy, Jake had taken care of her, and Dan would now if she let him. She looked for a place to rest her cup, but the dresser top looked too clean, and she didn't want to leave a ring. In fact she didn't want to leave any trace that she had been here. In a lower dresser drawer she found and rejected the neatly folded blouses in pink, white, and mint green. The other dresser contained a tangle of the man's blue jeans, T-shirts, and sweatshirts. She put on one of each, and even the jeans weren't a bad fit when she cinched them at the waist with the most worn of three leather belts. She draped her muddy clothes over the side of the bathtub and wondered if this guy was accustomed to women who dressed as though every day was their wedding day and who never got smeared with creosote or fish guts.

She managed to retrieve her coffee from the plywood floor without spilling it. Another room opened off the living room and was probably supposed to be the bedroom, when it wasn't torn down to wall studs. In the middle of the room, balanced on sawhorses, was the curved wooden skeleton of what looked like a boat. Back in the kitchen, she found the man cooking. He placed items on the newspaper-covered table one at a time, and each thing glowed as it passed through a shaft of sunlight: plates, forks, two glistening jars of jelly, a stick of yellow-white butter on a cream-colored plate.

"You've got to be hungry." He held out his hand and shook hers. "I'm Michael. Mike Appel. I've lived here for a year, and other than the guy next door, you're the first person from the neighborhood who's been in my house. You'd think on a river, people'd always be socializing." He gestured with the spatula. "But look at you—you get house guests, you run off."

"I'm Gwen. Gwendolyn."

"That's a pretty name." He repeated it wistfully. "Gwen-do-lyn."

The way he laughed as he talked made Gwen want to say more, to add, "It was my mother's name too," but then she might end up trying to explain to a stranger that her mother left a husband and daughters, six and eight, and never even wrote. Michael pushed aside several books that lay open on top of each other and set a glass of orange juice and half an omelet in front of her. Gwen was careful not to put her glass down on the pages or the covers. One book with a library sticker was called *Building Bookshelves*. A paperback was called *More Greek Mythology*.

"What do you do over there at that little house?"

She shrugged. "I fish." Gwen thought the omelet, with mushrooms, onions, and peppers, was the best thing she'd ever tasted. Next time she was in Confluence, if she had money, she'd buy eggs. She had only six dollars and some change left.

"I've never fished," he said. "Don't even know how to fish, but I'm building a boat."

"Fishing is easy," said Gwen.

"Maybe you can give me a lesson, tell me what tastes good out of this river. Hell, I don't even know how to bait a hook."

Gwen shrugged and lifted the edge of the omelet to look inside at tiny cubes of green pepper. There wasn't anything to teach, really. "I should have put tomatoes in this," he said, "but I forgot to buy them. I work for the power company, so I know you've got no power over there. Have you got a generator? A phone?"

She shook her head no. The fishing dog lay under the table so Gwen worked her bare feet beneath him. She had left her shoes in the boat.

"It's incredible you live like that." He chewed, swallowed. "And you don't have a job?"

Gwen shook her head. A half-sheet of paper on the table read "Overdue book notice."

"Your house looks like a hideout, you know, like a place in a movie where criminals get away from the cops. Would you be the gangster's girlfriend?" He lifted his eyebrows. "Or his daughter maybe? You could be completely innocent, after all."

Did he know something? A sickly knot began to form in Gwen's stomach.

"You don't talk much. Now, Danielle, she could talk." He pointed a fork at Gwen. "And yet, she never thought to mention she was sleeping with my best friend. Funny. Of course, he didn't mention it either. But they're in love now, so everything's swell."

Gwen clung to silence. Why was he telling her this?

"I moved up here from Kalamazoo a year ago for my job. Where're you from?"

When she saw he was going to wait for an answer, she said, "Snow Pigeon."

"That's forty, fifty miles up the river. Did you grow up right on the water?"

She nodded yes and watched out the window. Dan was messing around on the dock.

"When Danielle was here, I hardly noticed the river. Now it's all I think about."

As Gwen finished her toast, Dan got into his boat and pulled away, and Gwen watched him grow smaller as he headed upstream. When he was out of sight, she took the last bite of her omelet and let her fork drop onto her plate. The clank startled her. "I've got to go," she said.

"Can't you stay a few minutes longer? I promise to stop complaining about women. Here, I'll make you another piece of toast."

She sat back down but kept her weight on the balls of her feet. She felt she was stretched across the river like a shock cord, ready to snap back.

"You act like a girl who was raised by wolves." He smiled. "They don't like to be in enclosed spaces."

"Thank you for the food." Gwen stood and hurried out the kitchen door, leaving the toast to pop up behind her. She broke into a run across the yard, and by the time she reached her boat she was panting, Out in the middle of the river, she felt a momentary sense of freedom, but upon reaching her dock the first thing she noticed were rotting catfish heads still nailed to the big oak. Then she remembered she had meant to buy matches. With her second to last match she started a fire in the wood burner, but she dozed off on the floor before it really got going. When she woke up, the sky was fully lit, so she moved to the dock for the sun's warmth. She looked down and was surprised to be wearing Michael's clothes. After his Jeep rolled away across the river, she pressed her face into the clean sweat shirt.

When darkness muscled in again, she used her last match to light the kerosene lamp, but it only seemed to intensify the darkness outside. She heard a sampling of rain, and it occurred to her, as if for the first time, that Jake really wouldn't be coming back. She thought of her dad's trailer in Snow Pigeon and the shoulder-high stacks of wood her father must have already cut and split, which Paula must have stacked by herself against the trailer for the winter. Her own winter supply was about two armloads of broken branches, and once the river iced up Gwen would have no transportation. She ought to cross while she could, walk to the road, and hitchhike someplace warm, Florida, maybe. All evening she watched the lights in Michael's house: the kitchen, the hall, the bedroom that was supposed to be a living room. His silhouette sat hunched over the table where they'd eaten. She wondered, had girls really been raised by wolves?

Even though it was late, she had to get out of the cottage for a while.

She pulled one of Jake's stretched wool sweaters over Michael's sweatshirt and carried her quilt to the boat in case it got really cold. Past Willow Island, almost to Confluence, her engine sputtered out of gas and died. She didn't protest, but let herself be pulled back down river. If she fell asleep out here, and slept long enough, she would wake up in Lake Michigan. The river was quiet and dark. The herons were asleep in their trees. Nobody danced on lawns, no stars shone, and cold rain began to pour down on the river. By the time her quilt became soaked through, she realized she should have kept rowing to reach Confluence to buy matches and boat gas for her next trip. And some food too, a burger and fries for starters. Instead she'd be stuck in a dark cabin with cans of beans and oily sardines. She reached into her pants pocket to feel her money and found nothing—she had left it in her jeans on Michael's bathtub. She drifted with a numbing sense of her own stupidity. Rain water collected in the boat and pooled around her feet. Instead of going to her own side of the river when she rounded the last bend, she pulled up at Michael's oil-barrel float. Surely he'd loan her matches, and maybe he even had gasoline in his shed. She tied her boat and tucked the oars inside but found the shed locked. With the blanket around her, she approached the house and looked in through the sliding glass door. At first she could see only the glowing numbers on a digital clock. As her eyes adjusted, she saw King lift his head from the floor at the foot of the bed.

As quickly as King began to bark, Michael was standing on the other side of the glass in shorts. His chest was as hairless as the chests of schoolboys she had known before Jake. She had fooled around with boys back home and had always been afraid of her father finding out.

Michael switched on a blinding light and slid the door open. "Gwendolyn? Don't you ever sleep in a bed?"

"I'm sorry."

"Well, come on in. Be sorry inside."

She stepped up and puddles formed on the plywood.

"Damn, I've got to finish this floor. I'm going to put down oak like in the kitchen."

Gwen hadn't realized how cold she was until she stepped into the warm house.

"This blanket's soaked--let me put it in the dryer. I'll put your other clothes in there from this morning—I washed them. Talk to me, Gwen."

He looked at her until finally she said, "That omelet was good."

Michael laughed. "Take a shower now, and you can thank me for that tomorrow." Gwen closed her ears to his babbling and followed him to the bathroom. He started running the water, and she remembered only after she had peeled off her shirts that she shouldn't undress in front of a stranger. Michael looked away and abruptly left the room. Gwen hardly recognized the thin, dirty creature in the mirror. Her once dark, soft curls were matted, and her complexion was ruined with scratches and poison ivy scars. Three times she shampooed her hair before the water rinsed clean. She put on the dark terry cloth robe which hung on the back of the door, then padded across the hall to the room with the boat skeleton. It looked too big to fit through the doorway. The room didn't even have a view of the water, so it was no wonder he didn't sleep in there. She returned to the living room and lay with King on his rug. Michael came in and sat on the foot of the bed and looked amused. "Maybe you really are a wolf girl."

"I watch King fish from my house."

"Why do you call her King?"

"Her?"

"I never had a dog before Renegade." He stroked the dog's head. "It was the craziest thing. When I closed on this house the old owner asked if I'd keep her, because she loved the river." Mike tugged on the dog's ear and her mouth opened as if in a smile. "You sleep in my bed, and I'll sleep on the floor. I haven't got a couch."

"We can both sleep on the bed," said Gwen. "It's big." Still wearing the bathrobe, she climbed in on the river side. Michael got in the other.

"What's that mysterious light at your house?" he asked.

"A kerosene lamp. I used my last match so I had to leave it burning."

"Did you come here to teach me how to fish?"

"I need to borrow matches. And I ran out of gas on the way to Confluence."

"Did you see my boat in there?" Michael waited for her to nod. "When

Danielle left, I decided to redo that room, but then I figured I'd rather have a boat. Then I could go to that island with the black willows. I'd like to live on that island."

"Why don't you buy a boat?"

"I want to build my own boat, the way I did this bed. I slept on mattresses on the floor for a month and a half until I finished this."

Gwen looked at the headboard, which was made of solid planks, nothing fancy. "How about a motor? You going to build that?" Her dad would have called her a smartass.

"Next door neighbor's got a two-and-a-half horsepower he'll sell me. I got my boat plan from a library-sale book from 1905. You have to bend the wood and use brass screws. You probably know all this stuff from living on the river. Maybe you can take me for a ride in your boat tomorrow."

Michael was propped on one elbow looking at her. Gwen had never driven a boat with a man in it, and it struck her as a fine idea that she'd take Michael up to Willow Island. Instead of offering, though, she leaned up and kissed Michael, and the kiss she got in return was so mild that she wasn't sure it had happened. When Jake kissed you, you knew you'd been kissed.

"Talk to me," he said. "I don't kiss just any girl who wanders in here. Who was that man at your house the other day?" When she didn't respond he said, "Tell me why you're out in the rain. What could a girl like you be afraid of out there?"

She couldn't tell if Michael was laughing at her, and she wasn't sure she minded if he was. She would've liked to tell him something—maybe that she'd seen the heron flying with a little snake—but then he'd want her to talk more. His arm lay above the blankets, small compared to Jake's or Dan's or her father's. This arm couldn't hold her down or put her any place she didn't want to be. A girl could even stand and fight against an arm like this, instead of running away. The light dimmed across the river, then flickered and went out. Michael started to talk several times but stopped himself. Gwen felt sorry for him, for his being unable to overwhelm a woman. She turned to face him, then pulled him against her with what felt like somebody else's strength.

"I'm not afraid of anything," she whispered. Even if it was a lie, she liked saying it. She wrapped a hand around the back of Michael's neck and kissed him hard. She pushed her fingers through his hair, then felt along his bone-and-muscle shoulder with her hand, wanting suddenly to touch as much of his skin as possible. She leaned across him and felt the curve of his back and his buttock, then continued down his leg until she felt him shudder and move toward her. Fresh air trickled through a window not quite closed. King sighed on the floor. From the end of the hall she heard the clothes and blanket in the dryer turning around and around, softly falling on each other.

She woke alone to light pouring through the sliding glass door, luxurious on her clean skin. Her own cottage had no southern exposure, and she usually slept with her clothes on. Gwen pulled herself up and noticed her quilt and her jeans and red T-shirt folded on the end of the bed. Money was folded on top. Her heart thudded hotly before she realized that it was the bills and change that she'd left in her pants pocket. In the kitchen she found Michael wearing a tie and a name tag.

"Do you want to stay here while I'm at work?" He leaned against the sink counter. She tried to remember his warm, bare chest, but his body seemed stiff and small beneath the white shirt, and she couldn't imagine him naked.

"I'm going home," she said automatically.

He handed her a cup of coffee. "How old are you, Gwendolyn? I'm thirty-one."

"Eighteen." She pushed aside three clothbound books and an old *Mother Earth News* and rested her coffee on newspapers. King sat on the floor beside her.

"You wouldn't lie, would you?" he said. "If you're sixteen, I could be arrested for statutory rape. God, I had no intention of doing that last night. I don't even know you." He stared at Gwen in a way that seemed rude, so she refused to look up at him. He raping her—what a joke. She sipped her coffee and stroked King's head. The dog had the most glorious eyes, as warm as fire. As the silence expanded, Gwen let herself settle into it. Silence was a game that she felt comfortable with, the only game he knew she could win. She didn't even consider saying that she'd trade the whole river for coffee this good every morning. Instead, she pretended to be out in the boat with her father or Jake, pushing thoughts out of her mind so she wouldn't be tempted to express them.

"I'm sorry," Michael finally said, sitting across from her, giving in as suddenly as he had last night. "I just don't know anything about you. For all I know you're some lost heiress or a girl who just killed her whole family and buried them in the garden."

Through the window Gwen watched an old man in a limp fishing hat troll downstream.

"Or maybe I'm dreaming you." His voice grew quieter. "Because, believe me, if I dreamed, a girl, she'd be just like you. She'd have beautiful shoulders like you. She'd be smart, and she'd even smell like you."

What could she smell like? Gwen wondered. She'd just had a shower.

"Except this girl would talk. She'd argue with me. And if I was lucky, she'd be an heiress with an island in the river."

Gwen still kept his words on the surface. She wasn't a wolf girl or a murderer or an heiress. Or a dream. She was Gwen, trying to figure out what to do next. Give her some matches and gas and she'd be fine for a while longer. King pushed her head beneath Gwen's hand until Gwen resumed petting her.

"But maybe that guy you live with will come back and cut me up and use me for bait."

Gwen thought that was the first sensible thing he'd said. "Don't worry about him."

"So he's gone for good?"

Gwen shrugged and tried not to think about Jake coming back. He could be found innocent. The judge could let him go.

"Are you going to live in that cottage year 'round? Keep warm with wood?"

"I'm thinking about going south this winter. Florida, maybe."

"The herons go to Florida. You'll fly south like the birds, eh?"

As if seeing through clear water, Gwen imagined Jake and Dan coming downstream in the boat, and her stomach knotted. The thought of Jake's body near hers made it hard to breathe. Suddenly she couldn't stand Michael's laughing talk. "I have to go."

"Will you come back tonight?" Michael's eyes were as brown and hopeful as King's. Jake's eyes were deep blue. "We can eat dinner or something. I could come get you in the Jeep."

"There's no road."

"And I don't have a boat yet, so I guess it's up to you, Gwendolyn." He folded his arms and watched her stand and drain her coffee and walk to the door, just as he'd watched her row away with his dog on the day they'd met.

Gwen sat cross-legged on her dock and watched Michael pull out of the driveway. She felt the tug of King and Michael and the house, solid even without its floors and walls and baseboards. Even the road onto which Michael turned pulled at her—it led to Confluence, Roseville, and Snow Pigeon, and all the towns on other rivers. Maybe she could go to Michael's house during the day to be with King or bring the dog over here. Or maybe, thought Gwen, she would just hitchhike away from here and find a new place, where people would let you start over again without asking a lot of questions. A heron dropped from the sky and settled out of sight downstream. Two female mallards drifted near shore, one not quite full grown. Gwen wondered if this was all that remained of a dozen chicks that the momma hatched this June. Maybe this girl was the only one who survived the fat raccoons who hunted at the water's edge. Gwen lay back on her dock, her hands behind her head and her knees up, and fell asleep.

Late that afternoon, a pale car pulled into Michael's driveway, and Gwen knew immediately that the woman who stepped out of it was the owner of the white underthings. She disappeared behind the house and, shortly afterwards, King bounced down to the water. Was she intending to take the fishing dog away? As soon as Gwen considered the possibility, she reeled in her line, dragged the outboard motor off the boat without taking any care to protect the propeller, and rowed into the current, rowed so hard that she landed upstream. King ran to her but bowed playfully and tossed her head instead of climbing into the boat. "King!

Come!" Gwen barked. "King! Come!" As the dog jumped in, the woman appeared from inside the house. She wore a white sleeveless turtleneck. Gwen could imagine her holding a glass of champagne, looking over at Gwen and not inviting her to the party.

"What are you doing with Renegade?" the woman yelled. Her hair had the color and shine of caramel melted onto apples. Her bare arms were long and clean.

"She's not yours!" Gwen yelled. "You left her!"

"I'll call the police, you freaky little tramp."

King began to whimper, and as she rowed out into the river Gwen saw Michael stepping from his Jeep. The woman stomped toward him, yelling and pointing at Gwen, and Michael crossed his arms. Gwen looked away, but soon she heard Michael shout, "Rene-gade!" At the call, King jumped from her boat—nearly tipping it over—and swam back. Gwen stopped rowing and put her head in her hands. Upon reaching land, King followed Gwen's boat along the shoreline until Michael called her again. Then Michael shouted her own name, "Gwen-do-lyn!" She knew she should pick up her oars and row, if not to Michael then back to her own cottage, but she didn't have the will to fight the current. Instead, she let her boat be swept past Michael's house and everything that was familiar.

She glided past solitary black fishermen with bottles twisted in paper bags and the green heads of willows weeping beside them. Turtles and blue racers sunned themselves on fallen trees, sliding into the water at her approach. A heron fished silently at a tiny inlet, one bulging banded eye on her as she passed, wary, but not alarmed so long as she moved with the current. She was tempted to row and approach it but decided instead to leave the bird in peace. The river widened. Men steered speedboats around her, and she tossed side to side in their wake. Her hands rested on the oar handles, but she dipped her oars only to right her downstream course. At times she let herself twirl in the current like a twig. She saw a tree which resembled first Jake and then, at closer range, her father, with her father's brooding face and big arms upraised.

After she'd floated for hours, houses began to appear more often on either side of the river, a sign that she must be approaching Lanakee and the harbor, but she didn't feel ready to see all those strangers and their houses and yards. She wished she could see her sister Paula, and maybe Michael, but they were both behind her. By finally taking hold of the oars she stopped herself and tied the boat up at the ruined dock of an abandoned fishing cottage. She climbed onto the dock and lay carefully on the boards to soak in the last light before continuing. Downstream, after the river flowed under some traffic bridges and past boat slips, lay Lanakee Harbor and, beyond that, Lake Michigan—the coldest, darkest place she'd ever been. She knew what happened when the river met the lake, that the river emptied at a lighthouse which perched at the tip of a long tongue of concrete. The lighthouse winked red, then white, then red. Gwen found herself drifting beyond the lighthouse, dark water pressing on her from all directions. But from the heartless depths emerged the fishing dog, now paddling toward her boat, eyes as bright as fire. Upon hearing a splash beneath her, Gwen awoke.

As though part of her dream, a great blue heron flew up in front of her. Gwen held her breath as the bird spread its wings in slow motion, its feathers almost brushing her leg as it took off from under the dock and flew over the river, against the current. As the bird left her, Gwen felt herself shredding from the inside out. She wished she had been awake to see the heron close up, to stare into that clear, savage eye, to see the drops of water on his crest and witness the neck feathers roughen and smooth out. The motion of those wings reminded her of being with Michael in his bed--the feathery blankets. The night air through the window, his skin warm in her hands. She leaned back and let herself imagine the flush of wings again, the swoosh of air, as soft as her clothes turning in the dryer, falling upon themselves. She longed to hear the steady breathing of the fishing dog.

The sun was setting over houses where people were eating dinner. Paula was probably cooking Daddy macaroni and cheese. Paula had turned sixteen this summer without her, and maybe she'd finally learned to cook fish. If Gwen filled both gas tanks and had money to refuel in Confluence, she might be able to motor all the way to Snow Pigeon. She would sneak in and remind Paula not to feel bad, remind her that there was no pleasing Daddy. Jake was sitting in a jail cell, probably eating with a bunch of guys complaining about the food. Maybe Michael had cooked that woman dinner, or maybe he was eating alone or bending wood. Gwen's stomach hurt from hunger. She hadn't brought along fishing gear, and once she hit Lake Michigan the water would be empty and the tide would pull her out and away. She did not want to go. She did not want to starve to death in a cold, bottomless place. Somehow she would have to row back upstream.

To lessen the current, Gwen hugged the edge or the river as closely as she could without scraping bottom, dipping her left oar shallow. She faced backwards toward a fuming orange sunset, and as the color faded, her eyes adjusted. She rowed steadily, seeing the dark cottages and ancient trees only after she'd passed them. The hair stood up on her arms when she heard a whippoorwill cry. Farther upstream, a nighthawk made a crazy flutter as he stabbed the air for insects. Muskrats and other night. hunters slid into the water and rose alongside her boat. When a quarter moon appeared, Gwen pulled herself up to a snag. Her arm muscles burned and her hands were raw from the oar handles. She felt the night pulling at her boat, luring her into the dark, easy current. If she gave up this time, it would carry her all the way to the blinking light at the entrance to Lake Michigan, where there were no herons, no dogs, nothing for her. She fell asleep leaning against her boat and awoke stiff and cold with no moon in the sky. The thought of working her muscles again brought tears stinging to her eyes, but resting wasn't helping, so she pushed off again and rowed. The river curved and narrowed until she could make out occasional irrigation pumps and boathouses on the opposite bank. She focused on a line of three bright stars until they disappeared behind trees. Blisters formed and ruptured on her hands, but she didn't let go of the oars, for fear she wouldn't be able to make herself grab hold again. To warm herself, she conjured up a picture of Michael's yellow-and-white kitchen, cluttered with books and jars of jelly.

She needed to stop rowing, to rest under her covers, even if there was sand in the bed. But when she finally caught sight of her dark place on stilts, she remembered that she had no matches, and she knew how the pockets of coldness would be trapped between her blankets long after she tried to curl up and sleep without a fire, And she'd left her warmest covering, her quilt, folded on Michael's bed. She headed instead across the river, to Michael's oil-barrel float. She misjudged the distance from shore and stepped out into thigh-deep water. Her fingers no longer worked well enough to make a knot, so she wound the rope as many times as she could around a crosswise support piece. As she worked, her aluminum prow clanged against the metal barrels. The noise must have woken King, because a light came on in the bedroom, and King jogged out into the yard and over the plank to watch Gwen at eye level. Gwen petted her, face to face.

When the kitchen light came on, Gwen suddenly noticed her legs were numb in the water, as though she'd fallen asleep standing. She staggered to shore. If that white underpants woman was gone, she and Michael could empty her dresser into the river. Gwen would like to drag out all of Jake's huge pants and flannel shirts and release them alongside the perfect brassieres. She and Michael could watch pieces of clothing twirl and dance on their way to Lake Michigan, sinking and resurfacing, grasping at each other before disappearing for good.

Michael opened the door before she knocked. King stayed beside her.

"Can I have some matches?" she asked. She thought deliriously of swallowing a box of wooden matches, having them fall to the bottom of her empty stomach.

"You're late for dinner." The clock behind him said 4:10. "Come in, though."

Gwen clenched her teeth, locking her jaw against the cold. She could survive in the cabin across the river, or in Florida, or anywhere. She asked, "Are you by yourself?"

"Don't worry about Danielle. I can defend myself against her."

"I brought King back. She came out to find me."

"Come in, Renegade," he said, stepping aside, but the dog didn't move. Michael looked into Gwen's face. "Did somebody do something to you? That guy with the speedboat?"

Gwen stopped her shivers by hunching her shoulders. Inside were coffee and butter and clean sheets. Food and hot water awaited, but she now wished she'd brought Michael something. She should have stopped at the cottage and gotten those three beers she'd taken from Dan. Or sardines. She was finally hungry enough to eat canned sardines. "That big island upstream," she said. "It's called Willow Island. I'll take you there if you want."

Michael leaned against the doorway. He crossed and uncrossed his arms, smiled, and said nothing.

Gwen felt drunk but blinked her eyes open. "What's your favorite bird?" she asked.

"My favorite bird? Let's see. How about the great blue heron?"

"There's herons on Willow Island." Gwen was dizzy from standing, "A campment of herons, living way up in the trees." She put one hand against the doorframe to steady herself. "Hundreds of them. One came so close it brushed me with a wing."

"I don't suppose you know the story about Leda and the swan?"

Gwen wondercd if she'd get used to Michael.

"Your fingers are pure white." He took her free hand and held it up in the kitchen light. "They're so cold. And you've got blisters broken open. We should clean your hands with peroxide and bandage them." He tugged at her wrist but stopped when she resisted. "I forgot. You want to stand right here in the doorway. Well, I bought you a can of gas. Matches are right here on the stove. I'll hand you everything so you don't even have to come in."

"'What if your boat doesn't fit through the doorway?" Gwen's teeth clacked together, breaking up her speech.

"Then I'll cut out the doorway with a Sawzall." Michael pulled her other hand off the doorframe and held both of them. In Gwen's blurred vision, it seemed that Michael's arms were fusing end-toend with her goose-bumped and bruised arms, stretching into an impossible length of skin. "Come in, Gwen. Renegade's going to get cold out there waiting for you. I'll make you an omelet. This time I've got tomatoes."

Before she stepped through the doorway, Gwen looked behind her, across the river, toward the dark little house. She would row across tomorrow when her hands stopped hurting and close it against the raccoons. Beyond that, she didn't know yet what she'd do. King followed her inside.

Contributor Bios

ADEN ALBERT is a writer, martial artist, and father. He lives in South Carolina with his three best friends—his wife, daughter, and son. He blogs at adenalbert.com and publishes photographs at sameghost.com.

JODI ANGEL is the author of two story collections, *The History of Vegas* and *You Only Get Letters from Jail*, which was named as a Best Book of 2013 by *Esquire*. Her work has appeared in *Esquire*, *Tin House*, *One Story*, *Zoetrope: All-Story*, *Electric Literature Recommended Reading*, and *Byliner*, among other publications and anthologies. Her short story, "Snuff," was selected for inclusion in *The Best American Mystery Stories 2014*.

BRADFORD PHILEN writes and teaches in the Philippines where he lives with his wife, kids, and dog, Bear. He is the author of two books of fiction. His full list of publications can be found at bradfordphilen.com.

JEFFREY BYREM—A retired educator, Jeffrey Byrem (pseudonym: Jeff Lee) devotes his creative energies to his blogs (www.educationandfreedom.com and www.growingupboomer.net) and to writing fiction. He has independently published five novels, a collection of short stories, and he is currently nearing completion of his sixth novel (see www.jeffleenovels.com for more information).

BONNIE JO CAMPBELL is the bestselling author of *Mothers, Tell Your Daughters*, *Once Upon a River*, and *American Salvage*, among other works. She was a National Book Award finalist and a Guggenheim Fellow, and the *Guardian* named her one of the top writers of rural noir fiction. She is six foot tall and rides a donkey.

RICK CAMPBELL is a poet and essayist living on Alligator Point, Florida. His latest collection of poems is *Gunshot, Peacock, Dog* (Madville Publishing). He's published five other poetry books as well as poems and essays in numerous journals including *The Georgia Review*, *Fourth River*, *Kestrel*, and *New Madrid*. He's won a Pushcart Prize and an NEA Fellowship in Poetry. He teaches in the Sierra Nevada College MFA Program.

K.B. CARLE lives and writes outside of Philadelphia, PA and earned her MFA from Spalding University's low-residency program in Kentucky. Her stories have appeared in *Homology Lit., CHEAP POP, genre2, Jellyfish Review, Milk Candy Review*, and elsewhere. She can be found online at kbcarle.wordpress. com or on Twitter @kbcarle.

SHELBI CARPENTER—is a creative writing graduate from the University of Arkansas. Outside of her literary projects, she enjoys hiking and climbing around the Buffalo River with her partner and dog.

EMILY CHILES' work has appeared in *The Masters Review* (New Voices), *Blackbird, Copper Nickel*, and elsewhere. A recipient of the *Sonora Review* Short Short Fiction Award, she was recently named a finalist for *Narrative*'s Fall Story Contest. She teaches at Northern Virginia Community College and lives in Northern Virginia.

MARISOL CORTEZ is a creative writer, community-based scholar based in San Antonio, Texas. Current projects include a novel entitled *Luz at Midnight; I Call on the Earth*, a chapbook of documentary poetry; and *Deceleration*, an online journal of environmental justice thought and practice. For more information on previous publications and current projects, visit her website at marisolcortez.wordpress.com.

RICHARD JAY GOLDSTEIN has been writing fiction and non-fiction for almost thirty years. He lives with his wife and kids and grandkids in the mountains east of Santa Fe, New Mexico, where it's still pretty quiet, thanks. He's a lapsed ER doc and has published sixty-something stories and essays in the literary and fantasy/sci-fi/horror press, including a number of anthologies. He's also had two Pushcart nominations, but neither got in.

MERRILL ELIZABETH GRAY's writing has appeared in *Grain The Journal of Eclectic Writing, Temenos Press, Silver Birch Press, Birds we pile loosely, S/Tick, Blue Skies Poetry, Worth Architectural Magazine, Crazy Pineapple Press, Fieldstone Review, Four Ties Lit Review, Spring vol viii, Misfitmagazine, Sugar Mule Literary Magazine, CBC Canada writes Stranger than Fiction and Joy, Interrupted an anthology on motherhood and loss*. Merrill is a mother to three children and two granddaughters. She lives in Calgary, AB. Canada.

EMILY HOOVER is a poet, fiction writer, and literary critic based in Las Vegas. Her poems have most recently been featured in *Levee Magazine* and *Bending Genres*, her fiction has most recently appeared in *Gravel* and *BULL*, and her short

242

story "Angelo Loves Tammy" was nominated for Sundress Publication's 2018 "Best of the Net" anthology. Emily's book reviews have been published by *The Los Angeles Review*, *Necessary Fiction*, *Ploughshares blog*, *The Rupture*, and others.

BOBBY HORECKA blurs the lines between fact and fiction with his story based on actual events from his early childhood. A veteran Texas news journalist, he and his wife Jennifer reside on his family's farm in rural Lavaca County, where he also writes for the four county newspapers. He holds an MFA in creative writing from the University of Houston-Victoria and a BA in English from Texas State University in San Marcos.

DEBORAH JOHNSTONE's writing can be found in numerous online and print publications and has been nominated for a Pushcart Prize. Her story, "Pray for Rain" was selected as runner-up finalist for *Light and Dark Magazine*'s Flash Fiction Contest and recent work was anthologized in "Addiction and Recovery" by Madness Muse Press and in *Ethel Magazine*. She is a graduate of the MFA program in Creative Writing at Goddard College.

JEN KNOX's story, "Lost Her Way," first appeared in Junked. The story is about sisterhood, freedom, and what it is to tease out a life philosophy when sandwiched between extremes. "These characters took me places," says Knox. "In fact, this story was one of the first that lead to *Resolutions*," a collection she now calls a *Family in Stories*.

LOUISE MARBURG is the author of two collections of stories, *The Truth About Me* (WTAW Press, 2017) and *No Diving Allowed* (forthcoming from Regal House Publishing, 2021). Her work has appeared in such publications as *Ploughshares*, *Narrative*, *The Southampton Review*, *The Chicago Quarterly Review*, and many others. She lives in New York City with her husband, the painter Charles Marburg. You can find her at louisemarburg.com.

LOU MORRISON currently resides in South Korea. He has recently published non-fiction in the journals *Fleas on the Dog* and *Nowhere*, who nominated his work for a Pushcart Prize and *The Best American Travel Writing 2020* anthology.

MAUREEN O'BRIEN has tinkered with this story so long (is 30 years long?) it shows both her craft and tenacity and her insane inability to let go. She is deeply relieved and honored that "The Whiskey Monkey" has found a home here with other runaways. Her poems have appeared most recently in *3Elements Review* and *Tiny Seed*. She is the author of *b-mother* (a novel), and the forthcoming nonfiction book *Seeking Psalms* (Franciscan Media).

ERICA SOON OLSEN was born in Hollywood, California. She is the author of *Recapture & Other Stories* (Torrey House Press), a collection of short fiction about the once and future West, and *Girlmine*, a microchapbook (Bull City Press), where "Daphne: The Aspen Version" previously appeared. A graduate of the University of Montana MFA program, she lives in northeastern Utah.

BRETT RILEY is the author of *The Subtle Dance of Impulse and Light* (Ink Brush Press) and *Comanche* (lmbrifex Books, September 2020). His short fiction has appeared in journals such as *The Baltimore Review, f(r)iction, Solstice, Folio, The Evansville Review*, and many others. His nonfiction has appeared in *Role Reboot, Rougarou, under the gum tree, Green Hills Literary Lantern*, and others. Follow him on Twitter and lnstagram: @brettwrites. He lives in Las Vegas.

MAURICE CARLOS RUFFIN is the author of *We Cast a Shadow*, which was published by One World Random House. The novel is a New York Times Editor's Choice. Ruffin is the winner of several literary prizes, including the Iowa Review Award in fiction and the William Faulkner–William Wisdom Creative Writing Competition Award for Novel-in-Progress. His work has appeared in the *Oxford American, Garden & Gun*, and *Kenyon Review*. A New Orleans native, Ruffin is an assistant professor of creative writing at Louisiana State University, and the 2020-2021 John and Renee Grisham Writer-in-Residence at Ole Miss.

MICHAEL SIMPSON is a retired technical writer living in Charlotte, NC. He has a master's degree in English from the University of Maine. His story, "Reading Herzog" was first workshopped at the Wildacres Writers Workshop in 2013.

MISTY SKAGGS was born and raised in the backwoods of eastern Kentucky, a region held tight in the grips of poverty where the first thing most folks want to do when they get a little grown up is runaway. For some reason, this author, artist and activist decided to stay. She writes and lives and exists at the end of a gravel road off the beaten path. The themes in this anthology and in her contribution are a rural route reality. Her poetry collection *Planted by the Signs* is currently available from Ohio University Press and you can find her on Instagram @mistymarierae.

MELANIE RAE THON's most recent books and chapbooks are *Silence & Song* (2015); *The 7th Man* (2015); *The Bodies of Birds* (2019); *Lover* (2019); and *The Good Samaritan Speaks* (2015). She is a recipient of a Fellowship in Creative Arts from The John Simon Guggenheim Memorial Foundation, a Whiting Writer's Award, two Fellowships from the National Endowment for the Arts, and a Writer's Residency from the Lannan Foundation.

RANDALL WATSON's first book, *Las Delaciones del Sueño*, was published in a bilingual edition by the Universidad Veracruzana in Xalapa, Mexico. His *The Sleep Accusations* received the Blue Lynx Poetry Award. He is also the editor of *The Weight of Addition, An Anthology of Texas Poetry* published by Mutabilis Press and *No Evil Is Wide* (Madville Publishing), a revised version of *Petals*, submitted under the heteronym Ellis Reece, which received the 2006/07 Quarterly West prize in the novella category, judged by Brett Lott.

THE EDITORS:

LUANNE SMITH lives in New Jersey and works in Pennsylvania, but she is a born Kentuckian. She is an Associate Professor at West Chester University outside of Philadelphia where she has taught creative writing and film for nearly 30 years. Her work, usually short fiction, has appeared in *Puerto del Sol*, *The Oxford Review*, *The Texas Review*, and other literary journals.

MICHAEL GILLS is the author of eight books of fiction and nonfiction including the novels *West* and *Emergency Instructions* (Raw Dog Screaming Press), and the short story collections *The House Across from the Deaf School* and *The Death of Bonnie and Clyde* (Texas Review Press). Gills' work has won numerous prizes. His undergraduate novel writing workshop has been featured on *USA Today*, and several of his students have gone on to publish books of their own. Gills teaches for the Honors College at the University of Utah.

LEE ZACHARIAS is the author of three novels, *Lessons*, *At Random*, and *Across the Great Lake*, a 2019 Notable Michigan Book, as well as a collection of stories, *Helping Muriel Make It Through the Night*, and a collection of essays, *The Only Sounds We Make*. Her work has rtwice won the Sir Walter Raleigh Award, she has won the Phillip H. McGath Post-Publication Award. She has held fellowships from the National Endowment for the Arts and the North Carolina Arts Council. Her work has been reprinted and frequently cited in the annual volumes of *The Best American Essays*.